KILLING REDEMPTION

Faith or family - one will burn

JOEL CUTTER

CMD R
PUBLISHING

CMDR Publishing

4025 Postal Way, #50894, Myrtle Beach, SC, 29579

www.cmdrpublishing.com

Credit and special thanks to Charis Tenney for amazing work shooting the photos and contributing to the cover art for this book. Her services can be booked at **www.charistenney.com.**

Credit and extra appreciation to Darwyn Walker for his skill in capturing the essence of Protean as our model for the cover shoot. His work can be found on Instagram at @darwynwalker.model.

And finally, credit and special appreciation to Angela Robertson for her time and dedication to the proofreading process.

Cataloguing in Publication Data:

Names: Cutter, Joel.

Title: Killing Redemption / by Joel Cutter.

Description: CMDR Publishing trade paperback edition | Summary: Killing Redemption is an Action Drama that follows the story of an ex-gang member turned youth pastor who gets pulled back onto the streets when his 10-year-old brother is shot in a drive-by.

Identifiers: ISBN 978-1-7355876-3-9 (paperback)

Subjects: Crime Action & Adventure. | Crime Fiction. | Crime Thriller & Suspense.

PREFACE

This story is a work of fiction sourced from the experiences of real current and former gang members, gang detectives, and their families.

The author was directly involved in a high-profile, multi-year case against a gang composed primarily of teenagers and found people are still people, and nothing is as simple as it seems.

CHAPTER ONE

Damarion bunny-hops the curb with his BMX bike, jostling the Glock pistol tucked in his waistband.

"C'mon Pro. I see something," he calls back over his shoulder.

Fourteen-year-old Protean Williams stands up on the pedals of his black spray-painted bike, swerving at the last second to take the slanted driveway into the gas station. He is acutely aware of the hard metal object precariously concealed in his pants and is careful to not bounce it loose.

"Hold up," Pro calls to his 16-year-old brother in a low voice, "whatcha got."

At 3AM, even the tumultuous South Side of Oklahoma City is pretty quiet, and their low voices carry on the hot night air.

Damarion "Trey" Williams the Third is comfortable at night. It feels right, like his home, his natural state of being. He rolls into the deep shadows at the corner of the gas station and puts his feet down, waiting. The choking odor of rotting garbage from a nearby dumpster mixes with something sharper, assaulting his nostrils.

1

The younger boy rolls up and stops beside him, balancing on his bike. "Gaw. What's that smell?"

"Piss. Pretty sure you are standing in it," Trey answers with a snicker. He does not look at the ground, though; his eyes stare intently into the distance. "Quit bitchin.' Check this dude out."

Protean pushes up his beanie and follows his brother's gaze. They are tucked up behind a badly aging gas station a block off the main drag — bars on the windows, doors locked after dark type shit. The gas station occupies the corner, and the next building over is a strip mall. At least, that's what it used to be. What the boys look at now is depressed and used up, with badly cracked pavement, most windows boarded up, spray-painted scrawling letters, with more spray-painted in un-matched colors on top to half-hide the gang graffiti.

"What dude?" Pro asks.

Out of a dozen, only a solitary floodlight in the center of the parking lot is still operational, and Protean's initial scan yields nothing of interest.

"In the back. Tattoo place with the black light. Shhhhh. I think he's looking this way," Trey's voice develops a note of hesitation. "Yeah, he scoping us. Maybe we skip it."

Now Protean can see it. About 50 yards away, a shiny low-rider truck, gleaming quietly in the deep shade on the back-side of the long building.

Niiiice.

His pulse increases as he imagines rolling in that thing.

Ride all night, sell it before dawn.

The thought of handing Mama a stack of cash feels good. Electric is off again at home. Nothing but a jar of relish in the refrigerator.

. . .

The orange glow of a cigarette springs to life by the front of the vehicle. As more visual information reaches his brain, Protean realizes a man is standing in the shadows under an awning between the hood of the truck and the concrete block building,

"Yeah, he's peeping us for sure. Probably strapped." Trey pulls the front of his bike around, ready to look for another target. Trey is a daring opportunist, but running the streets since 11 has given him finely-honed survival instincts.

"Hold up," Protean urges. He moves slightly back into the light and lays his bike down in the half-visible part of the station parking lot. He unslings his backpack and starts rummaging in it.

"What the hell you doin'?" The older brother hisses. His adrenaline is spiking, and he begins wheeling his bike in the opposite direction as the shiny low-rider. "Let's ROLL."

Protean pulls out a cylindrical object from his dark blue backpack and starts shaking it with a loud rattle. "HOLD UP, LEMME TAG THIS FIRST," his voice is loud and clear in the night air.

Trey flinches involuntarily from the sudden burst of sound. "What the F-" He drops his bike at the edge of the building and moves quickly toward the younger boy, "You crazy?"

The 14-year-old ignores him and stands in the most visible spot in their vicinity, shaking the can loudly. "Crip the Fuck up, bro! Ima tag this shit." His voice is again loud and clear, and he steps toward the battered green metal dumpster. He sprays a huge "C" on the can, expertly making the pattern in the dim light.

Fifty yards away, the orange glow of the cigarette flicks down to the pavement, then goes out as the half-visible man steps on it.

Trey grunts, catching onto his younger brother's ploy. "On the Set. Yeah, tag it up, Crip." That part was loud, for the benefit of their target, but he follows it up with something almost a whisper, "Keep going. I got 'im."

The shorter boy continues spraying, going through a mental list of gang graffiti while his older brother watches the truck out of the corner of his eye.

Wielding the spray can like a weapon, he paints *"FUCK 12, BK, HK, and LK,"* disrespecting the police, and claiming to kill Bloods, Hoovers, and Locos. With that done, he starts on an elaborate playboy bunny to represent his gang, South Side Playboy Gangsta Crips. The movement of his arm causes the 22-caliber gun in the loose waistband of his jeans to move around. He jams the muzzle of it into the tight elastic of his boxer shorts and stuffs the edge of his shirt down the front of his pants to help secure the object. He is running short of both inventive ideas and room on the dumpster when Trey finally whispers, "Booom, he goin' in."

It worked! Protean quickly adds a stylized 'Pro' at the far edge to sign the tag, then stuffs the can back in his backpack.

By silent agreement, the boys quickly climb back on their bikes and pedal across a dirt patch between the gas station parking lot and their target. Once on the cracked asphalt, they roll down the slight downhill, coasting toward the truck in near silence.

Trailing slightly as they approach, Pro is momentarily captivated by the truck. It is some sort of sparkly metallic purple, riding on lowered suspension and gleaming 20-inch chrome wheels.

It's gotta be worth 30 grand at least. His mind spins as he starts to think about who they can sell it to. A unique ride like this, you don't want to stay under that kind of *hotbox* long.

Trey brakes suddenly, coming to a stop near the driver's

door of the vehicle. He hisses a whispered curse as a mentally preoccupied Protean almost piles into the back of him.

Wordlessly, Trey pumps his arm, finger extended, toward a steel door under the awning. The only nearby illumination is from a small black-light fluorescent 'Tattoos' sign above the metal awning, but Pro picks up on the gesture.

Working smoothly in concert, the younger brother positions himself on the hinge side of the door, keeping a lookout while Trey goes to work.

No windows. Easy. Pro looks back at the truck, wondering how someone with a hole-in-the-wall tattoo shop could afford a nice ride like this. *Gotta be drugs.* He inhales deeply, catching a faint, sickly sweet scent of what must be in the building — *marijuana, weed, green, tree.* Whatever you call it, they must have it stacked up inside.

Protean's reverie is shattered by lights and sound.

White flashing, blinding. Sound piercing the silence.

HONK, HONK, HONK!

Adrenaline slams through his veins, but before he can process what is happening, much less react, darkness and pain slam into his face.

"HEY, YOU LITTLE SHIT!"

He instinctively pushes the hard metal surface away from his face.

The door! He was on the hinge side of the door and realizes it had slammed him in the face when it flew open. Clamping down on the pain signals, he tries to get his bearings.

The headlights of the truck are repeatedly flashing, the horn going off continually.

HONK.

"MOTHERF-" A smacking sound punctuates a stream of curse words.

HONK.

"Pro!" His brother's voice cries out in pain above the

racket, and Protean steps numbly around the front of the truck, moving as if in a dream.

HONK.

Like the flash of a camera, the headlights blind him again, and he shades his eyes against the glare. When the lights cycle off, he sees a figure in the dim shadows, white tank top, hands against the truck, leg swinging violently.

"Help-" A sickening smack turns the wounded cry for help from the figure on the ground into a groan.

HONK-FLASH.

Trey! Everything is suddenly clear. The truck owner, a burly Hispanic male, covered in sleeve tattoos, is wearing steel-toed boots. Boots that he is slamming mercilessly into the teenage boy writhing on the ground.

"Try to steal my-"

HONK-FLASH.

Without thinking, Protean charges, slamming into the side of the larger man. But the stocky adult is easily 250lbs., all muscle and sinew. Protean's 120-pound frame knocks the man momentarily away from Trey, but then he easily keeps his feet and turns toward his new assailant.

"Yeah? C'mere!" Turning toward Protean, the man cocks his fist back.

HONK-FLASH.

Pain explodes in Protean's face for a second time, and he feels his knees going soft. Suddenly unable to support his weight, he staggers against the truck and begins to slide down. The zipper of his backpack scratches down the door panel, making a slight squealing sound next to his ear.

The man uses one hand to pin Pro's shoulder to the truck, pulling his fist back for another crushing blow.

"Get off my brother!" A battered Trey tries to get up from the ground, surging into the man's knee. His effort succeeds in getting the man's attention but little else.

HONK-FLASH.

"You little shits are gonna pay," the man threatens. Still holding Pro against the truck, he pivots to aim at Trey and smashes a fist directly into his eye, stunning him.

Through a roaring in his ears, Protean hears Trey gurgle something that sounded like 'run,' but his instinct rebels at the thought of leaving his brother. The man lets him go so he can focus his rage on Trey, and Pro's mind races for a way to gain the upper hand. He tries to move forward to tackle the tattooed man, but his backpack hangs up on the mirror behind him, tearing loudly and arresting his forward momentum.

A sickening thud, then another, as the man let his boots fly into Trey. The teenager is flat on the ground now and groans as he tries to crawl away from the beating.

"GET YOUR GUN!" Trey's desperate words punch through his fog of pain and adrenaline, and Protean suddenly can feel only one thing – the metal object at his waist.

HONK-FLASH.

He hears a 'snick' sound and sees a gleam of something metallic in the hand of the bigger man. A menacing shape barely illuminated by the soft glow of the tattoo sign.

Knife. The thought registers as the man swings to fully face Protean again, and the whole world goes into slow motion. He fumbles against his shirt as the man's hand comes up.

Gonna die.

Then the 22-caliber pistol is in his hand.

HONK-FLASH.

POP. The noise sounds both loud and far away at the same time, and he feels the small gun pushing back against his hand. He thought it would be like the movies, a sudden flower of blood appearing on the man's chest. Instead, it seemed like he wasn't even hitting the guy. He just kept coming, knife first.

POP, POP, POP. Panicking, he repeatedly fires at point point-blank range.

HONK-FLASH.

The light illuminates the scene, showing a surprised look on the Hispanic man's face and several small dark holes in his white tank top. He grunts, and the arm holding the knife sags down to his waist.

"Let's go!" Trey is on his feet, slipping on the asphalt, scooping something up off the ground.

The man staggers another step toward Protean, and the teenager's finger jerks instinctively once more.

POP.

"C'mon!" Trey grabs his younger brother by the shoulder, shaking him. "Get your bike!"

The man has stopped all forward movement now, and as the boys scramble to get their BMX bikes, he slowly drops to his knees. He stares straight ahead as they pedal toward the edge of the parking lot.

Gasping for breath, the boys pedal furiously toward a dark wooded area next to the parking lot, ducking branches and weaving through the thick underbrush.

Red did start spreading then, staining the kneeling man's white shirt, but no one was around to see it. His labored breath came in a ragged wheeze, and when he coughed, his lips were stained crimson.

The car alarm finally reached its 60-second time limit, and the parking lot descended back into quiet darkness. In slow motion, the man toppled face-forward onto the pavement. He did not move again.

CHAPTER TWO

10 YEARS LATER

Pro lies back, chest heaving. "Fricking amazing, on the Set."

Liz looks at him with half-lidded eyes, still breathing heavily. "What does that even mean?"

Eye roll. "You are so white. It's like *On God,* but I'm swearing on my Set, my gang."

"I went to school with plenty of black kids, and they never said that."

Protean looks over at her with the kind of disdain only poor kids can have for rich kids. "What, a bunch of privileged lightskins in Edmond? You ever come down to Hillcrest you'd hear it."

She sits up in bed, not bothering to cover herself with the sheets, and leans over him with a playful smile. "OK, OK, you convinced me. You're a hood N-" She stops when he frowns. "What? You say it!"

He shakes his head, "Naw, that's not cool babe."

She leans over further, putting her chest right in front of his face. "That's stupid." She sways back and forth. "You want to play with these, but I can't say what you say?" The corners of her mouth quirk upward. "That's stupid, *on the Set.*"

He groans and sits up, his well-muscled physique easily pushing her athletic but lighter body out of the way. "Oh, my Gawd, just stop."

She pouts, "I'm just trying to learn your language, honey."

"I'm not -*we* are not like a quirky subspecies to be studied and laughed about." He faces away from her, and the powerful muscles across his back tense up. "And I'm not hood anymore, so if that's your thing..."

With him facing away, she drops the pout and adopts a more neutral tone, "C'mon Pro. Culture is what I do, you know that."

He stands to his full six-foot-two inches and turns to face her, every one of his muscles on full display. "Oh, I know what you do," he raises an eyebrow, "and you do it well."

She smiles and moves as if to crawl across the bed toward him.

He grabs a nearby towel and wraps it around himself. "But it's not just like learning Arabic or one of your other languages. It isn't just something funny to say, either. It has meaning, every bit of it." He looks down at a poorly done tattoo on his upper left arm, a stylized 'S' inside a money bag, "And getting it wrong, like false claiming my set," he throws two fingers and a thumb out and holds them in a particular symbol with practiced ease, "could get you killed."

Turning from her, he pushes open the accordion doors of their shared closet, forcing aside memories of his youth with the same motion. The closet is neatly arranged into his-and-hers sides, a selection of designer dresses and high heels on her half, and neatly pressed shirts and slacks hanging on his. The closet's center is much more similar, with their Army National Guard OCP Uniforms hanging side-by-side. The primary difference is that hers have Captain bars on the front, while his display Sergeant's stripes.

He reaches for an ensemble fresh from the dry cleaners, a dark grey wool matching suit, and a sky-blue shirt. When he tears off the thin plastic wrap, a pleasant scent of cleanliness reaches his nose. It smells like success, like being on the up and up.

"You coming today?" He asks her as he reaches for a silk tie with a discrete swirl pattern.

Lounging on her side in the sheets behind him, watching the muscles in his back tense and ripple, she bites her lip. Her response is quick and playful, "Oh, I already did..."

Still facing away, he rolls his eyes but can't help a little smirk. "You know what I mean."

She doesn't reply right away, and he thinks she will say no. She is a devout atheist and often makes use of her Sundays for Yoga or a lengthy run. He likes to go together, to feel like a family but finds it hard to argue against anything that keeps her body that well-toned.

"Yeah. I'll come," she says.

Wait for it, he thinks. A highly intellectual woman, Elizabeth Myers has a reason for everything she does.

"I want to see the dispersion between those who sing devoutly or just go through the motions."

Turning to head toward the shower, he stops mid-stride and looks at her. "Are you kidding me?"

She stands from the bed and walks almost directly at him to reach the closet, displaying her considerable charms unabashedly. "I think it is delineated by age. There is a certain demographic in the middle..."

Irritation with her words overcomes his desire to watch her walk, and he steps toward the bathroom. "Just stop."

She continues with her theory as she selects clothes from

the closet. "I'm serious; generational transference of belief is dying out."

Looking in the large bathroom mirror, he tries to shut her words out, but a flash comes to mind of him and all his siblings sitting in a pew when he was younger.

Mamma cries, hands raised towards Jesus. His twin sister Phaedra sings earnestly - while Trey pulls a joint out of his pocket.

He looks in the mirror at a clean-shaven, clean-cut 24-year-old face. It's the visage of a college-educated, military man, a man who has struggled mightily to make good. He tries to leave the past in the past, but the memory is strong, and it takes over.

A younger version of himself, bored during the sermon. Mama praying because Pop is freshly locked up again. Him half-praying in his head, 'Let my dad get out soon.' No answer.

Standing outside the church, looking at the tall white building. It becomes nighttime, and he is up close to the wall, tagging the white expanse.

Trey laughing beside him. "Crip, you in church on Sunday, but always on the Set."

P ro and Liz get to the large Baptist church 20-minutes early, and he parks the newer Impala in the side lot. Liz makes him keep it running until the soft-boiled music of her latest favorite *Monsters and Men* song ends.

He can't help looking back at the immaculate car as they walk toward the brick building. Gleaming 20-inch wheels, jet-black paint. He can't see the 15-inch speakers in the trunk, but knowing they are there brings a bump of joy to his heart. The stuff Liz plays on it these days is hardly worth turning the amp on for, but he still bumps it every now and then when he's alone.

Beside him in a long white dress with thin red stripes and

red high-heels, Liz sighs theatrically, "I swear you like that car more than me."

"I do," he jokes.

He used to tell her not to wear red around him but got tired of being called a Neanderthal. A light blue Carolina Tarheels vanity plate on the front of his car subtly broadcasts his Crip roots. But there's no one else around who cares about gang colors, and he feels silly for giving them meaning.

The building side-door has a number-pad next to it, and he effortlessly punches the code in from memory. Inside, they find themselves in a long foyer and see a middle-aged man in slacks and a slightly rumpled shirt materialize from an interior door.

"Protean!" He pushes his hand forward for a firm handshake. "Wow, looking sharp." He hesitates as if trying to figure out how to say the next part.

Knowing what he is thinking, Pro smooths the front of his suit with his left hand and counters the unspoken assertion. "I think it's important these kids learn attention to detail, and this makes for a great conversation piece."

The man pretends not to wince at Pro's crushing grip when they shake hands and smiles a bit uncomfortably. "If you say so." While his expression is guarded, the assistant pastor looks like he wants to go tell mommy the diversity pick is out of line again. "We like to keep it casual with the youth group. You know kids these days..." he trails off, and Protean wonders what he could possibly know about the subject. "Young people are hard to keep in church," the man finishes unhelpfully.

Young people don't like douchebags. Pro manages to keep the observation to himself. He pours on the affability instead, spreading his even white teeth in a wide grin. "Just mixing it up a bit, Bob." He puts his hand on Elizabeth's arm. "Unconventional warfare, that's what we do. In our day job, right babe?"

His girlfriend could have been a powerful and disarming ally in that moment. A quick smile, stepping forward to draw the sheltered man's attention. She could have easily put them in the winner's circle. *A power couple.*

Elizabeth is both situationally aware and intelligent enough to easily grasp the nuance of the conversation and play off of Protean's gesture. A single word from Captain Elizabeth Myers would have cemented both their alliance and mysterious technique in simple Bob's mind, but she follows her own agenda.

Staying well away from the man's personal space, remaining aloof and unalluring despite her beauty, she addresses him like a researcher, "Bob," her tone is factual and dispassionate, "do you find that adolescents between the ages of around 11 and 17 do not sing along with the hymns?"

"What?" His eyes swing toward Elizabeth's face. Halfway toward going along with Protean's methods of leading the Youth Group, his momentum is now derailed by her question.

Groaning inwardly, Pro tightens his grip on her arm while keeping the grin fixed on his face. "Hey, Liz, looks like the coffee bar just opened."

Barely interested in the exchange in the first place, she is more than happy to take the hint. "Ooooh, coffee!" With a mischievous wink at Pro, she makes a beeline down the hall as if caffeine has suddenly become the most important thing in her life. Having completely skipped using her sex appeal as a weapon in conversation, as soon as she moves past the man, she lets her hips sway seductively as she moves down the hall, distracting *him* instead of Bob.

C'mon, Liz.

It's always like this with her. The two both enjoy a high

level of intelligence and being in a relationship with her is like playing chess. Sometimes she lets him win, but even then, she manages to remind him he owes her one.

"What's she talking about?" The less mentally agile man is still trying to get up to speed.

"Don't worry about it," Pro says. "She was raised by hippies. Still trying to figure out how church works." He lets his voice carry down the hall after her and is rewarded for his efforts when a hand at her side, half-hidden by the folds of her dress, discretely extends a middle finger.

Pro puts a hand on the man's shoulder and guides him in the other direction. "Let's talk about my idea for Wednesday night."

"I bet you're thinking basketball. Am I right?" Without waiting for confirmation, the man continues, "We need something big so they will invite their friends. I bet you are really good at basketball..." He trails off when he sees the look on the larger man's face.

"I don't even play basketball," Pro lies, deadpan. The silent implication hangs in the air between them. *Racist.*

The man looks confused and embarrassed all at the same time. "Uh, I thought..."

Pro doesn't offer forgiveness or even acknowledge the man's misstep; he just moves smoothly on to his plan. "Fortnite, Bob. We are going to have a Fortnite championship."

As they walk into the sanctuary, Pro tries to explain to Bob what the immensely popular game is. The lead pastor, Michael Jensen, raises a hand in a friendly greeting from where he performs sound-checks on stage, and Pro waves back.

He is accepted here. Respected, even. A valuable member of the church. While not a paid pastor like the older men, he is ordained into the ministry and helping modernize the entrenched Baptist institution. They love him for it and are always happy to show off their diversity on the printed programs each week, new member welcome packets. His face is everywhere.

Future of the franchise?

Stopping for a moment at the back of the sanctuary, he imagines his younger self in the front pew, bored and trying to stay awake after running the streets all night. With long practice, he forces away thoughts of the streets, focusing on his mother's face instead. Scared and furious at the same time, her words had pierced his soul. *You gotta get right, Protean, do good. Off them streets, no more banging, I mean it! You took a life. Now you owe one. You owe God a life, Pro.*

His mind snaps back to the present, half a state and a decade away from that fateful night. He smooths his suit and walks toward his church boss with a smile.

I'm doin' it, Mama. I'm doin' good.

"See, Paul, he was an OG – an Original Gangster. He was running around killing Christians, getting that street cred, getting that paper from the Romans."

Fifty teenagers stare back at him with rapt attention. *NOT.*

Two 15-year-old boys are twisted in their chairs, trying to flirt with a cute redhead high school senior. She is irritated by their antics but young enough to be flattered even by unwanted attention. About half of the kids, which is to say a whole eight souls, stare at their phones like zombies. One girl holds her hand under her chin for a moment while she smiles beatifically, then immediately resumes her slack expression while she posts the picture.

#Churchselfie

Pro takes a deep breath and tries to draw strength from the four or five youth who are at least half listening. He continues the inner-city parable, trying to keep them interested.

"Now if God was on the *South Side*," for emphasis, he briefly twists his index and pointer finger into a curve, the stylized 'S' repping his old neighborhood. *Like these rich kids would know. I could throw sign language, and they would think it was gangster.* Reminding himself not to hate them, he continues. "If God was a Loco, he would have been rolling up on Paul for revenge."

Maybe one or two more have looked up to watch his hands, and he tries to capitalize on it. Shaping his hand like a gun, he holds it sideways and makes a popping noise at them, "POP! POP-POP!" The sound is loud in the room, and he feels a jolt of adrenaline. Rap lyrics spring to mind, and he punctuates the gunshots with "Mother–" before catching himself.

That gets their attention, and he moves quickly to sink the message while their heads are up. "But God had a plan for Paul, and it wasn't to hit him up. God *forgave* Paul and used him to reach countless people."

Using words like God and forgiveness turns off a light switch behind their eyes, and their attention visibly moves back toward their phones as if by a powerful magnetic force.

Maybe you should have just gone ahead and cussed at them.

A sudden flashback rips through him, guns blasting, noises. *Blood. Fear.* This time there's no purple truck, though. Instead, his family is lined up in front of his gun, and he just keeps firing no matter how much he wants to stop. He shakes his head to clear the images, shivering despite the layers of his suit. The images fade, but a sense of sadness lingers.

His own phone starts buzzing in his pocket, and he frowns. Anyone who might be calling him should be in the main service. *Did I run over on time?* He pulls it out to silence the buzzing and stops when he sees the message.

"Mom needs you."

It is from a number he doesn't have saved as a contact, but the 405-area code means Oklahoma City. A mixture of emotions well up, anger among them. Anger at his old life for always coming back to haunt him.

He almost slips the phone back in his pocket. If mom needs money again, it can wait another few minutes. The device buzzes again, and it feels jarring in his hand, warning.

"CALL NOW!"

"Hey, Pastor Pro, thought we were supposed to be off our phones in here." It's the redhead, taking a shot at him for being a hypocrite.

He only half hears her, his mind racing to conjure up worst-case scenarios. He hammers out a quick text. *"Who is this?"*

"Fade. CALL MOM."

His twin sister. They hadn't spoken much since he joined the Army and moved three hours away to Tulsa. They had words. It had gotten ugly. Fear wells up inside him about why she would be reaching out like this. Before he could reply, her next text came through.

"It's bad."

Mumbling something about an emergency, he heads for the door to the room. He scrolls to a contact named "Mama" and hits the call button. Fade may have switched numbers, but hers should be the same.

The hallway and foyer are deserted except for an older lady cleaning up the coffee bar. The drink station is at the far end of the hall, and he decides the distance between them is enough privacy. He leans against the wall, heart rate climbing. The ringing tone seems to go on forever, and he realizes his left hand is clenching open and shut.

She picks up on the fourth ring, but the sound he hears is

confusing. It sounds like a wounded animal, but none he can readily identify.

"Mama?"

"Ahhhhhhwwwwghhh!" The sound is horrible. Angry, piercing, but most of all mournful. There is cursing and crying in the background, but the wail drowns everything out.

Alarmed, he half-shouts into the phone, "MOM, What's wrong?" The elderly lady looks up questioningly from her cleaning cloth, but he ignores her.

The wail becomes words, "MY BABY'S DEAAAAAAD!" The last word draws out, using the last oxygen in her lungs, degenerating into a heart-rending cry.

Pro's heart stops, and the walls around him suddenly seem like a prison trapping him, collapsing in. "What?" Denial was automatic. Anger and grief surge, but his mother has several children who still bang. He is desperate to know which one she means, "WHO?"

She takes in a gasp of air and then lets out another wail, "Tommmieeee!"

NONONO! His mind rebels against it. Tommie is too young to even be hanging around with the gang, let alone get caught up in some bullshit. "NO! He's only nine. He ain't even out there like that!" He yells it into the phone, trying to convince his mother.

A voice in the background of his mother's wailing gets louder, "That Pro? Let me talk to that–" A second later, a man's voice, surprisingly not Trey, comes on the phone, high-pitched with grief and anger, "They hit us up, bro! We were headed out to church, and they rolled right up on us! They got him, bro. They hit up Tommie..." The man's voice is overtaken by emotion, and he can't finish the thought. But the truth of the situation passes into Protean even as he wills it not to.

Denial of the nightmare surges. "No! He's just a kid!" *Was a kid.* Hot on the heels of unacceptance, anger roars out of the base of his skull. Anger at whoever shot his kid brother blending with rage at his family for staying in that life. He had left the gang behind him, but they were all still right there. *And this happens.*

Helplessness blends with the anger, and he paces blindly in the hall. He squeezes his eyes shut and lets the anger surge through him. "GOD DAMN IT!"

A sharp intake of breath causes him to open his eyes, and he sees the elderly lady rearing back from him in horror.

He grimaces in apology. "Sorry." My brother just died." The impossible words crash out before he can stop them.

The judgment in her eyes shifts slightly towards pity, and she nods as if she understands. But saying the words out loud causes an even bigger avalanche of anger and grief to well up in him. Feeling horrendously trapped, he bolts for the front door of the house of God before exploding in a burst of profanity and violence. He loses himself for a bit, screaming through blurred vision at the neat rows of cars in the parking lot.

"You have to come back," his twin says. Her voice is quiet and controlled but with depths of emotion reverberating in it. "You are, right?"

The question is half an accusation, as if she expects him to say no even though it is only a three-hour drive. Sitting on the curb at the edge of the church parking lot, he watches the people streaming out of the building towards their BMW SUVs and high-priced minivans. Tears blur his vision, and he idly compares his slick black whip to their vehicles. Rims, slick paint, beats. His mind desperately needs something safe to think about.

"Yeah, of course," he pretends like there is no decision, even though a part of him doesn't want to go, "For the... you know." He can't say the word *funereal*.

The Impala pivots in his mind to rolling down the streets of the South Side. In the parking lot here, people look at it as a curiosity, *or a nuisance, to be honest.* But in that low-income area, it will be both a symbol of wealth and a target. *A man could build a Set around a ride like this.*

"Good..." She says that word but her voice quavers before she can say anything else. Phaedra has always been a hardass. Her name means bright, but her life has been dark ever since she was 12. The substance of that darkness threatens to boil into his present thoughts.

Don't. Pro punches those surfacing memories in the face and stuffs them back in a box. *She's the strongest person I know, a warrior, not a victim.*

"I'm coming. I got you, Fade." He knows his twin will not say she needs him now just as surely as he knows that she does.

"Hey!" A female voice calls across the parking lot, and he sees Liz heading his way with a confused look on her face. As she moves closer, she looks a question at the suit jacket lying crumpled beside him, half hanging in the dirt.

"I gotta go," he says hurriedly into the phone. The desire to be strong surges. Broad shoulders. Handle anything. Invincible.

"What?" Phaedra's voice rises an octave, and the plaintive tone makes it even more clear she needs him.

"I'm coming," he reassures her. Liz is almost to him, and he hangs up without waiting for an answer.

A playful smile dies on her lips when his girlfriend of two years gets close enough to see his face. "Oh my god, are you OK?"

The genuine concern replacing her familiar smirk is a

hammer blow. For the briefest of moments, irrationally, he thought he might be able to preserve his world. Maybe he and Liz could go out to lunch and leave his family in the past?

Tears flow. Wailing. She sits beside him on the curb, soiling the creamy color of her dress. He feels bad about that, like it's his fault. She puts her hand on his shoulder and rubs his back while he cries. It feels good, comforting, like Mama telling him everything is going to be alright. But he hates himself for the small amount of good it makes him feel.

His baby brother is dead. *Nothing will ever be right again.*

CHAPTER THREE

A roomful of detectives crowd around a long table. A massive map of Oklahoma City occupies the wall at one end, but while a few look at it, most are engrossed in their phones.

The door opens, and an older man in a tan suit strides purposefully in. A black leather folder and two cell phones are balanced in his right hand, and a tall coffee cup is carefully cradled in his left. He expertly nudges the door closed with his foot and starts talking before he even reaches the empty chair at the head of the table.

"Homicide this morning." He plops the stack of items in his right hand on the table, then subconsciously uses the same hand to guide the Glock at his hip around the armrest of the chair as he sits down. "Hillcrest."

Several people speak simultaneously, the loudest of which is a mid-30s male slouching in his chair with an amused expression. "Fricking *Hillcrest again*?" He smiles and nudges the man next to him. "Just let 'em shoot it out for a while. They kill enough of each other, and it'll die down."

Tan suit looks reproachfully at the man.

He is unrepentant, laughing and spreading his arms. "You know I'm right, Cap'n."

"It was a kid, Conners," the supervisor states flatly.

"Oh, damn." Detective Conners mutes his jovial attitude into something almost approaching guilt and dispassionately condemns the slaying, "Fricking animals."

A female detective leans forward. "How young?"

Captain Barnes sighs heavily and cracks open the black folder to read his sparse notes. "Nine. Officers on scene are saying drive-by."

"On a *kid*?" The woman's eyes narrow in disbelief.

Captain Barnes looks at the information in front of him, "Vic is Tommie Williams. The family is completely unhelpful. Refusing to cooperate, basically."

"Sounds like Hillcrest," Conners' voice is happy, almost joyful. "We sure it wasn't accidental? Maybe they were high and playing with their gats? Probably accidentally cranked one off and are now trying to say, *oh, it was a driveby!*" His voice goes into a falsetto at the end, and he waves his hands at shoulder height in mock dismay.

Barnes grunts at the nearly empty page in front of him, then picks up his phone to scroll back through some texts. He raises his eyebrows and then quotes from the phone dryly, "Forty bullet holes and counting... shell casings scattered up and down the parking lot... yeah, I think we can rule out accidental." He looks pointedly at Conners.

"Look, I'm just saying it wouldn't be the first time," the man says defensively. He snaps his fingers as if remembering something. "Williams. Last name Williams, right?" Without waiting for a reply, he starts volunteering information, "We got a gang member last week. Crashed out in a pursuit. Was leaving the vicinity of a drive-by on the Locos. Last name Williams, a confirmed Crip. Maybe it's related?"

Barnes shrugs. "You tell me, Mr. Gang Unit. You want

this? I was about to give it to Contreras." He nods at the woman who asked the victim's age.

Conners physically backs his chair away from the table, palms raised in front of him. "What? Hell no. Williams is a common name, and that pursuit was nowhere near Hillcrest." Perhaps realizing that his empty excuses sound exactly like what they are, he switches tactics, "Cap, I've got a dozen active gang cases right now, all shootings. Even if this does turn into something we can follow, which we both know it won't, I don't have time to run it."

The woman leans in front of Conners, making herself the obvious choice. "You've been promising me a Murder One," she says to Barnes, indicating the heavy charge this crime warrants, "and I grew up near there, maybe the family will talk to me?"

The Captain hesitates and looks around the room as if to consider other options. Everyone else is playing the gray-man, though, carefully avoiding giving any indication they want the heavy workload associated with a murder case. Several would typically jump at the chance for a homicide, but everyone in the room knows this one will likely go unsolved, especially with the family playing hard-to-get.

Barnes' eyes come back to rest on Contreras and briefly alternate between her and Conners, considering. They stop on Contreras. "You got Primary. See if you can get the family to give you something to go on. If they don't, there's a reason, so canvas the neighbors not only about the shooting but about the family."

She nods and makes a show of writing that down. She knows if she lets on why she really wants this case, Barnes won't let her anywhere near it.

Barnes is still talking. "No matter how many people get shot there, we know Hillcrest won't shell out the cash to put in video surveillance. But maybe we'll get lucky, and some of the stores nearby will have a vehicle coming in and out of there."

She writes that down, too, without giving any indication that was already in her plan. Sometimes it pays to be a good listener.

Barnes turns toward Conners. "I'm putting you on it as secondary." He raises his hand to stop the detective from objecting, "I know it was before your time, but I got my start in gangs. A Crip gets arrested after a drive-by, and now a known Crip apartment complex is getting shot up? C'mon, you know it's gang-related."

"It's Southwest OKC. Everything's gang-related!" Conners blurts out. His face is a little red from the Captain's treatment.

"And a kid is dead, Marshall," He uses the man's first name, trying to reach him on a personal level, "probably not the intended target, but he's still dead. So we are going to do our best to get him justice, right?"

The question is rhetorical, and the man moves his eyes to continue issuing orders to the rest of the room. "Crowe, Gomez, Vassar, Griggs, you are all on standby to support." He tips his head toward Detective Contreras. "If Isabella gets a lead and reaches out for help, helping her becomes your new top priority."

The boss's phone starts to buzz, and he looks displeased when he sees the caller ID. "Shit. The Major. The news must already be on it." He cradles the ringing phone in his hand, using the first couple of rings to squeeze a few last moments out of the meeting. He addresses the last part directly to Isabella, "Get your boot in some asses," he nods almost imperceptibly toward Conners, "Whoever's asses need it. Let's bust this thing open and make a case of it."

The man stands, answering the phone as he leaves the room, "Yes sir, already have a team assigned... Yes, sir..."

The room bursts into motion as everyone comes to their feet. Most are just making a beeline back for their office, relieved they did not catch the case, but Conners sighs heavily.

"Don't worry, I'll do all the hard work," Isabella says peevishly.

He frowns and looks at his phone, more to avoid eye contact than because there is any reason to do so. "That's not it."

He does not elaborate, so she starts toward the door. "Whatever. I'm going to pee while I have the chance. Take my car?"

He agrees testily. "Sure, I'll ride bitch."

With her gone, he is the last person in the room. He grumbles quietly to the air, "Already am, anyway."

In the bathroom, Isabella's control shatters, and she rushes into a stall and starts heaving. She doesn't even get the stall door shut and barely manages to pull her hair up in time.

Tommie Williams. A vision of a kid at her boyfriend's boxing match comes back to her. His kid brother rushing up to give him a hug after he won. *Couldn't have been more than two or three then.*

Sagging weakly against the metal wall of the stall, she fights back the tears and hopes it's not the same kid.

The age is right, though. Hillcrest. Has to be him.

With a seven-year-old son of her own, the last thing she wants to do is go look at a brutally murdered child, but she knows closing a case like this is next to impossible. You have to actually care. To want it bad enough to go the extra mile. The memory of the grinning toddler comes back to her, of her shaking hands gravely with the little man.

I got you, buddy.

She gathers herself, drawing strength from her imaginary deal with the boy. She has to keep her emotions in complete control because if Captain finds out she knows the victim's family, he will pull her off it with a quickness. Make some slap-dick like Conners Primary to avoid a conflict of interest.

Conners. He is probably wondering what happened to her.

Her hair is in disarray now, and she pulls it into a ponytail at the bathroom mirror. She makes some emergency fixes to her makeup and heads out the door. Ready to go that extra mile.

I care, Tommie.

"You sure you don't want me to?" Liz sits on the bed, arms wrapped around her bare legs, wishing she could help. "I should be there."

Pro takes a pair of pressed jeans off a hanger and places them neatly in the overnight bag. He controls his movements just like his emotions, calm on the outside while screaming inside his head.

"Naw. It's good, babe. I have to do this alone." He feels guilty for excluding her, but he doesn't want her anywhere near his old life. *His old self.* "It's going to be really small, just family."

She chews on her lip, not knowing what to say.

He knows what he wants to say but doesn't dare to. *You are my good life, Elizabeth Myers. Stable relationship, good jobs, a future.* He glances at her dress, now lying in a heap in the corner of the room with the dirty patch from the curb visible. *I can't let you get wrecked too.*

"I love you." She says it as a statement, but he knows it is also a question. She needs affirmation. Needs to know that he is not running away from her.

He steps closer to her, and on impulse, leans over and scoops her up in his arms. She is built like a gymnast, with no more than 115lbs in her lacy underwear, and he easily picks her off the bed. He kisses her like he means it before replying simply, "I love you too."

She feels good in his arms and visibly melts with an eyelash fluttering smile. Unable to bear the beautiful moment of wholeness and warmth in his current state of mind, he wrecks it. He mischievously uses the hand under her back to unsnap her bra.

She squeals and scrambles to capture the garment as the elastic causes it to snap away from her like a rubber band. He uses the opportunity to dump her unceremoniously back onto the bed.

"Stop it!" She complains.

He moves back to the bag, placing a few last items in before he zips it shut, using the time while she regathers herself to try to swallow the lump in his throat.

She refastens the undone clasp and rearranges herself at the head of the bed, then pulls one of the large pillows in front of herself for extra protection. But he is done playing, and when he throws the bag over his shoulder and looks up, she realizes he is about to leave. Neither of them says anything for a moment, and when she speaks, it is very softly and gently. "I'll be here when you get back, K?"

He tries to give her a roguish line, but it comes out closer to a mournful note, "You'd better be." The lump comes back, and unable to say anything else, he takes a backward step toward the bedroom door.

Either realizing he isn't going to attack her again or feeling a sudden urge to entice him back, she tosses the pillow aside, giving him a good look at what he is leaving behind.

That earns her one last small smile, then he is gone.

He walks to the Impala without looking back. It feels like he is leaving his home, budding youth ministry, career, the love of his life. Leaving everything behind and heading into an old darkness. He pictures Liz on the bed a moment before.

I need you here. Guarding my good life.

The past he has run from pulls him back into sadness, into death. Draws him dangerously close to old feelings, old sins, and he needs something pure to return to.

Guarding my redemption.

Elizabeth's spineless pop music drifts on low volume from the powerful sound system as he hits the highway. He turns it up a bit and lets it flow, reminding him of her. He holds onto the feeling of her in his arms, tries not to remember what it was like the last time he hugged Tommie.

When he accelerates up onto the interstate, a wave of loneliness and trepidation hits him. The road is straight as an arrow, stretching into the distance. His hands start shaking on the wheel as the thought registers in his brain that he is physically headed straight for Oklahoma City now. He sees Tommie as a baby, then a toddler, running around their apartment in a diaper.

Guilt for not going back more often piles up and fills the Impala's passenger seat, clawing at him accusingly. Looking for relief, he flips the radio over to something harder, lands on a classic rock station. Not the music he grew up with, but ACDC makes it hard to be sad.

After *it* happened, he had grabbed on hard to what his mother had said. He was always a bright kid, he started sleeping at night instead of banging the streets, going to summer school to catch up to where he should be. His hard work and determination paid off, and he managed to start on time as a high school freshman in the fall.

Everyone in Hillcrest knew a couple of kids had shot a dude, but the grainy surveillance video from the nearby gas station wasn't good enough to actually provide a suspect. That night he and Trey had ditched the gun and torn backpack in a culvert in the woods. When they got home and told Mama, she had made them swear to never tell anyone else.

You owe God a life now, Protean.

Trey never ratted Pro out, and in time began to let people believe *he* may have been the mystery shooter. Trey wanted that body, wanted that notoriety, and was happy to take it after the homicide investigation had long since gone cold. Over the next few years, Trey followed in his father's footsteps, banging Crips even harder, while Protean did his best to steer clear and focus on school.

Right before reaching adulthood, Trey had gotten caught up with some older gang members and picked up his first batch of felonies. Weapons, drugs, assault and battery, the list grew steadily, and soon he did his first year in the Prison, but Trey reveled in the prestige. With Trey in and out of lockup and Pop doing twenty-to-life for a shoot, things got rough at home. Mom got an abusive new boyfriend, and Pro tried to stay away from home as much as possible.

When Pro turned 16, he found an outlet for his anger and frustration in the boxing ring. A smart fighter, he punched his way right into the Golden Gloves, and people started to think his nickname Pro was because of his talent in the ring. He met his first serious girlfriend, a fiery female Latina fighter.

The miles roll by under the Impala as he lets the memories flow. Remembering his late teen years gets his blood pumping. Bouts in the ring and nights with his First. He rolls down the car window and turns up the rhythmic music. It feels good. Feels young and free.

P haedra Williams huddles in the bedroom with her two girls, arms around them, shaking silently. Half a dozen holes are visible in the wall that faces the parking lot. There is a thick black blanket covering the window, but glass from the shattered portal sparkles on the carpet.

Selena and Seriah don't say anything; just let her hold them. At 7 and 4, they are still in shock at the terrible events of the morning.

She squeezes, then releases them, and kneels on the stained carpet. They are sitting on the edge of the bunk bed they share, only a few feet from her twin bed in the cramped bedroom. A toppled pile of folded clothes occupies part of the floor, further diminishing the available space.

"Y'all OK?"

They both nod silently, looking sad in the unsure way of children who know something bad has happened but don't know how to process it.

Of course they aren't OK, Fade, she silently admonishes herself. *Their uncle, who they were playing Minecraft with just last night, is dead outside.*

"Mama loves you, you know that right."

They nod again, and this time the youngest, Seriah, responds in her baby girl voice. "I luv u, Mommy."

Heart full, she hugs her baby again, then straightens. "I have to take care of some things now. I want you to go be with Gina for a while, OK?

Selena digs her hands into the threadbare comforter and moans, "I want youuuu."

Her heart is breaking, but Phaedra really needs them outside, needs them gone. "I'll give her money for candy, K? You can walk to the store with her." Thinking about how she doesn't want her girls walking down the street, she revises her promise, "Actually, she'll go get some."

The girls protest more, but it is non-negotiable, and they are running out of time. The cadence of authoritative voices out front is like a ticking time bomb.

Her bribing proves sufficient to secure the little ones'

cooperation, and she spirits them out the back door. She holds Selena's hand and carries the 4-year-old on her hip, expertly navigating the dirt, trash, dog feces, and occasional furniture in the narrow space between the back doors to apartments and the dilapidated fence at the property line. The expected alley smell mixes with tendrils of marijuana smoke coming from several residences.

Her throat is tight as she takes the girls to hand them off, wanting nothing more than to be close with them right now, but an invisible urgency drives her.

Gina Han was the owner of the once-proud Hillcrest Apartment complex. An immigrant from China, she and her husband had somehow located the property and bought it sight-unseen when they moved to America. They probably thought it was a great deal, not understanding the neighborhood it was in. A tough couple, they had never turned their back on the American Dream, and Mr. Han had been a meticulous repairman while Gina managed the books and harangued the residents for rent. When her husband died, part of Gina died with him, and the complex fell into disrepair she was largely helpless to prevent. Now the rent is negotiated by unit, in some cases lowered drastically for damaged amenities or a particularly persuasive tenant – like Phaedra. Each year more units become uninhabitable, and many already sit empty.

When Gina comes to the back door, she is pissed. "You bring this shooting?" She waves at the parking lot in front of her unit. "I tell Damarion no shooting here!"

Fade ignores the griping about the obvious problem, working quickly to try to solve the unobvious. "Gina, my girls need to stay with you while *they* are here." She nods her head obviously at the parking lot, indicating the cops.

"What?" The savvy old lady is not a hint-taker.

Damn it, you old hag. After all the money I pay you... Fade tries again, speaking clearly, trying to lay out the benefit to the woman, "Gina, I will pay you twenty bucks if you let my girls stay here all day until I come to get them."

"Tweny dollar?" The woman's eyes narrow.

"We are gonna have candy. Mama said," Selena makes her stake in the matter clear.

"Candy!" Seriah echoes happily.

If possible, Gina's eyes narrow even further. She loves the girls but can't help but haggle – it's what she does. "Twenty not enough for babysit and candy."

Sensing the deal is already going south, a low moan starts in Seriah's throat as Phaedra sets her down. "Idonwannna..."

I don't have time for this! Phaedra reaches into her bra, expertly extracting two twenty-dollar bills while leaving the rest of the money hidden. "Here. Babysit *and* candy," with no time for haggling, she practically forces the money on Gina, "All day, OK?"

Gina's eyes un-narrow slightly, and she cracks the sliding glass door to let the girls into her neatly organized apartment. "OK. OK, girls, you lika watch cartoon?" The youngsters sniff with a slight uplifting of spirits and step around a maze of small potted plants to get into the back door.

Phaedra smiles encouragingly at them when they look back, but as soon as the vertical slats of the curtain fall into place, she bolts back toward her own apartment. Dodging through the narrow space, she bumps against an old and broken washer someone has thrown out back. A faded and cracked plastic bin full of rusted tools sways precariously on the lid of the appliance, and she worries momentarily that it will clatter to the ground and betray her position.

Re-entering the house, she looks at the collection of people mourning in the living room.

Mama is a mess, which is pretty close to her baseline anyway. She slumps on the couch, crying and moaning steadily despite a double dose of Xanax and a valium. Aliyah, Tommie's 10-year-old half-sister, sits in complete shock next to her insensate mother, staring straight ahead as tears slowly stream from her face.

Poor girl hasn't said anything since…

Both 17 years old, Deuce and Jiggy crowd the room, cursing and pacing. Deuce has one of his guns, a silver semi-auto, in his hand and taps the barrel at an angle against his forehead. "My lil-G, bro!" He looks toward the front of the house, and his voice twists in grief and frustration as he repeats the words, with extra emphasis, "My LITTLE-G!"

Ice sits motionless in the kitchen, watching the tableau with a black pistol in his lap. He is her full brother and actual family but is known for never showing emotion. Their older half-brother Damareon "Four" Williams is the leader of the gang set, and even with him locked up, his set still treats her family's small apartment like home. *And Tommie like family.*

It's chaos, and she wants to start barking orders, but she can't control all of this. *Focus on what you can control, Fade.*

Deuce slams a heavy hand into Jiggy's shoulder. "Our lil gangster bro!"

Jiggy, a solid 275 lbs., rocks listlessly from the blow, head hanging. The only white member of the gang has stains on his Tupac shirt, marks from an earlier flood of tears. His voice is tortured, "It's fucked up bro…" he looks angrily at the front door, shifting his hoodie to put his hand on his own gun. "An these pigs don't giva shit."

Ice looks at her, his face betraying no emotion. "They good?" His head moves imperceptibly in the direction of the back door, indicating his nieces.

"They good," her response matches his style of speech. She points at the two big men in the living room. "Handle them? The cops are right outside."

Ice looks at Deuce, who is getting loud and moves as if to head out the front door, "Bitches won't do *shit!*"

"I have shit to do," Phaedra hisses to Ice, "and I need the cops to stay out."

Eight years younger than her and only 16, her younger brother is an old soul and well aware of her activities. He understands immediately and rocks to his feet to try to get the other guys under control.

She rushes back into her bedroom, closing the door behind her, keenly conscious that the cops could try to come in at any minute. She stands on the edge of the girl's bunk bed, screwdriver in hand, and quickly unscrews the vent above their bed. Reaching blindly up into the hidden space, she retrieves a small red fishing tackle box.

Trapping it between her knees with practiced ease, she quickly replaces the vent cover. She opens the container briefly, making a visual inventory of the contents organized in their compartments.

35 Xanax, in 4mg bars. The yellow anti-anxiety "Xanibars" are a staple of her business, selling especially well among the younger crowd. At $10 per pill or better, the stock equated $350-500 in sales depending on who was buying.

12 Oxycodone, in 10 mg pills. The small white circles were expensive to get but top-dollar products. With the pain pills going for $40 each, the tiny bag contained almost $500 worth of product.

She removes the top tray to get to the larger bottom compartment. Green leafy buds are clearly visible in two vacuum-sealed bags and a clear glass mason jar. One bag is opened but still mostly full, so she can easily estimate the amount of marijuana remaining.

An ounce of Kush and almost a half-pound of Reggie. The medical-grade Purple Kush would go for about $22 per gram.

Reggie was much cheaper, but the "ditch weed" was still going for $7-10 per gram.

Satisfied everything was still there, she snaps the lid closed and secures the brass latch. Freshly stocked with a street value of over $2,000 of weed and close to another $1,000 in pills, this box is their lifeblood, and the only way she could ensure there would be money for rent, utilities, and food.

Tucking the box under her arm, she opens the bedroom door.

"We just need to come in for a minute and get everyone's information." The officious voice at the front door is a warning klaxon in her mind. She immediately shuts the bedroom door again and locks it.

Shaking, she sits on her daughter's Frozen blanket with the box in her lap. *Prison, Fade. They will hook you up with trafficking charges for what is in this box.*

Emotions that she has been holding in check all morning threaten to spill over, and her hands grip the plastic container. Her arms protect it like it is the sibling she just lost. It doesn't seem fair. She has never shot anyone, never committed a violent crime of any kind, but risks a 7–20-year prison sentence for her efforts to provide for her girls. Keeping a low profile has been sort of easy, with everyone's eyes on the gang, not her. But now the police are right outside, and the bullet holes in the wall behind her mean they are coming inside.

Tears threaten to overwhelm the necessary iron control she exercises, but a knock at the door saves her from that indignity.

"Fade. You good now." The voice belongs to Ice, and she knows she can trust him.

She swings into action, opening the door a crack. His lean face speaks urgently from the other side. "I told them we don't want no visitors right now, but I think he's coming right back."

It may be her only opportunity, and they both know it. She nods a silent thanks as she opens the door fully and makes a beeline for the back of the apartment for a second time. Her mother sees her moving and cries out after her, "Faaaade, come here babeee."

Ignoring her mom's drug and grief-altered cries, she rushes back out into the smelly backside of the complex. There are no fences keeping anyone from entering the ends of the narrow byway, which is why it is great for her customers. But now, the easy access poses an immediate threat, as all it would take is a nosy cop from out front to walk around the end of the long building, and she would be caught.

She moves quickly back toward the old broken washer. When she reaches it, she quickly hefts the heavy tray of rusted sockets and tools and places it on the ground. The musty interior of the appliance smells like mold, and the red case barely fits in end-wise next to the plastic center agitator in the machine.

"Whatsha got there?" The voice behind her makes her jump and give a little cry, and the metal lid of the washer drops shut with a loud clang as she spins around.

"JEEZ- Dale! What the hell!"

The renowned drunk peers at her through leaky red eyes, his lids barely open. "Shiiii, girl. 'S my porch." His words are unsurprisingly slurred, and she wonders if he will even remember this conversation in 10 minutes.

Ignoring him, she reaches down and grabs up the plastic container of tools, placing it back on top of the appliance to weigh the lid down.

"Whatsha got?" He repeats his question, swaying on his feet but laser-focused on what she is doing with the tools.

"Nothing."

"Hiding yer pills?" His beady eyes bore into the side of the washer like X-ray vision.

She grits her teeth at how perceptive the drunk is. Alcohol is his drug of choice, but like any addict, he has a powerful ability to sniff out anything that could make him high. "You stay out of here, Dale."

"Uh-huh, sure." His tone is agreeable, but he totters a step forward as if drawn by an invisible force toward the stash.

Movement out of the corner of her eye splits her attention, and a quick glance back toward her apartment shows Ice beckoning frantically with both hands.

I don't have time for this, she thinks for what must be the twentieth time. "Dale!" She has mere seconds to figure out exactly what needs to happen to keep the man in line. "You stay out of here, or I'll have my brothers kicking in your door." As she is speaking, she takes out her phone and snaps a picture of the random jumble of tools in the plastic container atop the washer, "And if a single piece is out of place in here, I'll know you moved it!"

The picture and the threat register dimly with him, but he licks his lips unconsciously, eyes clearly already working on how he can get around the tool bucket.

Swinging a stick at someone who lives on the bottom doesn't always work, and she reaches for a carrot to sweeten the pot. She makes her voice friendly, "You're a war veteran right? How 'bout you guard this for me. If no one touches it, I'll give you an Oxy."

"Three," his reply is unhesitating, his brain surprisingly agile despite his obvious inebriation.

This dude. Anger rises. "My little brother just died, you piece of shit." Her voice isn't friendly anymore, and she steps directly at him.

A few houses down, Ice is now urgently and loudly whispering her name. *"FADE!"*

"Two, and I keep Ice from shooting you." She says it with a note of finality, knowing she is out of time whether he agrees or not.

He grunts an agreement, and she bolts toward Ice. When she reaches him, she sees his usual calm demeanor is stretched to the breaking point.

"They said they gotta talk to an adult, and if we don't let them in, they are writing a search warrant!" His hand moves subconsciously to the illegal gun weighing down his pocket. She curses, realizing she has an additional round of critical problems to deal with.

She points toward her brother's bulging pocket and beckons impatiently with her fingers. "Quick, gimme your strap."

CHAPTER FOUR

"**Y**ou pretty much grew up in Hillcrest, didn't you?" Lounging in the passenger's seat of her unmarked car as she drives, Detective Conners intends it both as insult and bait.

She tries to ignore both undercurrents, but irritation creeps into her voice, "No, Conners, I did not grow up in the ghetto."

"You told Cap you grew up around there. No need to be embarrassed about it," his tone is one of camaraderie, but the edges of a smirk betray the fact he is indeed poking at her.

She sighs, realizing he will not let it go without some clarification. "I went to US Grant, like 5 blocks from Hillcrest, but it's a big school. My parents had a nice little brick house in a quiet neighborhood nearby."

"Quiet?" He scoffs. "I bet."

"It was a cul-de-sac!"

"Sounds nice," he says it like he is sure it was a shithole.

She takes a breath. "Can we talk about the case? What gang was this Williams guy from the pursuit in?"

His expression becomes guarded. "Crip."

It's her turn to scoff now. "Oh yeah, a Crip? I bet he lived in Oklahoma too. Great intel there, Gang Unit." He looks pissed at her sarcasm, but she doesn't let him off the hook. "I grew up in the ghetto, remember?" She makes air quotes when she says ghetto, "I know Crip is just a broad term. I'm asking what *Set*."

A bit of grudging respect creeps into his expression. Most cops don't even know what a gang set is. He rolls his head sideways to look out the window, trying to decide whether to give her the brush off or actually start going into the detailed tangle of gang structure that is his specialty.

"C'mon, partner," she steps on her pride and makes herself sound like a young girl who wants to be impressed, "I know you are like a walking gang encyclopedia. I know you think it is connected. Share your secrets!"

Flattery works on his type. He tries to look bored but launches in, secretly glad to parade his knowledge. "We got a bit of gang war kicking up. It started a few months ago when a South Side Loco named Sneezy got killed in a drug deal gone bad."

She laughs involuntarily. "Sneezy. Like the dwarf?" *You can't make this stuff up.*

"You want me to tell you are not?"

She changes lanes, dodging through traffic. "Sorry. Please continue."

"So, this dude gets popped, and our snitches say it's the Rollin' Sixties." When he sees her blank expression, he sighs and expands on the background, "Rollin' 60s are the biggest contingent of Neighborhood Crips out here. Nipsy, OG of all Crips back in Cali, he sanctioned 60s here as being legit."

She stays quiet and nods, trying to keep up. In high school, kids talked about Crips and Bloods, wore red or blue, and made signs with their hands. As a cop, she heard about the violent South Side Locos plenty, but didn't know what was fact and what was urban legend.

His brow furrows slightly. "But then we hear that S-Loc, the local Rollin' 60s leader, didn't order that Loco hit and is trying to figure out who did it. So then we start looking at the YGs; they're always trying to make a name for themselves. By far the most dangerous."

"What gang are the YG's?" She asks.

He shakes his head. "Not a gang, a generation. Young Gangsters. These kids are born into it and start out as Baby-G. Around seven to twelve, they graduate to Lil-Gangster, like a hang around, wanting in the gang. Then at around 13-14, they are normally getting jumped-in -officially initiated- then they are a YG, a Little Homie."

"So, you think a 13-year-old kid shot Sleepy the South Side Loco? I thought they were supposed to be hardcore?"

"Oh, they are, trust me," he says. "Very violent, very territorial. Fewer in number than the 60s or GBC, but really volatile. But YGs start hitting 14 and 15 and want to prove themselves. They won't rank up again until about 18-20 unless they put in some serious work, and even then they normally have to do prison time."

All of this is new information to her, and she realizes the man truly is a walking library. Her head is starting to swim with the detail though, and they are only 10 minutes away from Hillcrest. "OK. Let's focus here. How does all of this have to do with Williams, and why do you think it's connected?"

"I was getting to that," he complains before mentally switching gears, "OK, basically we start hearing about a click, a mixture of different gang sets. All Crips that have been involved in a series of back-and-forth retaliatory drivebys over the last several months with the Locos. See, since Sneezy, there have been several more. We get a lead that one of this group is a South Side Playboy Gangsta Crip, a subset of the 60s nicknamed "Four," and that he is planning another move."

In the turn lane for SW 59th Street, approaching Hillcrest, she looks over at him as he names the gang set, but it means nothing to her. She is getting impatient that his wealth of information isn't getting her any closer to understanding the connection.

The gang expert rolls his eyes. "Of course, *I* know that *Hillcrest* has been the home stomping ground for Playboy Crips for at least a decade." He shakes his head as if his intel is pearls before swine. "And I also remember that we had a drug bust, with weapon charges, less than 6 months ago, and the main guy was a certified gang member, a Big Homie the other guys called Four."

They pull onto 59th, and she wrinkles her brow. "I thought you said Little Homies were doing the shootings."

"I said that's what we originally *suspected*, but this new click was of slightly older guys. Smarter but just as violent." On final approach, with only a few blocks to their destination, Conners finally connects the dots on his tale. "Anyway, before we have a chance to dig deeper, we have another drive-by come out, South Side Loco territory. Couple of Gang Unit guys happened to be nearby, already wearing vests, so they head into the area. Three guys bail out of a suspicious car when they see the cops, all running in different directions. But my boys in the Unit are able to chase down the driver."

She turns on her signal to pull into the only entrance of the large, run-down apartment complex. Her mind is already shifting from him to the crime scene they are entering.

He delivers the punchline. "Driver has the word 'Four' tattooed across the front of his neck in huge letters. Admits to being a South Side Playboy Gangsta Crip. Damarion

Williams, address on file in Hillcrest, unit one-hundred-something."

They pull into the looping parking lot and bank right, heading towards several police cruisers and zig-zagging yellow crime scene tape.

"Huh!" Conners smiles broadly beside her, pointing toward the numbers on the apartment door that police are pounding on. "Damn, I'm good."

Irritated that he is happier his hunch proved correct than sad that a kid is dead, she opens her door with unnecessary force and steps out.

A sergeant walks forward with a clipboard in hand, and she absent-mindedly signs the crime scene log.

The cracked and faded numbers on the apartment are 119. A police raincoat is forms a makeshift shroud over a small shape on the ground nearby. Shell casings are scattered across the asphalt, and she makes a mental note to put a yellow marker by each. *Gonna need a lot of markers.* Pockmarks are on the sidewalk and the side of the building. *Looks like at least twenty rounds fired, maybe fifty. Amazing only one person got hit.* The kid is lying close to the sidewalk, and she sees a small pair of clean sneakers and fresh jeans sticking out from under the raincoat. There is blood on the sneakers. She looks away.

P ro's phone is connected to Bluetooth, and a digital ringing sound resounds through the car as he tries to call Phaedra back on the number she called from earlier.

"C'mon, answer me." After three attempts, he steels himself and dials his mother's number. When she doesn't answer either, he starts to worry.

As he crosses the distance between Tulsa and Oklahoma City, the initial shock and grief give way to cold logistics. He needs to plan the nuts and bolts of his stay.

Can I stay on the couch? Do I even want to? Do they need money for the funeral? Probably.

After dwelling for a while on the same cycle of thoughts, other thoughts begin to creep in, mostly unwanted ones. The problem with making something of himself is it meant running away from who he was. He always knew he had run far in the back of his mind. But now, the distance between him and his family feels like the Grand Canyon.

When he graduated, he had gotten a partial scholarship at Oklahoma State University, an hour away in Stillwater. At first, he had come back on weekends to visit his mother and younger siblings, but that soon became only holidays and not all of them.

The real divide happened when he found a way to pay for college. An Army recruiter had found him in his sophomore year and talked him into the National Guard.

One weekend per month, 2 weeks a year, that's it!

The part-time military idea sounded magical initially, and it called to his desires for adventure, to get *out*. But by the time he spent the next two summers doing Basic Combat Training and Advanced Individual Training, his family seemed like another life.

Another life where his youngest brother Tommie, the baby of the family, was growing up without him. Mama would send him pictures and videos sometimes, but the reality was he barely knew the kid.

And now I never will.

The guilt settles on Protean like a heavy, cold blanket. His heart reaches for memories of the young boy, for shared times together, but they are horrifyingly few. He feels like he abandoned the little boy, left him to his fate while he went and played soldier, got a cute girlfriend, a nice car.

You left him to die, Pro. He wants to reject the thought, but there is too much truth in the self-blame. *You left them all to die in that life.*

Anger surges, and he reaches for the radio. The rock and roll station does not feel right anymore. The Oklahoma City skyline hovers in the distance, and his old favorite station seems like the obvious choice. He finds 103.1 on the dial, and Snoop Dog slides into the car with his new hit.

"Vato, you won't believe what I saw..." The sounds of gunshots mix with the lyrics on the track and Pro turns it up.

"Yeah, here we go," he lets his head start thumping with the music and turns it up. The 15-inch subwoofers in the trunk are happy to finally be set free and start thumping in good earnest as he turns off the Interstate.

"I saw these guys, and they acting real hard."

Slowing as he swings out onto 59th St, he rolls down the windows and shares the wealth.

The music thumps, his heart beats, and the familiarity of the neighborhood starts to pump through his veins. He tries to forget why he is back and just look at what has changed in the last decade. Not much has.

T rying to act like they just started knocking instead of having been pounding for several minutes, Phaedra lets the dam holding her emotions back crack and opens the door to their apartment.

The cop on the concrete front stoop looks polite but pissed. "Ma'am. We need to come inside."

She sniffs, worried briefly the flood of tears won't come in time. Seeing the still form just beyond the man, she is instead overcome with emotion.

"Noooooo," she starts to wail, giving herself permission to feel the impact of what she knows happened. She stumbles forward half a step, leaning toward the cop, who catches her out of instinct. "Tommieeee," she lets herself cry loudly, both acting and grieving at the same time while the boys hide their guns.

"Jeez." The man supports her weight and looks over his shoulder for help from another nearby officer.

The other officer wears Sergeant stripes and steps forward with a firm voice. "Get her back inside, man. She doesn't need to see this."

Falling apart with grief and in no hurry to get inside, the grieving big sister makes a scene of it in the doorway. "I wanna seeee hiiim," she wails. She is dimly aware of two more people approaching, a man and a woman, wearing guns but not in uniform.

The man stops and peeks under the raincoat. He speaks quietly to himself, "Yep. Dead."

The woman scowls at him and walks past the body to reach the hysterical young woman. She stands between the woman and her dead family member, blocking the view, and engages her with a gentle voice. "Ma'am, I am Detective Isabella Contreras, and I am truly sorry for your loss."

The grieving woman collapses in the door frame, sitting crossways with her feet against the jamb, shaking and crying. Isabella uses the opportunity to consider the other woman. A young black woman, about her age, attractive despite her current state.

It's her all right. Pro's sister, Fade. Isa's worst fears are realized, but she keeps the recognition to herself. It has been a long time, and it's possible the family won't recognize her.

The detective crouches down and puts a hand on the woman's shoulder. "What's your name."

The woman makes a visible effort to stop crying. "Phaedra," She sniffs, and when she exhales, a small keening cry comes with the air, "Phaedra Williams."

Despite her acting, the compassion in Isa's voice is quite

real, "Miss Williams, I'm so sorry to *meet* you under these circumstances. let's go inside, OK."

A brief look flits across Fade's face, and Contreras wonders if the woman will play along or out her on the spot.

Saying nothing, Fade instead turns her head to look through the half-open door as if she is looking at someone Isabella can't see. Anxiety blooms on her features, plain to any cop who is used to dealing with people who have something to hide.

Conners has come up behind her, and he zeros in on the woman's hesitation. "Ma'am, we can smell the weed all the way out here. Trust me, we don't care about any of that right now. We just need to talk to everyone that was here, collect any bullet fragments we can find, take some pictures."

Pheadra's face hardens, and she stands under her own power. Storm clouds of anger gather plain as day on her face. The tears still fall, but sharp words fall with them, "You bastard! My brother is dead, and you come up here accusing me of some shit?"

Isabella wants to punch Conners in the face for being so blunt and confronting, but she also knows he probably hit the nail on the head and tries to play the middle. "I can't smell anything, but he's totally right; if there's something you are worried about, trust me, we don't care about that. We are here for Tommie."

Phaedra hesitates, knowing better than to believe that line but also knowing she has to let them in, or it will start to look even more suspicious. She wants to glance behind her to get the sign from Ice that the boys have hidden all the guns out back but instinctively knows she has to keep her eyes forward.

Isabella sees the hesitation and doubles down on her line of persuasion. She leans forward and lowers her voice conspiratorially. "I'm sure *if* you had anything, it would be *medical* marijuana. We don't care about that anymore."

Well, you are not wrong, Detective, Phaedra thinks. Her mother's medical marijuana card is her greatest source of supply. Technically having it is legal in Oklahoma, at least for her mother. Of course, selling it is still a felony, but this woman seems to be willing to let any suspicion of that go in favor of investigating the shooting.

She sends up a silent prayer that Ice has the gun situation straightened out and slowly backs into the apartment, allowing the female detective to follow her. She wishes it was just her, but the asshole male detective follows.

The cramped living room and kitchen are suddenly over-flowing with people. Half zooted on meds in the corner, Mama is motionless and numb. 10-year-old Aliyah leans heavily on her mother, with her arms wrapped around her and her head down. Jiggy and Deuce sprawl across chairs in the kitchen, looking very uncomfortable with the entrance of the cops. Ice stands at the sliding glass door at the far end of the kitchen as if he just came in.

Fade looks a question at him, *are we good?* But his face is inscrutable as always.

Isabella's voice is polite, trying to build rapport and hoping none of the rest of the family recognize her, "Quite a family you got here..." She pivots slowly in the confined space. Her visual sweep stutters for a moment when it reaches across the chalk-white teenager in the kitchen. "Ah, family and friends?" The question mark hangs in the air, and no one rushes to explain the noticeably different genetics of the gang member.

The silence lengthens, and Mama lifts her eyes with an effort. "We all family here," her speech is slow, but the tone dares the detective to imply differently. After a pregnant pause, she asks her own question with a voice devoid of hope. "You gonna find them that killt my child?"

Isabella leans down to talk to the older woman, "Mrs. Williams? I am so sorry this happened. Do you have any idea who might have done this?"

The woman stares straight ahead, at the wall her son lies dead on the other side of, saying nothing. A single tear rolls down her face.

When she realizes the woman will not speak further, Isabella straightens and addresses the room as a whole. "Does anyone know? I want to help, but we need something to go on."

Stony eyes and closed lips stare back at her.

"We were just going out to the car to go to church." Bitterness runs through Phaedra's voice, "We're getting killed out here, and you cops don't do anything."

Ice tries to reinforce his older sister's statement, "We didn't do nothing."

Before Isabella can respond, Conners takes them all straight off a cliff. "OK, I'm not buying this crap." He makes a show of breathing in *real* deep and looking pointedly at each of the three boys in the kitchen. "That Green smells so thick in here, I'm pretty sure *I* am getting high. We got a room full of gang-bangers here," he nods unceremoniously at the three young men and twists his hands in a series of specific symbols that they clearly recognize, "Playboy Crips, am I right?" When the two at the table scowl but Ice doesn't, Conners zeroes in on him, "What's up Cuz? Yeah, I know who you guys are."

Isabella is stunned, mouth hanging open. She feels she should stop the man, but he is on a roll and continues to push the issue.

Conners steps past his female partner and moves into the

kitchen, barking questions rapid-fire, "You guys strapped up? Should I pat you down? Where's Four?"

"Fuck you, 12," Jiggy spits out. With both of his parents locked up on drug charges and years of running away from shitty foster parents, he hates cops.

"Uh, Conners," Isabella tries to get his attention.

Ignoring her and unperturbed at the white gangster, Conners smiles broadly. "OH! That's right, Four is not here because I locked him up last week!"

The boys are clearly incensed at his barrage and arrogance and lean toward him, surging to meet his attack with a violent response.

"Conners!" Isabella steps around him, getting between him and the boys. "What are you doing?"

"Four didn't do nothing! Go find who killed my little brother!" Ice barks.

The gang detective talks mildly to his partner while maintaining eye contact with the gang. "See? Look how pissed they are at me. Told you it was the same group." To Ice, he says, "I'd love to! You gonna help us out? Gonna tell me which Set wants you dead? Was it a drug rip, or they just mad because your boy Four shot at them?"

The boys fold their arms and stare stonily, cursing under their breath instead of answering.

Conners presses harder, "You want us to catch these killers, be honest. They picked your house for a reason. You shoot them. They come shoot you. Come on, this isn't my first day on the job. Who have y'all pissed off recently?"

Pheadra, watching events in the kitchen spin out of control, begins to yell, "WHAT THE HELL IS WRONG WITH YOU?" She jostles past the detectives, trying to get in between them and the boys before someone says something dumb. "Stop interrogating them! They are minors!"

Conners snorts at her and points at Playboy Bunny tattoo

on her brother's cheekbone. "Minors with gang tats. Give me a break. You want us to solve this, give us something to work with, or we are done here."

"My brother isn't in a gang! You fuckers are always trying to pin some shit on him!" She gets right up in the man's unflinching face. "Shouldn't you be out talking to people, looking at video surveillance or something?"

Isabella coughs. "We could canvas the area…"

Conners crosses his arms and addresses Phaedra. "Best lead we got is the one standing behind you. Your little brother here is a jumped-in gangbanger, and he knows exactly who did this." He moves his eyes around, addressing everyone. "You may not like me, and I don't give a shit if you do. But I do know that this is a gang shooting, and it will NOT get solved if you guys try to blow smoke up our ass." He puts his hands together in a praying motion. "*Please* give me something. Tell me what set it was, where they hang out. Give me a car description, and I will gladly go to *their* turf and harass them instead of you."

His words echo in the room, and Phaedra hesitates. Isabella thinks his aggressive method may be about to work. The one by the glass door starts to open his mouth, but then a strong masculine voice bellows behind her, "HEY! What's going on in here?"

A few minutes earlier, Pro had turned down the music as he turned into the apartment complex. Fear gripped him, fear of pain. He rocked slightly in his seat, breathing increasing like before a fight in the ring. But it is not physical pain his mind anticipates now, but deeper-cutting psychological pain.

It is hard to find a spot in the parking lot with the police cars and crime scene tape jamming up the corner by his mom's apartment. The yellow tape is like a barrier he doesn't want to see past.

He is out of the car, moving quickly, vision tunneling toward a black lump on the ground. He knows what it is but his mind rebels. *Nononono!*

A man in uniform moves quickly to intercept him. "Hey! You can't come through here, Sir!"

Pro disregards the smaller man and pushes forward, eyes locked on the source of his grief. His chest pushes against the man, whose eyes begin to look worried.

"STOP!" The man's voice has gone from polite authority to warning, and another cop peels away from the door to provide reinforcement.

"I'm family," Pro manages. His throat constricts, and he steps back. They give him space to pull out his driver's license and hand it to them as proof.

"Protean Williams," the first cop reads from the piece of plastic. His mind shifts gears, and he offers the card back with an apology, "I'm sorry for your loss, sir, but I can't let you go in there. It's a crime scene."

"I just saw two people going in," he says.

"They were detectives." The man looks at a sheet of paper on a clipboard in his hand, pointing at the list of names as if it explains everything.

Loud voices come from the apartment, and Pro looks over the shorter man's head, trying to figure out what is happening. The place looks the same as always but now is pockmarked with dozens of small holes.

Drawing on the self-discipline of his military training and the eternal politeness of being a pastor, he speaks respectfully. "What's going on in there? Why are they yelling?"

"Ah... not sure," the man with the clipboard admits.

The yelling intensifies, and he hears a familiar voice.

Adrenaline spikes, and a protective instinct starts to over-power his politeness. "I'm going in."

"You can't. Everything has to be controlled now." The man subconsciously waggles the clipboard again, and the significance of the document on it becomes clear in Pro's mind. *It's just like a sign-in roster in the Army*.

Before the man can react, he snatches the clipboard, pen and all, and signs his name across the bottom. *Monkey-see-monkey-do, follow the man in front of you*. Just like in the Army, he copies the way the person before filled it out and shoves the clipboard back toward the open-mouthed man.

The yelling intensifies. The man's eyes are turning down-ward to retake possession of the clipboard, and his backup has turned back toward the apartment, trying to ascertain the cause of the yelling. Light on his feet, Pro dances sideways and then surges forward with a sudden burst of speed.

"Hey!" The cop with the clipboard sounds indignant, but Pro is already past him. He blasts past the other cop before he can react and makes it to the open door in less than two seconds.

He takes in the scene all in a glance, like a tactical assess-ment. *Who are the hostages, and who needs to get shot? Red light, green light. Gogogo!* Mama is on the couch, head in her hands. A smaller girl he doesn't immediately recognize is hugging her. The action is in the kitchen. He steps further into the room and sees two people in nice clothes with guns on their hips cornering his twin sister in the kitchen. Some bigger kids are behind Fade, one of them kind of looking like a bigger version of his brother Caelan.

Of the two people with guns, the man is postured more threateningly and dominates the opening between the adjoining kitchen and living room.

Of all the things he expected to see upon arrival, all the scenarios of tears and hugs and sorrow, even his painful bouts with guilt and self-doubt, none of it had prepared him for this.

Indignation bubbles up, and he lets his voice roar from deep inside his chest. "HEY! What's going on in here?"

Everything happens all at once. The detectives whirl to face the loud noise, surprise and displeasure on their faces. Fade looks past the investigators, and a tinge of relief mixes with a silent plea for help on her features.

"Pro!" Fade motions toward the detectives. "They are harassing us!"

"Pro?" Detective Contreras says it as a question, her face stunned.

"How'd you get in here?" Conners face booms in an attempt to match Pro's volume, and his hand goes to the butt of his gun.

An apologetic uniformed officer materializes in the doorway. "I tried to stop him..." when he receives a withering look from Conners, he swings the clipboard up to defend himself, half-pointing toward Pro's signature at the bottom as if to show he was doing his job.

"I'm family. This is my house," Pro stretches the truth slightly. He looks toward Isabella and does a double-take. "Isa? What are you doing here?" He looks her up and down, taking in her athletic figure and stopping on the gun and badge clipped to the belt of her pressed slacks. "You're a *cop?*" He twists the word to make it sound like the ultimate betrayal.

Before she can respond, Conners, who is trying to regain control of the room, interjects. "Wait, you know this guy?"

Isabella bites her lip, fighting an involuntary rise of her pulse as her cover is blown to pieces by the man she once loved. Their past is suddenly fresh in her mind, very fresh. She has an insensible urge to go to the man, but that's impossible. Fractions of a second are flying by, and she knows she must speak to avoid a noticeable silence. "You look... well." She was going to say *good* but revised it on the fly, trying to bridge the gap between their past relationship and the current circumstance.

Get ahold of yourself, Isabella.

Conners is looking at her, then back at Pro, and groans when his investigator instincts intuit the pregnant look between them. "What the actual hell. You guys used to be a thing, didn't you?" He sounds disgusted.

Many things hang in that exact moment. Pro's gaze is continuing to harden toward his old flame, even as her heart rate elevates.

Careful Isa, they will pull you from the case, A voice in her mind reminds her. Followed somewhat belatedly by another thought, *and you are a married woman now.*

"A long time ago." She makes her tone icy, makes it sound far less important than it feels.

"Seven years." Pro's face looks serious, like he is silently taking responsibility for something. "I left."

Her chin wants to tremble, but she won't let it. "You did," she acknowledges, her tone flat.

Phaedra's irritation has grown by leaps and bounds during the unexpected exchange, and it spills over now. She motions a circle toward the two of them. "Are you fricking serious with this shit right now?" Electing to not betray that she knew Isabella, she instead fixes Pro with a sharp look that focuses on her most important question, *who's side are you on?*

Her twin understands and is already moving to remedy the situation. Conners is opening his mouth, either to rekindle the investigation or complain about Contreras' now obvious personal connection, but Pro starts taking control of the room.

"Whatever this is," Pro motions toward Conners and the cornered young men in the kitchen, "It's done." His face hardens into a mask. "Do what you need to do outside but get out of our house."

As he speaks, he moves sideways towards the kitchen, and Conners rotates to keep the larger man in front of him. The maneuver puts Pro on the same side of the room as his family, and by default, forces the detectives to step back into the living room.

Isabella sees his choice, sees herself being placed in outsider status, and tries to keep the investigation going. "I'm here to help, Pro. I'm here for Tommie."

Pro takes a step forward, and he senses rather than sees the teenagers behind him move forward with him. "You want to help? Go hit the streets! The shooter isn't in here!"

Conners tries his method again, tries to figure out how Pro fits into his equation. "So, *you* are the Big Homie? You are running shit with Four locked up? Tell us who to look for, tell us who y'all pissed off lately."

Caelan speaks from behind Pro, "See, they keep coming at us with this gang shit, trying to say we are Crips or whatever. They trying to catch us out on something, not find whoever did this."

"Shut up," Pro orders his younger brother. Looking at the male detective's demeanor, Pro is disgusted. "That right? In here interrogating minors instead of out solving the actual crime?" His voice twists into disgust, hatred even, "Sounds about right, *TWELVE*. Now GET OUT!"

Isabella looks confused when Pro uses the gang slang, but Conners understands. POLICE and OFFICER each have six letters, and gang members use the number 12 as a derogatory reference.

"We need to look for bullet fragments in here..." Conners tries to object. "We could write a warrant..."

"Come on," Isabella puts her hand on the man's arm while looking at Pro with a bit of sadness. "Come on, Conners, we're done in here. We can get ballistics from rounds outside."

Pro reads the interaction between the two detectives accurately. Conners trying to push the issue, Isabella surrendering the field. He takes another step forward and feels his family surge forward with him again as he does so. "GET OUT!"

The detectives give up all at once and go back outside. When they do, Pro immediately shuts and locks the door behind them.

CHAPTER FIVE

Back outside, Isabella stomps past the crime scene tape, straight back to her car. Conners follows her but waits to speak until they are inside the relative privacy of her vehicle.

When he gets in, she whirls on him. "What the hell was that?"

He shrugs unperturbed. "What, you mean the part where I almost cracked the case open for you? I had them about ready to spill it before your *boyfriend* walked in. What the hell was *that?*"

"Old history. Not relevant to this case."

He snorts, "Yeah? Let me just see what the Captain thinks." He pulls out his phone and puts it to his ear, pretending to listen to someone on it. "What's that, Sir? Oh, you want me to take Primary now that we know Contreras has a conflict of interest? You got it, Captain. Makes perfect sense."

"Asshole."

He takes the phone from his ear and speaks with a serious tone, "You are too close to this. You know that."

She grits her teeth and points through the windshield at the shrouded figure next to the sidewalk. "And you are too far from it! We got a dead little kid over there. You know what, sure, I met him one time, OK? Maybe I even dated his older brother for a minute in high school, but at least I want to find out who killed him! All you want to do is bully those kids in there, get gang information so you can act cool."

He regards her coolly, lets her speak before answering. When he does reply, she is surprised to hear him serious, not mocking or superior. "I care." When she raises her eyebrows to challenge him, he sighs and expands on his statement, "I have worked 47 murders since I started, and I cared about every single one. 193 shootings, tried to care about all of them too."

He leans forward in his seat, a hint of passion invading his voice as he wags his finger toward the apartment. "But it's always like this with these people. They never want to tell us anything, then complain that we aren't doing anything."

Her eyes narrow. "What do you mean *these people*?"

Glancing at her tan-colored skin, he senses dangerous waters and quickly rejects her implication he is racist, "I mean gang-bangers, obviously."

"Uh-huh."

Ignoring her, he continues his diatribe, defending his methods. "You have to hit them hard, use every bit of leverage, let them know you know what's up, and you aren't playing around."

"Like interrogating them when their brother just died? God, you are insensitive."

"Especially then, 'cause that's the only time they will talk."

She shakes her head. "I was building rapport with them. I could have got them to talk about it."

He scoffs. "Look, we already know what happened. We knew it on the way over here. They hit the Locos, so the

Locos hit them. The problem is, they can't actually say that without incriminating themselves. They don't trust us, so by default, they are always going to play innocent and tell us nothing."

Remembering the stony faces she got when they went inside, she grudgingly has to admit to herself they were already giving her the runaround.

He continues, "But by calling them on their bullshit, we can at least get pieces of the truth. They confirmed that Four is indeed part of their set. Did you catch that? I got them to indirectly admit that in less than five minutes, and they would have never told you."

"That doesn't help us, though. That does nothing for us," she complains.

He groans and starts reciting how she can write it in the report, "Family members and other apparent Crip gang members on scene admitted close relationship with known gang member Damarion 'Four' Williams, who was recently arrested fleeing the area of a drive-by on rival gang South Side Locos."

Her eyes narrow thoughtfully at his smooth recitation. "Well, that sounds incriminating, but that's a lot to pull from what little they said. Bit of a stretch, don't you think?"

He shakes his head. "Not at all. Not with the background of the ongoing gang war in my head. Gotta put the pieces together. This is what I do."

"But that still doesn't get us anywhere near criminal charges or search warrants. No specific suspect even. I take that to a judge, and he will laugh at me."

He nods his head as if she is finally getting it. "Correct. Which is why our report *needed* to say: so-and-so Williams admitted to being a Crip gang member and said that he believed the shooting was retaliation for a recent attack by an *unnamed Crip* on the South Side Locos, at an address in the vicinity of blah-blah, the residents of which are believed to have a black sedan closely resembling the one used in the new attack at Hillcrest. Williams stated that he saw several Hispanic males shooting from the black sedan, and while he did not know them personally believed from their tattoos and manner of dress that they were, in fact, South Side Locos gang members."

She stares at him as the smooth flow of fictionalized information flows from his lips. When he concludes, she speaks slowly. "Well... yeah, that would get us at least halfway to a warrant. Maybe further if we find that address and there is a black car out front."

He smacks the dash. "Exactly! And I was halfway there. I almost had them admitting it when your Big Homie Pro walked in and shut them down."

"He's not a gang member." She states it as fact. "I knew him for two years, and he never did any of that stuff. Plus, he moved away years ago. Went to college..." She trails off, looking at the front of apartment 119.

Conners isn't having it. "Oh no, he is. You see how they respected him? How they backed him up? These kids are born into this. They are banging in middle school. This apartment complex," he waves his hands at their surroundings, "we got two whole generations of Crips in here. Brothers, cousins, friends, they are all in it." He nods confidently, "He's in it, trust me."

She moves her eyes from the specific apartment to the rest of the units. There are several people standing outside staring, and quite a few more looking out from windows. "OK." She nods her head slowly, filing away everything her partner has said. She doesn't agree or disagree with his methods, just moves on to the next task. "OK. Let's start canvassing these people. Hopefully, someone will give us something."

They step back out of the impromptu conference room, and she looks at him over the roof of the car. "And you're still an asshole."

Inside, Ice, Jiggy, and Deuce mumble with macho expressions about pushing the cops out, jostling each other, and acting like it was they, not Pro, who turned the tables. Turning from the door to his mother, Pro kneels quickly in front of her vacant face.

"Mama."

Fresh tears form in the corners of her eyes and roll down her face unheeded. She stares through him, rocking slightly while the young girl hugs her tightly from the side. "They killed my babeee." The end of the simple statement degenerates into a quiet moan.

Pro doesn't know what to say and leans forward to gently place his arms around her shoulders. When he does, the girl he doesn't recognize releases her grasp and sits back to give him room.

"I know, Mama," he says simply.

She takes a breath, then releases the air in a quiet cry, "Whyeeee?"

Looking sideways from her shoulder, he sees the teenage boys jostling each other, faces grim with the loss but still trying to act tough. *Because y'all stay in this life.* He wants to punch whoever is responsible, but the cycle of violence has no clear beginning. To his mother, he says, "He's in a good place now, Mama. God's got him."

He imagines an angel coming down to Hillcrest, scooping up the boy, ascending to heaven. He tries to tell himself that it's a good thing, that everything will be beautiful for Tommie now, but it seems empty. "No more fear, nor more pain," he hears himself reciting to his mother.

"I want him baaaaack." The pain in her voice rips up the peace he was trying to feel, trying to share with her, and he stands up. Hardening in his spirit shows up on his face as punishing those responsible begins to occupy a greater portion of his thought. "I know," is all he can think of to say.

He turns toward Phaedra and the teenage boys. His twin stands motionless next to a bedroom door, her face a mask. "Fade."

He thinks for a moment that she is going to step forward and hug him, but then something crosses her face, and she doesn't. Once they were very close, like two sides of the same coin, but now a gulf stretches between them, a chasm of different circumstances and life choices. For the last several years, they have been living very different lives. The distance has never felt further than in this moment when he wants to connect with her, but she holds back.

Feeling an invisible rebuff and not knowing how to deal with it at the moment, he turns to the teenagers. He addresses the slimmest and perhaps youngest, who now he is sure is his brother. "Caelan? You have grown like crazy." He moves forward to greet the youngster, offering his right hand to shake while moving his left hand to a position to pull the boy into a hug.

Right before they make contact, the smaller male briefly holds the thumb and first two fingers of his hand out in a sign for *Neighborhood*, the universal Crip gang sign, before rolling smoothly into the handshake and hug.

"Sup, Cuz." The younger brother has clamped down on all emotion and is full-on acting hard. He breaks the hug almost immediately, making it more a formal greeting of respect and allegiance than mutual comfort. He stands back and tilts his neck slightly, showing off a Seattle Mariners 'S' tattoo peeking up from his collarbone. "The callin' me Ice now." The tattoo, of course, stands for Neighborhood Crips Rollin'

60s, the gang set of which their incarcerated father is a life-time member. With his long history of banging the set, their father rates the respect of an Original Gangster for the local Sixties, and his sons are born with a clear path toward membership.

He's trying to tell me he is a man. Pro understands. *To him, gang membership means he has come of age.*

In times past, Pro would have grinned and said something congratulatory as Caelen is expecting. A rite of passage deserves mutual respect, and Ice is presenting his credentials for manhood proudly to his older brother. Pro sees that the youngster is holding onto that expectation of respect even tighter with the fresh loss of their little brother, but from the perspective of his new life, it is a slap in the face of reason.

The automatic words of congratulation die in Pro's throat, and anger surges. He knows it is the wrong thing to say, but he needs someone to blame, and the words come out with angry edges. "Bangin' huh? All jumped-in and everything now?" His eyes harden as they move to Jiggy and Deuce, who crowd behind Ice in solidarity. "All of you straight Gs now, aren't ya?"

The anger that has been rolling around in his mind begins to focus on them, and he lets his voice slide into sarcastic gangster slang, "Lil bro-bro got a gat now?" He reaches out and flicks his brother's loose waistband as if looking for a gun. "Ya got a Glizzie with a Richard under there? You some big shit now, huh?"

He turns on the large white kid. "What do they call you, Diversity Hire?" He throws up his hands, clowning his own gang signs as his voice goes high and mocking on the confused-looking youngster. He throws a big 'C' with one hand, then in a moment of Crip sacrilege angrily twists the fingers of both hands against his chest to read 'Blood.' His voice is high and mocking as he throws what middle-school white kids think are serious gang signs, "Look at me guys, I'm a gangster!"

Jiggy looks genuinely hurt and is immediately incensed at the disrespect. "Fuck you, B!" He reaches for the front of his pants, pulling his shirt out of the way to draw his gun from its customary spot before remembering Ice took it earlier.

Deuce steps forward, hands raised in a loose fighting stance. At six feet and almost 300 pounds., he is only an inch shorter than Pro and, while not as athletic, a good 30 lbs. heavier. "The fuck outta here with that bullshit," He moves his hands around, hands half-closed in fists, "Or you 'bout to catch this fade." Pro hasn't heard anyone use 'fade' like that in a while but knows this guy wants to fight.

Sometimes it feels really good to fall back on what you know. Maybe this young man, wracked by grief, is eager to hit something. Pro gets it. It is all nerves and fear until you step in the ring, but life is simple again once you start trading blows. His fighter instincts come online, surging to the fore with lightning speed when the large man steps toward him in the small space. "Oh, now we wanna throw hands?" Without conscious thought, Pro is suddenly on the balls of his feet, bouncing like he is in the ring again.

But even as a smile breaks across his face and his heart leaps with temporary relief from the pain of loss, even as his anger at the endless cycle of gang violence roars, he knows he has to hold back. When the kid steps closer, finalizing the agreement to mutual combat, Pro jukes a shoulder left, fakes a jab, then drops his right hip.

While no doubt the veteran of countless fistfights, Jiggy has no boxing or MMA training. He clumsily over-commits to counter Pro's feint and predictably swings a big right hand full of rage, trying for a knockout blow.

Rebounding powerfully from his lowered right hip, Pro comes up like a coiled spring just outside of Jiggy's extended arm. He uses his rising motion to blast a powerful open-handed slap with his left hand to the charging youngster's belly, followed by a flurry of right-left-right slaps to the kid's head as he continues to step around behind the off-balance fighter.

None of the blows were hard, as he intentionally pulled any real strength from the precise strikes. Jiggy swings back around, enraged at the treatment.

Pro holds his left hand, ready for a jab in front of him while issuing a quiet warning with a pointed finger from his right hand. "Better sit down before I put you down."

A blast to the back of his head momentarily stuns him, and he staggers forward at an angle toward the now wide-eyed girl on the couch.

"STOP IT!" Phaedra comes around to his front, the large book in her hands raised above her head, poised for a second blow.

Did she just hit me with the family Bible? Pro's animal fighting instincts are derailed by the irony, and he fails to react as she lowers the book like a battering ram and slams it into his chest, pushing him back instead of striking him.

The back of his knees connects hard against something behind him, and he feels himself going over.

Jiggy, eyes blind with aggression, tries to capitalize on Pro's misfortune. But when he surges forward, Phaedra blocks him.

"Stop it!" She says it again and raises the massive Bible, eyes blazing, chest heaving, ready to smack Jiggy with it too.

His gaze catches on her defiant figure, and something changes in his expression. He pauses his forward movement.

No one moves for a long second. When the young woman speaks again, her voice is softer and twisted with disappointment and sadness. "What is wrong with you?" She says it to Jiggy but then turns to face her twin, including him in the question. A trembling arm slowly raises to point out the closed curtain. "Our brother is out there. Dead…"

When she trails off, no one dares to speak. Pro slowly stands to his full height but still feels small.

She looks around the room, spreading her arms to encompass their posturing and violence as she resumes, "And now you wanna do *this?*"

"Sorry, Fade." Pro feels ashamed and desperate to regain the moral high ground. He quickly re-configures his thinking to that of the mature, logical man he prides himself on having become. "You're right." He looks at the frightened girl on the couch next to his mother, realizing for the first time she is his half-sister, now much older. He speaks to her and his mother as one entity, "Sorry, Mama."

His twin makes no overt indication she has accepted his apology but does turn to focus her glare on the younger men. They look uncomfortable and mumble something begrudging that may have been apologies, but their scowls are anything but humble. She places the bible back on the shelf in its customary place, then looks back at them. "And y'all get off this gangster shit 'till the cops leave. C'mon, gotta be smart right now."

Pro cocks his head slightly, surprised that she doesn't have the same reaction he does. *You'd think with Tommie dead, she'd be screaming at them for banging, for bringing this gang war to her front doorstep.*

Before he can formulate how to ask about that, other questions force their way to the surface. "Where are my nieces." He looks at the bedroom doors, realizing no one is in the closed rooms, "And where the hell is Trey?"

A knock at the door interrupts, and when no one moves toward it, Pro goes to the door to represent the family. It's the cop with the clipboard from earlier. To his credit, the uniformed man lets that incident stay in the past and keeps the exchange professional and respectful.

Pro tries not to look past the cop to the man in the black jacket standing next to the form on the ground. The raincoat has been propped up to shield the body from the apartment, but the bold yellow letters 'Medical Examiner' offer a clear and painful explanation of what is happening.

He answers the questions mechanically. It feels as if he is watching a lifeless version of himself speak calmly to the man.

No, they did not have a specific funeral home in mind yet. Yes, he understood one could be chosen for them. Yes, they would consent to an autopsy if one was deemed necessary. No, no one in the house owned a firearm.

The cop looked like he didn't believe the last answer, but when he didn't produce another question, Pro shut the door in his face.

Turning, Pro walks purposefully to each of the two bedroom doors, just off the kitchen, and opens each. Seeing no one and ignoring Fade's irritated look at his casual invasion of her space, he went back into the kitchen and sat on the counter.

"Where's Trey?" He asks again. "Why isn't he here?"

No one immediately replies, so when he continues, his tone curves toward accusation. "He hiding? Is this over some shit he started?"

Jiggy clears his throat and looks at Ice. Deuce keeps his head straight, but his eyes dart toward Ice as well.

"He's chillin'," Ice says obscurely. He sets his jaw, his features locked into the expressionless mask that fits his nickname. "We call him Four now." While his face is solid, his eyes are stormy as he answers, the recent ridicule of his gang membership still fresh.

"Four?" Pro looks questioningly at his younger brother.

Ice holds up three fingers, then pops up a fourth. "He

caught another body." One finger goes back down, then up again as the teenager counts. "Three. Four."

Pro snorts. "*Another* body? He trying to say a *fourth* body?" He holds up four fingers, copying Ice, and chuckles, genuinely amused. "You know he was Trey because he was Damarion Williams the *Third*, right? What kinda bullshit has he been feeding you?"

Deuce frowns. "What do you know? You been gone a long time."

Jiggy nods, plugging for their absent leader. "Four's all about that life. Crip started young. On the set."

Ice looks ever so slightly uncertain, as if he may suspect Damarion pumps it up but then visibly makes the decision to believe his oldest brother over Pro. "Yeah. Lot has changed while you been off living that soft life."

"Off getting white." Incredibly, it is the white gang member who delivers this accusation, denigrating the color of his own skin as if it is something to be ashamed of.

Without looking away from Pro, Ice extends his knuckles toward his white friend and gang member. "On the Set."

Pro snorts. "Not that much has changed. Stupid still growing on trees around here."

Deuce interjects, "Bitch, even the trees around here is Crips. Harder than you, too."

"Ayyyy," Ice half-turns toward Deuce, raising his hand and cracking a smile at his friend's burn, "my man!" They smack palms together at waist height, then pull them apart and smack them together in exaggerated motions two more times, each more emphatic than the last.

Observing their antics and attitude towards him, Pro mentally takes stock of the situation. When he went to college an hour away, he was coming home every weekend. Going to church with mama, spending time with Isabella, the whole bit. But college was a different world, and his view of the fabric of life changed.

Things became strained with Isa. She was pushing for a stable relationship, talking about wanting a ring, but he was drifting further into his new life. He had offered to get an apartment to share with her in nearby Stillwater, but she said there was nothing for her there. His class schedule was demanding, and he took a break from coming home every weekend. The break stretched, and the next thing he knew, it was Christmas before he came back to visit. By then, something had happened with Isabella, and she was pushing him away. He tried to figure out what it was, to repair the gap, but she started dating another man and wouldn't return his texts.

Fade had a scholarship, she was at least as smart as he was, but she got pregnant and reluctantly took a gap year. Their once strong friendship grew strained as he followed his dreams and potential in college, and she was stuck at home. His mother sank further into substance abuse, and the new baby crammed the already-full house to bursting. Throwing a sleeping bag on the living room floor with eight people in a 2-bedroom apartment started feeling more like an obligation than a joy to come home.

When that Army recruiter gave him a path to pay for college, he jumped at the chance. One year rolled into the next, each new opportunity and step in his life keeping him by default from coming back to his family.

And now I am a stranger, Pro admits to himself. Seeing the easy camaraderie of the three almost-men in his mom's kitchen, then their stony expressions when they look at him, the change is obvious. He looks down at his nice dress shirt, thinks about all the bored white kids he was trying to impress with gang talk just this morning. *I'm an imposter here.*

Fade watches him quietly, her back against the wall

between the kitchen and living room. "Damarion is locked up."

Her statement has a sobering effect on the boys, who settle back into their chairs around the table.

Pro tries to pick his way more carefully into the details of their lives, more conscious than ever that they may shut him out. He nods toward the front of the apartment, his face serious. "You said Locos. Is Trey- *Four* tripping with them?"

Ice and the other two share sharp glances. Their looks at each other speak volumes, but they don't say anything out loud. Clearly, they do not trust Pro with what they know.

Pro looks to his sister. Growing up, he saw very few women who get directly involved with gang activity, especially the heavy stuff, and the ones who did were normally thrill-seekers, fast girls who wanted to stay high and have fun. Phaedra was the opposite, and while living with gang members, she got good grades and never did drugs. But something is off now, and he senses it. She is standing close to the men, and he realizes now that her presence is not only accepted by them but something more. *It's like she is guarding them somehow.*

"Fade?" He bores into her with the question, his gaze telling her that he can tell she knows more, and he isn't going to be brushed off. "I came. Don't shut me out."

She crosses her arms. The same way she used to when they were in high school, and she was lying to their stepdad. Her chin lifts, silently acknowledging his assertion that she knows more than she is saying but also proclaiming her independence from his influence.

Ice stands, interposing between the twins. He looks pointedly at Fade then back at Pro, trying to appear older than he is. "We're handling it."

"What?"

"We got a plan. We aren't gonna take this lying down." He

looks intently at Pro as he says the next part, "Are you gonna Crip the fuck up and get behind us? Or just sit there in your pretty-boy church clothes and judge?"

He means they are going to strike back. Pro's realization is alarming but not surprising. *They aren't telling the cops who did it because they want revenge, not an investigation. They don't want the cops here and probably don't want me here either if I am not going to help.*

Pro's pulse climbs as it registers that he is essentially being asked to participate. He's probably already sitting in the middle of a gang war. The South Side Locos are arguably the most violent gang in Oklahoma City, and his family, these kids, are on the front lines. Their gang pedigree with the Rollin' 60s is solid, but none of the older guys are in the room. And knowing how much of a free-wheeler Damarion is, there is a good chance that this is all happening unsanctioned.

The perspective of his new world would scream back 'no' to Ice's veiled question, but the gang way of thinking is ingrained deeply in him from childhood. He feels at a visceral level their need to respond to the slaying in kind. Straight out rejecting the idea now will cement their view of him as an outsider, reducing his influence in the matter to zero.

He crosses his arms, trying to get out in front of this ill-considered line of thinking, but from a gang perspective. "The OGs behind you on this?"

Their silence again speaks volumes. They are on their own, just kids striking back in the only way they know how. Gangs have a lot of power to coerce younger members to act, not a lot to keep them from acting, but something like this would have to be authorized. If they act without approval from the old guys, the Original Gangsters...

They are going to get slaughtered.

CHAPTER SIX

sabella is standing on the second-floor landing, knocking on another door, when Conners sees a shiny all-black Ford SUV with tinted windows roll into the complex.

"Boss is here," he grunts.

Detective Contreras turns from her fruitless knocking on the door to follow his gaze. If anyone is home, they aren't answering, a mostly universal response to their efforts to gather information.

"Crap." Captain Barnes will want an update, and she was hoping to have more by now.

The vehicle can't find a place to park and rolls to a stop next to her department-issued sedan. It sits there, blocking the street with the engine running, and she imagines she sees the man inside looking around for her.

"Better get down there before he tries to go inside," Conners comments. He immediately starts down the stairs.

Yeah. Don't want him seeing that shit show, she agrees silently as she follows. Out loud, she says, "Are you going to say anything about..."

He frowns and wags his head back and forth, dispassionately weighing whether to betray her secret. He pauses in the alcove at the bottom of the stairs. "Look, I want the gang angle. These guys," he jerks a thumb toward apartment 119, "run back and forth, shooting each other up, stealing cars, getting in pursuits, robbing convenience stores. They are a menace to society, and I am trying to build a RICO on them."

"A RICO? She edges toward the open air, not quite understanding and feeling the need to intercept the Captain before he enters the crime scene.

He grabs her arm, preventing her from breaking from the temporary screening of the alcove. "It's basically a big gang case. Get 'em all at once," he struggles to summarize and shakes his head in a nevermind motion, "I'll explain it later. Point is, it is hard as hell to get enough intel to put one together, but they are a big deal. Case of a lifetime."

Her voice is low and urgent, "OK. You hate gangs and want to throw them all in prison. What's your point?"

"My point," he hisses, "is that this dead kid is just part of a long continuum. I could give a shit less if you used to bang that guy in high school, you clearly have an in with this family, and I can use that."

Ignoring his vulgarity, she tries to focus on the positives of what he is saying. She is surprised he would cover for her, but given the older man's cynical view, realizes she probably shouldn't be. "Thanks. I really want this one. Want to solve it."

He holds a hand up. "I'm not done. I'll let you keep this homicide *if* you let me work the RICO."

"Speak English."

"Racketeering Influenced Criminal Organization. The Feds invented special laws to take down the Mob. It takes a ton of work to string together, a lot more hours than Captain ever wants to give me to work a gang case, which is why I haven't been able to do it yet."

She starts to understand. "But you think he will let you do it as part of this?"

"Have you ever seen him show up on something like this so fast? And the Major was already calling him before we left briefing. They know this is going to blow up big; it could be national media exposure. *Poor kid gets gunned down in OKC.* Shit, they'll have his best school pictures on the front page of USA Today."

The casual way he talks about the young boy's death as if he was a pawn in Conners' game is really pissing her off, but he charges on, oblivious. "The Captain will throw tons of hours at this. Whatever we need, follow up on all leads, blah, blah blah."

"You want me to milk the case," She says.

"I want you to be incredibly thorough, eternally optimistic, impressed with the leads we have, and always have an idea about what we are following up on next," he counters.

"You want me to milk it, so you can build your own 'case-of-a-lifetime,' a RICO," she uses the new word. The Captain is walking toward her crime scene, looking around as if wondering where his detectives are.

"I want you, as *Primary Detective,* to solve a nearly impossible drive-by case, one that will have the attention of the top Brass. I can, and will, help you far more than you know. You can have all the credit. Just let me work on my thing in the background."

She hesitates. It feels unethical to use the boy's death to pursue a hidden agenda, but she can already see from the events of the day that her odds of succeeding are way better with the experienced gang detective than without.

Seeing her indecision, he reminds her of his leverage, "Or

I can just walk over there and tell the Captain you are practically in-laws with the deceased."

They are out of time. She jets from his grasp and walks purposefully toward their boss. Conners follows, wondering if they have a deal. Barnes, walking slowly and casting his eyes around the apartment complex, is just reaching the crime scene tape and Patrol officer guarding it when she gets within comfortable earshot.

"Captain," she calls out.

He stops, hand automatically reaching for the sign-in pen, and turns toward them. "News crews are crawling up our asses," he says without preamble. "Our Public Information Officer has them corralled outside the complex, but if I don't give them a statement, they will start making stuff up."

He looks at her expecting a report, and she makes her decision. "I got some initial cooperation from the family but will need more time to build rapport with them. With Conners' help, I was able to determine they are a gang family, and we have a lead that the shooting may have been retaliation for another recent gang attack."

Barnes, face thoughtful, looks at the apartment door 15 yards away. "They told you that?"

Absorbing his concern that they may be overheard, she lowers her voice to address the direct question, "Not directly, but they gave us incremental indicators that support that theory. The family is in turmoil right now, but we suspect some of the members who are not active in the gang may be more helpful once things calm down."

She catches Conners nodding out of the corner of her eye. She is nailing it, and he is glad to stay in the shadows. Her boss is still listening, absorbing details, so she keeps on feeding him information. "The other gang-involved appears to be the South Side Locos, and we are working on a possible location of where the suspects may live, but it will take some finesse."

The older man has been running cases long enough to know when someone is starting to spin fluff. He starts asking her short, pointed questions. "Neighbors tell you anything?"

"Very little," she admits.

"Vehicle description?"

"Not yet," in a flash of inspiration, she remembers he already assigned other detectives to help, "I was about to call Hudson to start pulling footage from anything nearby."

"Lab coming?" He points at all the brass shell casings.

"Yeah, I called them," Conners interjects.

She notes he carefully chose to talk about an aspect of the investigation that paints himself in a mundane supportive role. He leaves it open for her to run with, so she plays off him. "I am going to have them take pictures of everything and run the cases and bullet fragments through ballistics."

Nothing earth-shattering there, but it is a preemptive strike to ensure that Barnes knows she is on top of it.

"Good. Looks like some rounds are probably inside. Family letting you search?" His voice turns up in an unhopeful question mark.

"No," she says slowly, the admission making her feel impotent.

He presses his lips together thoughtfully, nodding his head almost imperceptibly, unsurprised.

Hoping he will say no, she hears herself ask, "You want us to write paper on it?" She hates writing search warrants on victim's houses, but it is surprisingly common. People, even victims, just don't like the cops going through their stuff.

Everyone has secrets.

"Ahhhhhh," he thinks out loud, sighing as he does so. "No, let's not. A judge would sign it, but I don't think we need it. Let's err on the side of sensitivity to the family on this."

She is relieved at the decision, not wanting to go back inside and reaggravate the family. She feels a spike of guilt, remembering how Conners already got in their faces with accusations. She shares a look with her partner. *Yeah, we are all about sensitivity around here.* He absorbs her pointed look like a soft sponge, giving no indication her telepathy is working.

The man turns to walk toward his SUV, his mind clearly moving toward the next item on his internal task list. He summarizes the situation, practicing what he will tell the media, "While playing in front of his apartment in Hillcrest this morning, a young boy was struck by stray bullets from a shooting. Upon arrival, first responders found the boy clearly deceased due to a bullet wound to the head. The investigation is ongoing, but early indications show the shooting was targeted, not random, and tied to gang activity. Gang violence has been on the rise in the area, and Police leadership assure us they are aware of the problem and working overtime to keep our streets safe." When he concludes his monologue, he looks at her. "Sound about right?"

"They were on their way to church," she corrects.

He shakes his head with muted sadness and amends his first sentence, "A young boy was slain in Hillcrest this morning when a bullet struck his head as he and his family prepared to go to church." He nods as if satisfied he has what he needs. "Going to church. Can't make this stuff up."

The detectives are following him as he walks toward his SUV, and Conners coughs quietly behind Isabella. Taking the hint, she increases her pace to overtake the Captain. "Sir? This is turning into a spiderweb. Lots of leads..."

He is pulling out his cell phone and cuts her off with a wave of his free hand. "You need time, I know. Look, this is high priority. Work whatever hours it takes. Let me know if you need more people."

"Thanks." She is surprised at his unhesitating approval of what will be tens of thousands of dollars in overtime.

Standing at the door of his SUV, he punches a button on his phone screen and puts it to his ear. While he waits for it to ring through, he puts his hand on her shoulder and looks her in the eye for the first time since he arrived. "And hey. Good job."

Before he can elaborate, the party on the other end picks up. He starts talking to whoever it is as he gets in his vehicle, then he is gone.

The two detectives stand in the parking lot and watch their supervisor leave, then turn to each other.

Conners smiles and rubs his hands together. "Boom. We are in business."

She can see the wheels in his head already turning as he envisions building out the bigger case. She looks at the Medical Examiner ducking under the yellow tape to head their way and at the body a little further and feels a vast gulf is opening in front of her.

"We *are* going to solve this one, though, right?" She says, meaning the child's murder.

"Oh, 100%. These turds don't know what's about to hit them."

She can't help feeling that they are talking about two different things.

The evening air feels chilly, and Pro squares his shoulders in denial of the discomfort. He paces around his car, now parked directly in front of the apartment, taking the opportunity to call Liz while he waits for the pizza to arrive. The cops cleaned up everything and had finally taken down the police tape about an hour earlier, but the holes in the siding aren't going away anytime soon.

"How are you doing... with everything," she asks.

He kicks at a loose piece of the aging asphalt, trying to think of what to say. *Well, you know, Mom's a wreck. Family's off the rails. My sister is hiding her kids at a neighbor's house...* There is so much to say, but she feels too far away to tell it to. "I'm OK," he hears himself say.

She lets his response hang for a minute, trying to decide whether to call him out on it. Deciding to keep it neutral, she allows him to keep his lie. "Good, baby. I miss you." She uses the words as a generic replacement for something more meaningful.

He looks around the poorly lit apartment complex and hears a crash of an intoxicated argument in a nearby apartment. "I miss you too." His words are genuine, and he closes his eyes, remembering back to the way she looked when he left her this morning.

"So... when do you think you will be home?" Realizing that sounded selfish, she hurriedly adds, "Take all the time you need, obviously. I just want to know what to tell the Unit."

He sighs, trying to get his distracted head around the necessary things that will need to occur before he heads home. A quick phone call to his First Sergeant had been all it took to secure emergency leave authorization from his unit. Normally he would have to at least sign something, but it was the National Guard, and he was only three hours away, so no big deal.

"Some family members from Houston are coming up, so we are doing the funeral on Wednesday." His voice is flat as he suppresses emotion, pretending he is not talking about his own brother. So, I guess Thursday?"

She senses internal conflict in his voice and tries to be supportive. "You want to stay an extra couple of days? I can talk to Hicks, and I'm sure he'll extend you till Friday. You could just come back on the weekend."

He frowns. Her offer to talk to his Chain of Command is an easy one with her higher rank, but he worries making their relationship more obvious is unwise. "You sure that's a good idea?"

She snorts, well aware of what he is implying. "It's 2018, Pro. No one cares if officers and enlisted date anymore."

He doubts that is the case but is aware she has clearly convinced herself at least. She's probably right enough that it won't functionally matter in any case. Maybe just fuel whispers among the ranks. He's still torn, though, both aching to get back to her and the life he has worked so hard for and feeling a strong sense of duty to protect and guide his family.

Guilt.

Phaedra steps out of the apartment, and spotting him by his car, starts to walk over. The pull of his twin's presence tips the scales, the instinctual need to share the sibling bond he has had with her since before birth suddenly flaming brighter than the life he longs to return to. He smiles at her, motioning he will wrap up his phone call. She nods understandingly and looks out over the parking lot in a polite gesture of not reading his expression while he talks.

Feeling awkward despite his sister's manners, he turns and steps slowly down the sidewalk, trying to look like he is just roaming and not walking away from her. He speaks quietly into the phone, giving Liz an answer, "I want to come home so bad, but they need me here for a few days, I think."

She forces her voice to sound understanding, not disappointed, "That's totally fine, baby. Take the time you need. I'll be right here when you come back.

"Thanks." He did not expect a fight but still feels relief now the decision is mutual.

"You sure you are all right? You know, it's OK if you aren't."

Without warning, his throat closes around his answer. He cannot bridge Liz's world with the reality of what he just walked back into. Piling the pain of the day on top renders him unable to speak. He turns around and starts heading back toward the apartment, suddenly feeling lost.

"I should be there." She sounds like she's about to get in her mustang and start driving in his direction.

"No!" He quickly revises the tone of his spontaneous outburst to be more reasoning. "No, I mean, I appreciate it. You don't even know how much. But this..." he trails off, lacking words to describe it, "It is pretty bad," he finishes, quite truthfully.

Phaedra turns toward him, apparently hearing the last part. Liz takes a couple of breaths on the other end of the phone and then decides not to push further. "OK. I'll talk to Hicks. Let me know if you need anything. I love you."

"Love you too." He says it quietly, for some reason not wanting his sister to hear.

He ends the call and slips the phone into his pocket. His feet carry him back to Phaedra as he does so, and her eyes are heavy upon him. He thinks she is going to ask about who he was talking to, but instead, she looks at his car.

"Nice ride." She says.

"Thanks. Got subs and an amp." He loves his car and wants to tell her more about it. But he suspects she is just using it to make safe, idle conversation.

Her lips press tightly together, and she leans back against the faded vinyl siding of the apartment with her hands pressed against the wall behind her waist. He can't help but notice her two children have done nothing to diminish her striking figure. She has shed her nice going-to-church blouse from earlier, and a baby-blue tank top now hugs her figure above form-fitting jeans.

He purposely looks away, back toward the single entrance of the apartment complex, as if he suddenly must watch for the delivery driver to appear. "Food should be here soon."

"Thanks for doing that," she says.

"Of course. People gotta eat." He acts like it is nothing, but the abundant order of pizza, wings, and dessert rolls had topped $100. *A small price to feel useful to the family*.

She doesn't respond, and for some reason, appears antsy, like she is waiting for something to happen.

"Are you bringing your girls back? You know, to eat?"

She bites her lip, considering.

"It's probably safe, for the moment. They will be staying away for a bit after this." He attempts to reference the Locos without actually doing so.

"I'm more worried about their dad," She says. Seeing his confused look, she explains, "He's an ass, always looking for an excuse to take them away from me. Every time anything happens in Hillcrest, he is pulling the police report and having his lawyer file some crap saying I have them in an unsafe environment."

Pro looks pointedly at bullet holes next to her in the siding. *Maybe the dude has a point?* He keeps the thought to himself, but she guesses to some degree what he is thinking.

She groans. "I *know*. But you don't understand how hard I have fought this man. He doesn't give a shit about my kids. He just doesn't want me to have them. He's a narcissist who just wants to hurt me. He's always behind on his child support, making me pay for everything."

"You should move out," The words and accompanying decision are out of Pro's mouth before he knows it. "Get your own place, get you and your girls the hell out of Hillcrest."

She grimaces. "I... can't really do that."

Having voiced what he believes is the solution, he charges forward in problem-solving mode. "Sure you can. I'll help you. Help you pay a security deposit on a place close to your work."

"Pro."

He looks at the apartment next to them as if mentally trying to estimate her belongings through the wall. "Hell, I bet we could get you moved this week! I am staying an extra few days..."

He trails off as a middle-aged man approaches. Something about the man is off, and Pro stares him down. The man looks unwashed and moves oddly, almost furtively up the sidewalk. Pro is about to tell him to shove off and go around them when something unexpected happens.

"Sup." Phaedra is turned away from Pro, addressing the man with familiarity.

"Sup, Fade." As he finishes closing the distance, the man's face widens into a gross smile at the young woman, then he looks over her shoulder toward Pro. He cool?"

Am I cool? Pro still has visions of a new apartment for Phaedra in his mind and tries to switch gears to figure out what this ugly gremlin is up to.

"Yeah." Phaedra, still facing away from Pro, shakes hands with the man. With incredible smoothness, her right hand goes to his and passes off the small baggie with two Xanax in it, and her left reaches under to receive a $20 bill folded tightly into a square smaller than a quarter. Even as the exchange is occurring, she continues speaking. "He's my brother Pro."

From his position behind her, Pro doesn't see the drug deal. It is over in less than a second, and the man is already moving past his twin. On general principles, he stares the man down, though, and the guy steps off the sidewalk and drifts onto the asphalt in a subconscious effort to steer clear of the Fade's intimidating brother.

"What's with that guy?" As he watches, the man continues to arc around the parking lot toward an apartment in the far corner. His path had no reason to cross theirs other than the momentary meeting with Phaedra.

"Nothing. He's just friendly." She tries to dismiss the event, then when seeing that Pro is still fixated on it, reengages their previous conversation. "I can't just leave. Someone has to take care of Mama."

A massive spike of guilt lances through Pro when he realizes that he has left that task solely to his sister. "Is she... is it getting bad?" He was hoping her state of mental debilitation was solely because of Tommie but is aware that her decades of heavy drug and alcohol have to be taking a toll.

"She's better some days than others. The medical marijuana helps. I'm glad they passed that," she says, referencing the new law in Oklahoma.

"Uh-huh." He is noncommittal, both wondering how much Fade is trying to paint a good picture and trying to decide how to address the oppressive smell of weed in the apartment. "She doesn't smoke it around the kids, does she?"

This gets under his sister's skin. "You think we have a lot of options around here?" Her voice rises an octave and starts slipping into slang, "We barely making it. You off doing your thing, and that's fine for you. But we just *livin'* down here." She says *down here* like they are at the bottom of the ladder looking up at him, and he hates it. He also recognizes it as a defense mechanism.

He refuses to pity her. "I came from here, Fade. You think I don't know? Let me help you."

"Yeah? You want to help?" She points at his car. "How 'bout you let me drive your whip? We don't even have a grocery store within walking distance anymore. Did you know that?"

Not a chance. A deep part of him rebels against the thought, and he steers back around to his earlier suggestion. "Let me help you move. Maybe we can get you set up with your own car," he adds hopefully.

"You already forgot about Mama again?"

"No. Come on, let's figure this out," he pleads. "Where are you working right now? Is it full-time?"

"Oh my god!" She huffs angrily and rolls her eyes upward. "I didn't get to go to college, remember? I have two kids and a sick mother I take care of. You think I can make it flipping burgers part-time? We are struggling here, Pro!"

He narrows his eyes when something clear emerges from the tirade. It is the second time he has asked the question. *She's dodging it.*

She is wound up now, pent-up emotions suddenly slipping past her usual mask of control. "You don't like it? Fine. Go back to Tulsa, or hell for all I care." She steps toward him, eyes flashing as she looks up at him. She delivers her words straight from her heart, "I have things handled here. May not be your idea of perfect, but we are living. I don't need my big-shot brother coming in to fix everything."

He absorbs her anger. Searching her face carefully for guile, he finds none at the end of her tirade. He decides something is going on that she is not saying, but her feelings are genuine. Again, he feels like an outsider, the twin bond he had been hoping to rekindle denied to him.

Bright lights splash into the parking light, swaying first one direction then the next. Adrenaline spikes as Pro realizes it is the headlights of a vehicle coming quickly into the parking lot. His momentary instinct is that it is another drive-by, despite his earlier assertion that the Locos would stay away.

He shields his eyes against the painfully bright lights as they rush toward him. He is suddenly conscious that he and his sister are caught out in the open, unarmed and undefended. He starts to move in front of her, thinking to perhaps shield her body with his larger frame.

The car pulls up behind his Impala and stops. A white plastic sign sits atop the battered economy car, a hollow contraption with a light glowing faintly inside.

Fade snorts and steps out from behind him. "Watch out, Pro, it's the Pizza guy."

He feels foolish for a moment but then reprimands himself for doubting his tactical instincts. *It could have just as easily been the Locos. We need a way to keep them out. To keep anyone from just rolling up in here like this.* The stray thought seems ridiculous. It is not like Hillcrest is going to turn into a gated community anytime soon. But he can't shake the idea that there might be a way to make the complex more secure.

CHAPTER SEVEN

Although many of the houses are in disrepair, some of the small brick homes show clear hallmarks of pride-of-ownership. A carefully tended flower garden here, an impressive collection of garden gnomes there, perhaps a nicely polished 10-year-old car in the driveway. Some of the residents are old folks, predominantly Hispanic, who have been there for thirty years. But as the neighborhood ages, many houses are rented out to a younger generation who care more about putting fancy rims on their cars than doing upkeep on their property.

One car on the block really stands out, not by being brand new but because of extensive customization. An immaculate 1988 Oldsmobile Cutlass Supreme, riding on lowered suspension and gleaming wire-spoke wheel rims, squats on a cracked concrete driveway. Unlike the larger 20-inch 'dubs' often coveted as an upgrade, this car sports 13-inch undersized wheels to allow it to ride closer to the ground. What really makes it unique, though, is the intricate black and deep maroon pin-striping. The car's pattern is so detailed as to appear almost woodgrain up close, but the colors are so dark and similar in color that the vehicle could be mistaken for being all black from a distance.

The owner of this iconic vehicle is a 30-year-old man who is definitely not into garden gnomes. "Montana" Santos, a heavily tattooed Hispanic man, sits on the small concrete porch of his own home, beady eyes staring down the block. While he is often guilty of spending long hours staring appreciatively at his ride, he ignores it today. He is alert for signs of trouble and drinks a beer with his left hand, so his right stays available to his nickel-plated .45 ACP pistol.

His wife is yelling and carrying on in Spanish next to him, but he makes it less important than his next sip of beer.

A little boy! They are saying gangs!

He cradles his gun in his lap. He doesn't bother hiding it. Everyone on this block knows who he is.

Was that you? You killing kids now, Jose? Irritated that he is ignoring her, the animated woman puts her face in his line of vision.

The back of his hand flashes and collides with her lips and nose. "Puta," he calmly cusses her in Spanish, not even looking as she reels back in pain, "move."

She moves back out of reach, pissed but not surprised that he hit her. She continues giving him the business about the kid. *What if it was our child, Jose?*

"They hit us first." He looks in the direction of the garage with its three holes in the wooden garage door. Fortunately, the house itself was brick; no pistol was going to breach it.

She keeps at him, and he gets tired of her disrespect. Sighing, he picks up the pistol and points it in the direction of her head without bothering to look at her. She doesn't shut up until he moves his finger to the trigger. When she loses her nerve and goes back inside the house, he shakes his head slightly and takes another swig of his ice-cold beer.

He sees another Loco, his wiry friend Spider, emerge

from his house across the street and start sauntering his direction. Spider favors a small single-barrel sawed-off shotgun, and the way he is walking tells Montana the item is tucked in his waistband under his black shirt. Spider always dresses the part and has a black handkerchief neatly folded into a two-inch-wide flat strip draped over one shoulder. In gang neighborhoods, that is called a flag, and Spider never fails to fly his proudly.

As the other man reaches the driveway and starts walking past the car, Jose stands and tucks his own weapon in his belt, then steps forward for a handshake and one-armed hug.

After a brief greeting, Spider smiles. "You see the news? We smoked 'em good, Esse!"

Montana narrows his eyes and harrumps. "Just a lil baby-G." He looks disappointed. "I thought I got the big one."

His wiry friend is unperturbed. "One less soldier for them. Plus, I think we at least winged one or two of the other guys."

He narrows his small eyes to slits, considering. "They gonna be down for a minute for sure."

"You think they'll try and hit us back?"

"Probably, but brothers at County saying their Big Homie got locked up last week. They'll probably wait for him to get out."

Both men consider this. Spider is the first to speak. "Wanna hit 'im up on the inside? We got three locked up that would do it."

He shakes his head. "Fuck that. I want him dead, not just messed up, and County isn't the place for that." They both know prison would be easy enough for the right price, but while far from impossible in the Oklahoma County Jail, hitting somebody would attract a lot of attention.

The South Side Loco set leader continues, making his decision as he speaks. "Naw. We wait and watch for him to get out. They'll be on guard now, but by the time he bonds out, they will be feeling it more, start moving around."

Spider nods, listening while Montana lays it out, "Put the word out, I want them watched real close. Make sure they aren't getting froggy. If they start making moves, or when that *pendejo* Four gets out, we smoke them again." His gun is back in his hand, and he holds the large semi-auto sideways, jabbing it at the street repeatedly as he makes a silent 'pow-pow' motion with his lips. "And this time, we make sure we get them all."

D amarion "Four" Williams rages through his jail pod, blind with anger at the message. Everything is stainless steel and bolted down, but he smashes against the bed frames and the chairs in the open-bay jail cell, roaring in a fury.

"My brother, bro!"

The other three occupants of the cell watch the 27-year-old gang member warily, stepping out of the way whenever his rampage gets too close. One of them, an older Rollin 90's Neighborhood Crip locked up for the weekend after failing a surprise drug test on probation, makes empathetic noises. "That's some shit, bro. We got you. That's messed up."

The '90s are a smaller subset of Neighborhood Crips (NHC) and mostly live across town from Hillcrest but are allies.

Four comes up close to the man, eyes wild. "Yeah? You got me, huh? You gonna get behind me when I go after them? Cause I had nobody but my own set last time."

The man's look is guarded. J-One is in his late forties and is interested in seeing his fifties. He still claims the Rollin 90s, uses it for respect among the younger crowd, but he isn't banging anymore. Everyone he came up with is either dead or in prison, and with a nine-year suspended sentence hanging over his head and a new girlfriend 16 years his junior, the last thing he wants to do is go to war.

Four presses him, face twisted. "You an OG or a punk-ass bitch? You speak for the gang or just blowing smoke?" He subconsciously reaches for where he likes to carry his gun. "Cuz, I speak for my set, and we into some real shit!"

The older man crosses his arms, unruffled by Four's words or insults. Being an Original Gangster is a funny thing, and there is a reason not many guys reach that status. It is a very careful balance to maintain the younger generation's respect as they come up all full of piss and vinegar, trying to prove themselves. A careful balance of keeping the appearances of being full-on gangster while staying upright and out of prison. His current situation is a tough one because he got caught out on something dumb and is in here with this hothead who is demanding violence, but at the same time, a very real problem is brewing with the Locos, and they can't ignore such an obvious grievance.

"Into some crash-dummy shit, more like." He speaks flat and low, his voice having more impact by not raising it, "You come at me, it better be with respect. You into some real shit, huh? Bro, I been banging every neighborhood in the city since you were suckin' on your momma's titties."

"I'm quoted..." Damarion tries to reference his gang credentials.

"I know you are, off of 44th and Bryant," the man reels off the intersection where Damarion would have gotten beat up to gain gang membership, "I know that shit. Who do you think quotes 90s? ME. You wanna talk quoted? I took a couple years off from banging here so I could go out to LA. I went out there and did some *real* shit, got quoted all the way up to the top."

Gangs don't keep records, so the only way to prove gang

membership is to go ask the gang themselves, the Big Homies and OGs, about a particular person. If you are someone those guys will talk to, such as another gang member, then they will *speak for* the person you are inquiring about, vouch for them. If they know the person and know they are a real gang member, they are both honor-bound and ready to speak for them at any time. If your name is on the lips of the OGs, you are quoted. But don't get caught false-claiming a set because those same gang members are highly likely to kill you if someone comes asking, trying to confirm your membership, and no one ever heard of you.

Despite his rage, Four backs his attitude down a notch. "I got you, I hear you. Mad respect," he throws his thumb and first two fingers out in the over-arching NHC gang sign, "but I gotta know you are behind me on this. It's the Locos, bro, and they killed my *brother.*" His voice twists up at the end, emotion invading his speech.

J-One nods, thinking of all the angles. He would be busy planning revenge right along with this younger man back in his twenties, but now he sees the big picture. His girl is trying to start a clothing line; he has been buying some rental properties on the cheap. He has begun assistant coaching football at the middle school and fancies himself as an entrepreneur, a community builder. He had been quietly working with S-Loc, the leader of the 60s, to try to maintain a fragile peace with the other gangs in the city for the last two years. But these young guys are starting a war, and it is now reaching a level he and the other older guys can't ignore.

He walks a careful line when he responds. He balances his need to project power as an elder statesman of his own set, his desire to avoid another all-out gang war, the demands of the young set leader in front of him, and his own deep-seated desire for revenge for the slain youngster. "We'll speak on it."

"You'll *speak* on it? Are you fucking KIDDING ME!"

Four yells, unable to believe what he is hearing. He looks like he is about to say more, probably unload on the taciturn older man, but something in the eyes of the OG stops him.

"I *said*, we'll speak on it." His look is iron, and his eyes bore into the younger man. "In the meantime, you don't jump until S-Loc says. You do some crash-dummy shit *again*," he makes it clear he doesn't think everything Four has been doing is underwritten by the old heads, "you go dragging us all into some bullshit. You will have both gangs to answer to."

Four wants to argue, but he is smart enough to realize the man has made his decision, and it is a fair one. He is also intelligent enough to realize the precarious position his own set is in. The 60s and 90s together number more than 400 total across the city. But they tend to cluster in gang sets of no more than 20 and often, like his, as few as five. Only the OGs can unite them into an army, and even then, probably only for a short time.

He accepts the older man's words, "I appreciate it." He rapidly twists his hands to show an 'R,' then eight fingers and one thumb, followed by a circle with one hand and an 'N' for NHC with the other, fluidly stacking the gang signs for J-One's set. "The 90s are solid, on Crip."

The South Side Locos have been building steadily over the last 10 years and now number more than 600. It will take an army to face them. He just hopes his brother's death is enough to convince the OGs to give him that army.

After dropping Conners off at the station, Isabella drives north. the streets become better kept, the bars on the windows less frequent. Trees spread their branches in a welcoming arch over the small street she turns down, and middle-class cars mix with some nicer models in the drive-ways of houses she passes.

The day had been incredibly draining, and she absorbs these details as a general impression rather than individual observations. It's not Edmond, but the upper Northeast side is much better than the South Side.

Clean, prosperous, safe. Hello middle-class America, I'm home.

She pulls into the driveway of a small but well-kept brick home, hitting the button on her garage door opener as she approaches. Tony keeps the garage clean and clear of junk, so there is room to squeeze her department vehicle in next to the minivan he drives.

Her son's bike is up off the floor, on wall pegs to keep it from encroaching on her spot, and she smiles in anticipation of seeing him.

Edging between her car and the almost brand-new mini-van, she reaches her trunk and retrieves her go-bag with her body armor, extra magazines, and a folder full of different kinds of paperwork. She heaves the heavy container to her shoulder, holding it high to navigate back around the vehicles and get to the door leading into the kitchen.

When she enters the warm confines of the house, she is greeted by the sight of her husband turning from the stove with a smile and her seven-year-old son Brock running toward her with arms held high.

"Mama!" He hits her like a heat-seeking missile, wrapping both arms around her in a tackle that nearly causes her to lose the bag.

Tony abandons a spatula in a pan and steps quickly to save her, rescuing the teetering bag from her shoulder and setting it on the nearby granite counter. "Hey, babe, you hungry?" He leans over to give her a welcoming kiss over the top of the youngster. "I'm making breakfast for dinner. Eggs and bacon."

Evidence supporting his cooking claim greets her nostrils and mingles with the pleasant aroma of his cologne. She is beat and feels the sofa and a glass of wine calling to her but feels she owes it to him to engage.

"Sure, that'd be great." Telling her tired brain to mind its business, she smiles at her husband while crouching down to hug her son. Her voice takes on a joyful tone, "Hey buddy! Whatcha doing? Mama missed you so much!"

With the long and unpredictable hours she works, they had long since adapted as a family. With her bringing in the lion's share of their income, Tony had taken over responsibilities as a stay-at-home-dad. Her husband works from home doing web design to bring in extra income, and they are making a life of it, but she sure misses her baby boy.

The youngster babbles excitedly about a show he watched on YouTube, about somebody playing a video game. All she really understands is it is all *very* exciting. She smiles excitedly with her son and ruffles his hair as she looks up a little helplessly at Tony.

"He missed you," Tony says simply. Seeing her look change and knowing mother's guilt is never far from her mind, he changes the subject quickly. "How's the case? You said they finally give you a Murder-One?"

He hands her a plate of eggs, and she sags into a kitchen chair. She realizes she *is* hungry when confronted by the food up close. She doesn't want to talk about the case in front of Brock, but he tears off on a new adventure soon enough. Tony sits across from her, ready to listen.

Not for the first time, she feels lucky to be married to her husband of nearly seven years. Tony is a good man, a warm and loyal companion who unconditionally accepted her and her son. He had taken on the mantle of fatherhood with grace and love that she could never have dreamed possible.

She takes his hand now and smiles between bites, reminding herself she is glad to be with him instead of Pro. *He may not be tall-dark-and handsome. But he's about the furthest thing from a gangbanger.* The fact that he can easily pass for Brock's father has allowed them to raise the boy without awkward questions. She has built up a careful perception of normality around their life, a life she likes.

"Yeah, Captain gave it to me..." She has a vision of a grinning toddler coming up to her and Pro at one of her boyfriend's fights. "It's of a kid, though. And I know the family."

He makes a tsking sound, and his brow furrows empathetically, "Aw, that's terrible."

His look and presence is an open invitation to discuss the case, an unspoken understanding that she needs someone to share the weight with.

She talks a little more about the police details, the gang aspect, being teamed up with Conners. He nods along supportively. She attempts to casually slip in a tidbit about Pro, "Yeah, it's the craziest thing. I went to school with the family members on the South Side. Even dated one of the kid's brothers for a while."

Her vocal cords betray her casual tone, injecting unintentional emotion in her last sentence. The nervous chuckle she uses to try to hide it just makes it even worse, and Tony looks at her sharply.

Something inside him freezes, and he sits motionless at the table, pressing his lips together. They had met online and started dating when she was pregnant. She said the baby's father was from a gang family in her old neighborhood. She said he was no longer in the picture; he didn't even know he had a son. She may have implied that Pro was in prison and wouldn't be getting out. Tony had been gracious enough not to press for details. He was a good man and had accepted her decision to keep Brock from *that life*, agreed to keep him from knowing he had another father.

Now though, he grimaces. "Wait. Is it... him?"

She feels a piercing danger stabbing at her and wants desperately to deny the truth, to cinch her armor and keep her past from threatening the good life she has built with Tony. With no contact with Pro or his family, it has been easy to let the lie simmer, allowing Tony to think that she saved her son from gang life. She had lied to herself as much as him, though, with each day passing making it harder to admit that Brock should know his father.

It's far too late now. It would just wreck everything to tell Brock.

Her racing thoughts destroy any chance she had of possibly keeping the truth from Tony. He correctly reads her pause as his answer and is clearly hurt by her hesitancy to tell him.

He clears his throat awkwardly, eyes dropping. "Wow, that's crazy..." his eyes find an interesting spot on the table, and he rubs at it. "Guess it's good Brock isn't living there. Could have been him."

While his words are wise, she hates him for saying them. *Stop trying to defend me, Tony. Pro doesn't even live there anymore.* She wonders what Pro's life is like in Tulsa, what it would be like to be with him. She wants Tony to be mad at her for all she hasn't told him, feels guilty that he leaves the issue alone.

She reaches a hand across the table to where he is furiously rubbing the wood grain, arresting his agitated movement. "Yeah, thank God. We have a good life here." She uses the line of reasoning she has always used on herself. "*Brock* has a good life. You make our life good."

The subtext hangs unspoken between them. *I don't want that guy. I want you. You are my guy, Tony.*

He seems to understand, or at least accept their happiness at face value and takes her hand with a warm smile. "I love you."

"I love you too." She means it.

Her phone starts buzzing on the table next to her plate,

and she pointedly ignores it. When he raises an eyebrow, she grins, still looking at him. "The case can wait. We are having a moment here."

He laughs lightly and squeezes her hand, immeasurably pleased that she puts their relationship first. "No, you should answer it, babe. It's probably important."

She giggles, girlishly defiant. "Nope." A rush of warmth fills her as she commits again to the man who has made her life so wonderful. "Not as important as you."

He shakes his head and pushes her hand toward the insistent phone. "C'mon, it looks like Detective Protean needs your help cracking the case."

The name rolls unexpectedly off Tony's lips. It hits her like a lightning bolt, shattering her armor and sending the warmth she was feeling straight into outer space. She looks at the electronic device in horror, willing herself not to see what the caller ID reads.

Protean Williams.

"What?" Her voice comes out tight and high-pitched as she tries to figure out what is happening. *How is he calling me?*

Tony's eyes go from the ringing phone to her, and his playful smile evaporates when he sees the shock on her face. The phone rings again, and he makes the intuitive leap. "Wait, that's *him*?"

She snatches up the phone, suddenly desperate to deny the call, but the damage is done. Tony understands her intent. His features become a careful mask again, as he clearly chooses not to be offended about whatever is going on. "It's fine. Just answer it. I'm sure it's about the case."

She feels conflicted, half of her undyingly grateful to him for his understanding and graciousness, the other half angry at him for not fighting for her. *Don't let Pro back in my life, Tony.*

He can't hear her silent plea and is clearly done for now with trying to understand what she has going on under the surface. He stands, brusquely collecting her plate but showing no anger in the process. "Answer it." His voice sounds calm, forgiving, in control.

She wants to slap him, to be angry with him for not fighting harder, but answers the phone instead.

"How'd you get my number?" Her tone is accusing, needing to let Tony know this is a complete surprise to her.

"Isa?" Pro's voice is clear but hesitant. "I called in, and they said to call this number if I had any information. I was hoping it would be you."

That's what I get for being Primary on the case. "Yeah, it's me..." Her admission leaves her thrashing in deep waters, trying to figure out how to handle the call with Tony listening. She opts for the professional approach. "I'm at home now... Mr. Williams. Is this something that could wait until tomorrow?"

He tries to hide it, but she sees Tony look at her with a sideways glance from the kitchen.

"Mr. Williams? What the hell, Isa." He sounds hurt. "You want me to say Detective Contreras or something? I thought you might be going to help us..." He trails off as if reconsidering calling her.

Damn it, Pro. I want to help! She feels torn between opening up to him or ending the call quickly to put Tony at ease. "Can you come into the station tomorrow and discuss what you know with myself and Detective Conners?" Her request is not unreasonable. In fact, it's protocol, but she feels like she is slapping Pro in the face by putting him off.

He apparently feels the same way, and anger replaces the hesitancy in his voice. "Jeez. Went full cop, didn't you?"

"It would be better-"

"I'm not talking to that other asshole."

She thinks about Conners' plans to turn the shooting into

a big gang investigation and feels the need to warn Pro. *What can I say without compromising the investigation?*

"You need to be careful." The words leave her mouth before she can stop them.

"What?" He pauses, trying to figure out her vague warning. "Are you gonna help us or not?"

At that moment, Brock comes running back into the room, waving his tablet in the air to show her something. Tony looks from the boy to her, silently assessing if she cares more about being on the phone with her ex or paying attention to her son.

"Pro, I can't do this right now." She feels stretched in multiple directions, wanting justice for Tommie, trying to keep her relationship with Tony strong, and literally pulled downward by Brock's small hand.

"You have to listen! People getting killed down here, Isa. Gonna be a gang war." His voice is pleading, "Look, I know we ended bad, and I'm sorry."

"Mm-hmm." She tries to keep up her end of the conversation without betraying anything to Tony.

"We need you." She can almost hear him swallowing his pride on the other end of the phone. "Please help."

"I am helping."

"Good. Cause if you don't, they are going to-" He cuts off the end of his sentence.

He sounds on the verge of telling me about the gang. She knows what he has to say is critical but also that she can't absorb it right now. *Fricking Dispatch should have never given him my number.*

She makes her voice gentle but firm. "I will help. I am helping. But I need you to come in and talk to me at the station, Pro."

"Yeah, I got ya. Come in and get in a windowless room.

Let your partner bust my balls and accuse me of -you know what? I'll pass.

She winces at his clear distrust. *We once shared everything.* "I'm serious. Come in and talk to us."

"MOMMM!" Brock is becoming insistent, and Tony shakes his head disapprovingly.

"I have to go, Pro. I'm at home." She says it to Tony as much as to her Ex-boyfriend.

"Sure, sure. Thanks for nothing." He sounds betrayed.

She opens her mouth to say something more, to bridge the gap between them. But he hangs up, leaving her holding the phone like a broken link to her past. *Damn it, Pro...*

There is so much he could tell her that would help the case, so much she needs to tell *him,* but Tony is looking at her strangely.

What were you going to say, anyway, Isa?

She doesn't know the answer to her own question. She puts the phone in her pocket and turns her attention to the here and now, to her family.

She forces a smile as she finally turns her attention to Brock. "Yeah, baby, what you got there?"

"Look, mom, I'm cool, right?" He is wearing an oversized cap, cocked sideways. He folds his arms and closes his eyes halfway, trying to look tough. "See, I'm a gangster."

She snatches the hat away with more violence than she intended. "Not in my house, you're not."

CHAPTER EIGHT

His two small nieces stare at Pro over the top of their cinnamon toast crunch cereal. When Phaedra was sure the cops weren't coming back, that their names wouldn't end up in any reports, she had brought them back late last night.

Pro is used to being on an early schedule, but the rest of the family is still sleeping at this early hour. The girls' faces are solemn, and several spoonfuls of cereal disappear into their mouths with no one speaking a word.

"So, which one of you is the oldest?" He asks the question very seriously, brow furrowed as he looks between them as if he is trying to figure it out but can't.

They both giggle, and the smaller one points at her big sister. "Selena."

He narrows his eyes as if he doesn't believe her despite the noticeable size difference. "Are you sure? I thought you were the Selena."

She giggles again at his silliness. "No, I'm *Seriah*," she protests.

"Seriah," he repeats, making sure he is pronouncing it right.

He smiles inwardly but nods seriously as if he has gained an important piece of information. He places his hand on his chest and makes his best attempt at sounding regal as if introducing a prince, "and I am Pro. I'm your uncle."

The seven-year-old speaks, "We know that."

"Why don't you live here?" Seriah asks. In her world, everyone who is related lives nearby.

"Well, because I live in Tulsa. I'm a pastor up there."

Selena eyes him suspiciously. "Mama said it's because you are in the Army."

"Well, yeah, that too." He tries to think of how to explain the National Guard to the little girls. "I am in the Army part-time. Mainly I am trying to be a pastor, you know, to help kids get to heaven."

This mostly goes over Seriah's head, and in the way of a child, the four-year-old abruptly shifts back to what she knows about. "Tommie went to heaven."

She catches him by surprise, and he hears himself croak a weak reply, "Yeah, I know."

Selena's spoon drops into her cereal, and a moan escapes her throat. A sudden surge of emotion overcomes the seven-year-old, and her face erupts in tears.

Pro moves quickly around the table, tears of his own filling the corners of his eyes as he moves to put his arms around the girls. He kneels between their chairs, one arm around each, and pulls them close. Seriah sniffles, Selena cries, and Pro squeezes both for mutual comfort. That's how Phaedra finds them.

"I heard a noise," she says by way of explanation when she appears in the kitchen. She moves to rub Selena's back when she intuits what is happening. "I know, baby. It's gonna be ok, sweetie." Pro's twin still looks half-asleep, but the grief of her daughters is already infecting her.

This is going to be a long couple of days. The thought comes unbidden and registers in Pro's mind without resentment. But he refuses to accept misery and looks for an action to take, something to lighten their grief.

He releases them and stands up, clearing his throat forcefully. "We should do something today." He wants more than anything to cheer the little girls up. "Maybe go to the zoo?"

Phaedra looks at him over the top of her daughters' heads. She injects forced cheerfulness into her voice for the girl's sake. "Oh, the zoo would be fun!"

Her look at Pro is a question, one which he is happy to answer. "My treat."

She smiles, an expression of gratitude that is bereft of any real joy. Her phone makes a chirping sound, and she pulls in out of the waistband of her shorts.

"Shit," she says, half under her breath.

Little ears are finely tuned to detect profanity, even when they don't understand it. "Don't say the F-word, mama," Seriah admonishes.

"That's not the F-word," Selena corrects her younger sister.

"I said shoot," Phaedra defends herself distractedly while punching in a message rapidly on the electronic device.

His brow furrows. "What..."

She doesn't answer his half-formed question but immediately starts clearing items from the table. She grabs a salt and pepper shaker and puts them on the nearby counter.

"Finish your cereal, girls. Mama has to do paperwork." She disengages a child-safety latch on the door to a free-standing pantry cabinet in the kitchen corner, revealing a very professional-looking printer inside. She checks the printer paper with practiced ease and then pulls an expensive-looking laptop out of the cabinet and begins connecting it to the printer.

He stands, mouth agape at her sudden shift in demeanor and flurry of activity. The girls are less surprised and quickly scoop the remainder of their breakfast into their mouths before taking their dishes to the sink.

"Is Aunt Rae coming?" Selena sounds hopeful.

"She's not your aunt." Phaedra grabs a rag and rapidly wipes the table, scrubbing it like she is prepping a hospital room for surgery. "But yeah, she's coming."

Both girls look energized and run into their bedroom to change out of their nightgowns

Pro looks confused. "Who's Rae? And what's this?" He waves his hand at the workstation she is setting up on the now clean and dry table: pens, paper, a flat piece of cardboard, a magnifying glass.

She pauses in her preparations, looking embarrassed. "Look. You got a degree. You got the Army paying you the big bucks. You living that single life, without a care in the world."

"I have a girlfriend..." he trails off, suspecting that is not the point.

She continues, pointing vaguely in the direction of the parking lot, "You got a $30,000 Impala. You got health insurance." She turns on the computer and types a long and complicated password, then another, going through multiple layers of tight security.

Programs begin loading, and she takes the opportunity to face him directly, to offer an explanation. "You know what I got? I got shit on!"

He gestures toward the bedroom the girls just ran into. "Don't say that. You got two little angels-"

"Yeah. Two little angels that I can't afford to provide for. Their daddy never paying child support and always trying to take them away for good. No degree, no job. Was sharing a car with Four, but now he got it impounded." She works quickly, flicking back and forth between graphic editing programs on the laptop. The printer behind her whirs, and she spares him a glance. "You got a good-paying job. I got *this*. And I have a customer coming in hot."

"You do?"

"You wanna help? Go watch for a bright green car to come into the parking lot. A lightskin girl will be driving."

She goes back to typing, and he drifts toward the front of the apartment. Jiggy and Deuce left sometime in the night, but Ice is crashed out hard on the couch. Pro had spent the night in the recliner, and as he steps close to it now, he reaches down to fold in the footrest. He feels a reflexive need to clean up. *Company is coming.*

He peeks out at the quiet parking lot and finds himself relieved that his black Impala is right where he left it last night. Several low-dollar vehicles are nearby, some with plastic bags taped over broken windows or donut emergency tires. He sees one that actually has *two* of the small temporary tires on it and shakes his head —nothing bright green anywhere in the lot.

The girls come back out of the bedroom and pile onto the couch, heedless of the slumbering teenager. He groans sleepily and swats at them, but Selena pokes him and giggles. "Rae's coming."

He mumbles something about sleep, but when she repeats herself, he sits up. "For real?" He mutters a curse and looks around, then wipes his hands against his face and through his hair as if to clean himself up. Evidently realizing that won't suffice, and with a look of urgency flooding into him, the teenager stands up. He grabs a duffel bag at the end of the couch and starts moving toward the bathroom.

Pro's gaze moves from the boy's retreating back to Selena, one eyebrow raised questioningly.

"He likes her," the girl confides with a knowledgeable air.

Before he can answer, Pro hears squealing tires and looks back out around the curtain. A lime-green Dodge Challenger with thick black Daytona stripes shoots into the parking lot, decelerates abruptly, then swings in his direction.

"Uh, I think she might be here," He calls out

The car swings in a wide arc, almost hitting his Impala, then brakes so hard that it slides the last foot as it comes to a stop. The reverse lights flash on, and it backs up so quickly he thinks it will come right up over the sidewalk. He backs away from the window reflexively, but it slides in next to his ride like a knife going into a sheath, stopping neatly about an inch before the back tires hit the curb. The engine revs once, the deep throaty growl of an expensive Hellcat motor getting one last roar before the driver kills the ignition.

Niiice car. The thought has barely registered in his mind when *she* gets out of it.

Raeyanna Sallinger has long, straight, dyed-blond hair that frames a face aglow with the easy beauty of youth. Her skin is the color of a dark tan, and her halter top and tight shorts display plenty of it. Her face may be youthful, but her curves are all grown up and in all the right places. A mullato, or mixed-race girl, her type is heavily favored by black gang members.

She can't be more than 19! Pro wonders how she can afford to have such a nice car. Kids in Edmond, their parents might buy something like this as a graduation present for their daughter, but people on the South Side don't have that kind of money.

She walks toward his door, hips swaying, and he clears his throat. "Yeah. Must be her," he says loud enough for Fade to hear.

"Well, let her in!"

When he opens the door, the girl does a double-take. "Who the fu-"

Her eyes are open wide with surprise amidst long lashes, and he sees they are stunning green. A part of him feels like an uncertain teenager back in high school, but he capitalizes on his momentary position of superior knowledge to maintain an air of control.

"Come in," he steps back to let the door swing wide. He wants to say, 'we've been expecting you,' in a deep and mysterious voice, but it sounds cliché even in his head.

She hesitates, but then a small voice appears at Pro's side. "Aunt Rae!"

Recognition and relief dawn on the woman's face when she sees Salena. Her blond hair swishes as she darts a look over her shoulder at the entrance to the apartment complex. As her head swings back toward Pro, she is already stepping inside, her uncertainty about him overcome by wanting to get away from prying eyes.

"He's my uncle," the seven-year-old says before clapping her hands and jumping up and down. "What did you bring us?"

Fade calls out from the kitchen, "In here." A rapid clicking of keyboard keys emanates from the corner she has set up in.

Still a little unsettled by Pro's looming presence, Rae leans down to give both little girls a big hug. "Lemme talk to your mom first, then I'll show you." While she is bending over to hug them, she looks up at Pro, her eyes searching his face for some clue about him.

"Sup, Rae." Ice emerges from the bathroom, a cloud of Axe body spray from his freshen-up effort following close behind. He leans against the wall casually with his arms crossed and eyes half-closed.

Pro's chest spasms in a silent chuckle at the boy's obvious effort to both get ready for the girl but also be nonchalant about her arrival.

She moves past him, headed toward the kitchen and Fade. As she passes him in the narrowed space, she drags her hand lightly across his arms and chest. She sticks her chest out, turns her head toward him, and gives him the full benefit of her heavy lashes as she goes by. "Heyyy, Ice."

Pro finds himself following her but stops when he reaches his brother. He speaks low, out of the side of his mouth. "Tryhard."

Ice keeps his casual smirk intact and replies through his teeth in the same tone of voice, "Don't be jelly."

Rae leans down to hug Phaedra where she sits. "I heard. I am soooo sorry, baby."

Fade closes her eyes momentarily, putting one hand on the other woman's arm to acknowledge the gesture. She is suppressing all emotion, though, and happy to have an urgent task to work on. When her eyes open, she is all business and holds out a hand expectantly. "Paperwork."

The younger woman digs the car registration out of her purse and hands it over. Her teasing, flirtatious tone from a mere moment ago is gone. She also seems to intuit that her friend does not want to talk about yesterday's events and obliges her by focusing on the task at hand. "It's a Hellcat. Make sure you put that," she says to Fade.

"K." Taking the paperwork and scanning through it to find the Vehicle Identification Number, Fade deftly types it into her program with one hand. "When did you pick it up?"

"20 minutes ago. Some idiot left it running in the driveway."

"40 minutes left. You want me to roll with you for the drop-off?" Ice asks.

Leaning over the table to confer with Fade, she looks

back over her shoulder at him and smiles in a clear come-on posture. "You want to?"

"Yeah, I mean it's whatever," Ice tries and utterly fails to act like that wasn't exactly what he was hoping for.

The machine behind Fade starts making noise, and heavy, embossed paper issues from it when the item prints. "There's the title," the female twin says to no one in particular.

The little girls crowd into the kitchen, vying for Rae's attention. She smiles at them and kneels on the kitchen floor, digging in her purse. She pulls out a large gold watch and a $10 bill. "Ooooh, I got a Rolex and some cash."

Seriah reaches for the expensive man-sized watch. "Ooh, pretty."

Selena snatches the cash. "Oh, I'm taking that money." She runs off to the bedroom to squirrel her newfound riches.

Rae helps the four-year-old put on the watch, which is so big it slides all the way up her arm to her bicep. "There you go, a pretty armband," she says to the girl.

"I'm going to wear it to church next week."

While all of this is happening, Pro has been putting the pieces together. "Wait, your car is *stolen*?"

She looks up from the girl's new piece of jewelry, arching an eyebrow at Pro, then turns her head questioningly to Phaedra.

To Rae, Phaedra says, "He's my twin brother. He moved away and just came back for the... you know." No one wants to say the word funeral. Her eyes shift to Pro, and she keeps speaking, "He has been gone for *quite a while*. Guess he forgot what it is like down here at the bottom." She keeps talking but now directed toward Pro, defending herself, "I told you, this is what I got. I got skills, and I support my girls, but I'm no youth pastor."

Rae stands up, looking Pro up and down. Her eyes stop on the tattoo on his left arm, the one with the 'S' inside the money bag. "Youth pastor?" She snorts a laugh. "I thought you were fresh out of the Pen." She says, meaning newly out of prison, "You banging or false claiming?" She stacks signs fluidly, throwing an N, then rolling her arms over each other before coming up with five fingers and a thumb raised.

She's claiming Rolling Sixties and throwing it like she's actually in the gang. Female gang members are not unheard of, and while the initiation process is quite different, they can be some of the most cold-blooded members once in. "I'm inactive," he equivocates, "been away for a minute."

Fade's computer beeps, and she looks down. "Shit-yeah. Already got a hit on Craigslist." She frowns when she realizes she cussed in front of Seriah again and glances at her apologetically. "Sorry, lovey."

Rae crowds to look at the message on the computer screen, "Does it look legit?"

Ice smiles at Pro. "Never seen a hotbox before, bro? We moving like two or three per week."

Some guy in Midwest City already bit on the Challenger. "He says he'll do $8,000 if we have the title," Fade reads.

"All notarized and ready to go," is her typed reply. She looks at the document beside her. It proclaims itself to be a California certificate of title and has a notary seal already printed on it. Most Oklahomans will have no idea what a California title should look like anyway, but the laser-printed forgery is good enough to fool just about anyone.

At least until they try to register it at the Department of Motor Vehicles.

She picks up a black pen, signs a loopy flourishing signature for the notary, and exchanges it for a blue pen. She takes a moment to practice a signature on a blank piece of paper for the actual listed owner of the car and then smoothly signs 'Sasha Gomez' in the seller block. In memory, someone may wonder if Rae was half-Hispanic, and the name well help send their brain down that rabbit hole.

The man comes back with a place to meet, and Rae snaps the fingers on both of her hands at once. "Boom. We moving."

Pro can't believe what he is seeing. "You are going to go meet some rando from Craigslist? How do you know he's not going to rob you? For $8,000, he has to know it's stolen and that you won't call the cops."

Rae looks at Ice. "You got your strap?"

"Shiiih, I keep that thang on me, Crip." Ramping himself up into action mode, Ice dials up both his bravery and gang language.

The vivacious teen looks at Pro, confidence brimming. "I'm protected, see?" She takes a step toward him, her posture and voice changing none-too-subtly, "Of course, if a tall-dark-and-handsome like you wanted to ride along too, I might let him." Her lips are pouty, her eyelashes suddenly look heavy, and it is blatantly clear she is throwing her feminine charms at him, collateral against the value of additional protection he could offer.

Her perfume invades his nostrils, and the proximity of her ample chest is suddenly all he can think about. His hormones scream at him to say yes, yes to anything that involves her, but his brain successfully regains control.

"You're crazy." He steps back, putting distance between them. "The cops will be out looking for that whip, and it sticks out like crazy! You idiots are going to sell it in broad daylight?" He looks sternly at the girl. "What are you, 18, 19? Who's your Big Homie? Someone better pull you back."

Her eyes flash, and she immediately goes from flirting to looking ready to stab him. "I move around. But Four will speak for me." She makes the Playboy Bunny sign with one hand and South Side with the other. "We're all on the same team here."

Fade's urgent voice cuts between them, "30 minutes. Y'all gotta go." She addresses Pro specifically, "It takes at least 60 minutes from the time it is reported before the cops can get it entered into the system. We unload it now, and no one will be the wiser until it's too late."

"Told you, bro, like two *stolos* per week, sometimes more. We gotta pull together $15,000 to get Four back out." Ice says.

Rae nods, and as if a spring has been released, the two teenagers immediately start moving toward the front of the apartment. Pro feels a powerful urge to go with them, supervise the youngsters, so they don't get robbed, or worse. Everything is happening too fast, and he feels like it is headed toward a disaster he can't prevent.

He looks at his sister helplessly, his voice a hollow reproach, "Fade. I see like five felonies happening here. There's gotta be a better way. You are better than this!"

She snorts. "No, I'm not. None of us are." Her eyes grow hard, "You want to come back and pay your respects to Tommie, the family you left, then fine. But if you are here to judge us, then get the hell out."

The tense moment hangs between them as Pro looks for the right thing to say. Fade suddenly leaps to her feet, muttering a curse. She clearly wants to run to the front door, but she is all the way on the wrong side of the table, trapped by the computer cord and Pro's body.

"Stop them!" Her voice has gone from resigned confidence to fear, and he reacts immediately.

The Hellcat roars to life, and he rushes to the driver-side door, racing to stop Rae before she pulls out.

The car starts to move as he reaches for the handle, and

he desperately slaps the glass and metal on the side of the vehicle.

Hearing the thump, Rae brakes sharply. When she sees it's him, she rolls down the window with a smirk. "Change your mind, old balls?"

Old balls? What the hell, I'm 24! He pushes the useless thought aside. "Fade said to stop you," is his clever reply.

The woman herself rushes out of the apartment and joins him at the window of the car. Slightly breathless, she leans down to speak through the low window but is careful not to touch the car. "Babe, I forgot."

"What?" Rae glances at the parking lot, feeling exposed.

"Four got my car impounded, remember? Who's doing the pickup?"

Rae sucks in her breath, twisting her face in an expression of uncertainty. "Who else you know that has a car we can use quick?"

Fade is looking into the Challenger, and her focus is drawn to Pro's Impala parked on the other side of it. She turns toward Pro, her face starting to form the question, and he takes a step back, palms raised. "Uh-uh. Don't look at me. This isn't my deal."

From his position in the passenger seat, Ice speaks in an urgent voice, "Y'all, we 35 minutes in already. This box getting toasty!"

Fade stands up and looks him in the eye. "It's just a ride. They need someone to bring them back after the deal."

"No. Me and my car are going nowhere near this."

Rae revs the Hellcat to get him his attention. Her look manages to be both scornful and enticing at the same time. "What do you want, old balls, a blow job? Crip the fuck up!"

Before he can answer, she lets out the clutch, and the sports car surges out of the parking spot.

"I'm not old!" He calls after her as the car starts moving.

"And I'm not banging anymore..." he trails off as she is already 50 yards away and picking up speed.

Fade touches his arm. He looks down and sees that she's looking after the reckless pair, worried. At that moment, when she is subconsciously reaching to him for support, afraid that her already teetering world may topple completely over, he finally feels the connection he has been missing.

It's nice to be needed. He and Liz share something very strong, very mutual, but he knows she doesn't *need* him. She is an educated professional, an Officer in the Army. She does Crossfit AND Yoga and drinks dark beer if she feels like it.

But in this moment, with a ramshackle plan already going off the rails, he is acutely aware his family needs him. When his twin looks up at him, he can't say no again.

"Tell her she needs to change the meeting spot when she is almost there. Don't let anybody be settin' up on 'em." He moves toward his car, not quite believing the words are coming out of his mouth. "And the closest I'm getting is a block away."

CHAPTER NINE

"Not, it's not a steaming hot pile of crap," Conners corrects her, "It is a tangled web of crap. Much more useful."

They sit in the briefing room, surveying the evidence they have gathered so far. It doesn't look very hopeful to Isabella. "Oh. Why didn't you just say so? I feel so much better now. Why don't we go for an executive lunch and then knock off for the rest of the day since we are so far ahead?"

He ignores her sarcasm. "I didn't say it was going to be easy. We just have to put it together."

She smells her stale gas-station coffee, trying to decide if a sip of the no-longer-warm fluid is worth it, and decides against it. She puts the Styrofoam cup down and begins ticking off what they have so far, "Dark-colored sedan, probably a two-door, but also long and maybe a four-door. Color is either black, or dark purple, or maybe blue, or maybe forest green."

He grunts. "It's older, maybe classic. That's important."

She continues without acknowledging his comment. "Unknown race and number of people in the car. Fuzzy surveillance from a gas station on the corner gets us no closer on the car color and nothing remotely resembling a license plate number."

She shuffles papers in front of her, reading the initial lab report. "Shell casings are multiple .45, 9mm, and," she holds up a picture, "a single 20 gauge shotgun shell."

He refuses to be pessimistic. "Yeah, see. That's unusual. That could be a lead. Did you send them to OSBI for prints?"

"Of course I did, but you know that could be weeks, or even months before they get to it." She doesn't add that this type of biometric matching rarely yields a useful result, falling in the 'pulling out all the stops' category. It seems clever in training when everyone nods knowingly that criminals don't think to wipe their prints off of their ammunition. But the reality is that bullets are small, slippery, rounded objects, and a usable print is not very common.

He frowns. "Tell Captain to call up there and put a boot in their asses. If he tells them it is about the kid, they may move it to the front of the line."

It's a good idea, and she silently makes a note before going back to their sparse list of evidence and leads. "Motive? Possible gang connection with this guy Four. The few neighbors who would come to the door said nothing very useful..." She trails off, then comes back reluctantly, "I mean, unless we write paper on the house, I don't know what we do next."

"Screw that noise," He rejects the idea of writing a search warrant as he rocks forward and onto his feet, "By now, they have hidden anything important anyway."

"Then... steaming hot pile of crap," she repeats.

He grabs a dry-erase marker and walks over to the massive whiteboard that stretches across one side of the room. "No. A web. Let me show you." He starts drawing circles with names or question marks in them, connected by lines. Sometimes the lines get a small word or two next to them. "This is not random, it has happened for a reason, and that reason is related to these people and their actions."

Off to one side, he draws a triangle and puts People, Places, and Patterns, one at each corner of the triangle. "You learn trigonometry in school?"

"I'm a woman, not an ingrate."

In the barest of acknowledgments, he tilts her head that she has scored a point before jabbing at the triangle. "It's like that. If we know any two of the points of this triangle, we can figure out the third."

She regards the drawing critically and mentally applies it to the in-progress spiderweb of information he is scrawling on the rest of the board.

He moves several feet to the side and draws a large house symbol with 'SSL' inside, then a car and several circles connected to it, all with question marks in them. "So far, this end of the triangle is all unknowns," he writes 'dark' in small letters inside the car outline, "well, almost all unknown."

He steps back to his triangle and taps 'Patterns.' "But we do know one thing for sure, which is that they do drive-bys and aren't overly worried about hitting a kid." He bounces back to the Locos house symbol and draws a nearby square with 'drive-by' in it. "So now we have a pattern, a gang-related one, which already narrows our search."

She watches him, intrigued that the cynicism and grating attitude have disappeared as he draws on the board. *He really loves this stuff.*

He warms to the subject as he speaks, further confirming her realization. "Now, if these turds in Hillcrest had told us who was pissed at them, we would already have two points of the triangle and could start narrowing down a suspect location. Looking for that black/green/purple classic car." He writes 'classic, inside the car symbol. "But since they didn't, we have to reverse engineer that information."

"OK. But how if no one will talk to us?" She says. She hasn't told Conners about her phone call with Pro, but still holds out hope that he will come in and talk to them.

He chuckles. "Oh, they are *always* talking to us. You just have to know how to listen." He taps the triangle. "Don't listen for their words; listen for these three things. Work for them, so we can do our trigonometry." He writes out a list of things he extracted from the tumultuous exchange at apartment 119:

Person – Four, Pro, 3 male teenagers, crying female
Pattern – Gang Activity
Place – 119, Jail, moved away

Reading what he writes, she objects, "Pro wasn't involved. He has been gone."

"You don't know that. Do you know where he has been? Maybe he's just up banging with the 60s off Northwest 63rd and Lirewood. There's a ton of them up there."

The neighborhood designation means nothing to her, and she shakes her head, trying to keep feelings from the past from interfering with their current task. "No, he went to college and then moved away, Tulsa, I think."

He erases '*moved away*' and replaces it with '*Tulsa?*' "Well, maybe he's uninvolved, and maybe he isn't. If he *is* out of the life now, maybe we can use him. He may be willing to come in and talk to us, and even if by accident, help fill in our triangle."

"How does jail help us?" She points to Four's name. "If he did the last drive-by, there's no way he'll talk to us."

"Jail is awesome. Jail is our friend." He points at the triangle and then draws a replica next to Four's circle on the spiderweb. One corner of the triangle touches his name, another reads Jail, and at the third, he scrawls 'pattern?'

He steps back from the chart and goes into a monologue, explaining his process. "We have got nothing solid to go on for physical evidence yet. Normally we sit back and wait a couple months. See if the mighty Oklahoma Bureau of *Super-Slow* Investigation can magically produce a suspect from the shell casings, but screw that."

She grunts concurrence about the slow speed of forensic returns but lets him keep rolling.

"We need to be hot on this because it will go cold very fast. We have loads of intel to work with." He starts pointing at different sections of what he wrote. "And we have two sides of the triangle already filled in on several of our players. Patrol put the names of everyone in the victim's house in their scene report, and the kids confirmed Four is indeed their family member, plus we got your boyfriend, Pro."

She wants to tell him again that Pro isn't her boyfriend but suspects he is just needling her. She stays quiet while he continues his diatribe.

"So, we know *people* and *places*, or at least two places, for most of this set." He taps the Crips portion of the spider web. "All we need to do is use that information to gain visibility on their *pattern*, and they will lead us straight to their enemies."

"You think they will retaliate?"

"Oh, I guarantee they will," he says confidently. He places one palm over Pro's collection of information and the other over Four. "These guys right here are the key. If Pro is involved, he will lead the retaliatory strike. If he is not, then Four will do it when he gets out of jail. Either way, they will recon the neighborhood first, probably in the middle of the day."

She stands up, moving around to the board while shaking her head. "I'm telling you, even if Pro was in the gang years ago, he isn't now. He went good. What is Four's bond? Is he even getting out?"

He grunts and starts poking at his phone, pulling up the

publicly available county jail inmate information page. "Here we go, Damarion Williams." He chuckles at the book-in pictures of the heavily tattooed 27-year-old, "Look at this turd. Let's see, $150,000 for felony eluding, possession of a firearm after a former felony conviction, drug paraphernalia, three grams of cocaine, and obstructing an investigation."

She shakes her head again. "They are poor. There's no way they are going to be able to come up with $15,000," she references the 10% payment a bail bondsman typically charges. "And we can't watch him do anything while he's locked up."

"You'd be surprised what these gangs can pull together to get each other back on the street. A lot of times, they literally have bail funds stashed away and are back out in days." He dismisses the jail web page and starts scrolling through his phone contacts. "But Mr. Williams' public defender has already filed the standard motion for a bond reduction." He selects 'OK COUNTY DA' from his contacts list. "And lucky for us, I am used to working with the DA to raise and lower bonds."

She wrinkles her brow, catching on. "You are going to lower his bond? *Help* a dangerous gang member get back out just so we can watch what he does?"

"Absolutely. We do it with informants all the time."

She takes a step back and regards the whole board. There is almost no information on the suspect side, nothing much other than South Side Locos. But the Crip side of the board is a tangle of lines, symbols, and labels.

She summarizes his approach. "You want to investigate the victims. Do surveillance on them, figure out what their pattern is, so it will lead us to our suspects."

His phone is ringing, but he pulls it down from his ear to respond. "Told you I would help you solve it--" The District Attorney's voice comes from his earpiece, and he brings the device back to his ear. "Hey! Yeah, it's Conners. I got something for ya. Need your help on this kid homicide."

While her partner spins the deal, she looks at the tangle of intelligence from another perspective. She is amazed that he has pulled all this data directly from memory onto the whiteboard. *He could probably keep drawing lines and circles all day, connecting these people to other crimes and gangs.* Conners hasn't fully explained how a RICO case actually works yet. Still, this brain dump strikes her as a visual representation of what he is trying to build.

It's like a chart in an FBI movie, where all the strings lead to the Kingpin. She realizes if he starts adding criminal charges to each name as they commit them, ties them all together, this could be an enormous case. *But on who, the Locos or the Crips?*

By the drawing in front of her, she knows what the answer will be. They have far more information about the Crips, and Conners is already hot for them, especially this guy Four, who he is letting back out of jail.

She wants justice for Tommy. But Connors clearly is aiming his RICO gun squarely at Tommy's family. And it's Tommy's murder investigation, *her case,* that's loading the gun.

Her phone feels heavy in her hand, and she imagines herself looking through her recent calls, calling Pro, telling him to watch out. She feels like a traitor, forced into a position where she must choose between two lies to live. One path betrays her Ex-boyfriend and the family whose young child was murdered. The only alternative is to undermine her partner, profession, and possibly even her family.

"Hey Mama," Phaedra looks up, eyes solemn when her mother emerges from the bedroom a little after noon. Her quiet step-sister Aliyah is visible through the open door, staring at her phone on her own bed inside the bedroom.

The older Williams woman's voice bears an ocean of sadness as she replies, "Hey." She swallows hard and walks to the couch where Fade's girls are sprawled. She sits between the two little girls and reaches an arm around each of them to pull them close. "How are my babies? What you watching?"

The girls mumble something between a greeting to their grandmother and a vague description of the TV program but mostly just feel awkward and unable to process their emotions.

Seriah thinks of something and pushes her arm toward her grandmother. "Lookit my new bracelet."

The older woman does a double-take when she spots the $1,000-plus Rolex. "Whoa, that's really pretty, baby." She looks at her daughter questioningly.

Fade offers a single word as an explanation, "Rae." She rubs her fingers and thumb together in sign language for 'cash' and speaks in quiet sentence fragments, so the little girl won't pick up on it, "When she gets tired of it."

Mama Williams nods, understanding perfectly. Her phone is clutched tightly in her hand, and when it buzzes, she looks at it like a lifeline. A stream of condolences on Facebook demand her attention. She deals with a few of them and then looks at Fade.

The older Williams woman can't quite bear to make eye contact and talks sort of at her daughter's shoulder area instead. "My brother Joe and his wife are coming up from Dallas tomorrow. They are getting a hotel." The words hang in the air between them, evidence of but still not a direct reference to the subject's painful center.

She swallows, trying to find ways to talk about the logistics without talking about *it*, "The church wants $750 to let us have a wake there. Best they can do. They said it has to be a closed casket-" Her voice is overcome with emotion as if the realization she is planning her youngest son's last rites caught up to her and bit hard at the end of her sentence. Everyone wants to say goodbye, and a closed casket is another blow to her already battered soul. The harshest pain springs from a brief moment of visualization where she imagines *why*.

A speeding bullet. A small boy's head. It is too much, and her hands start shaking. No sound emits from her lips, but a silent wail constricts her chest until she has no air left in her lungs. The little girls, feeling her grief keenly but not knowing how to process it or their own, snuggle into her sides.

Fade doesn't wait to be asked and retrieves a Xanax bar from her room. When she pushes it toward her grieving mother, she is surprised by the reaction she gets.

"No!"

"What?"

"I don't want to just not feel." The words come in a strangled cry. Her mother is weeping openly, staring at the anti-anxiety medicine hungrily but exhibiting an unusual resistance to it.

Fade frowns. Not knowing what to do to help. The pill comprises four perforated half-milligram doses, and her mother has been taking one or two whole tablets at a time for years. Ever since Aliyah's father broke her jaw. Fade snaps the pill in half. "Here, just to take the edge off? Do your breathing."

Her mother sniffles and downs the fragment. She forces herself to breathe, four seconds in, hold four, out four, empty four, repeat. Over the next 10 minutes, her chest relaxes enough that she can breathe more naturally.

"My check doesn't come in for another week. Do you have $750?" She says.

The younger woman nods her head, reassuring her mother. "Yes. I sold some last night and this morning, and Rae brought a good car."

Mama looks relieved. She rushes on, trying to get the

words out before her voice fails her, "Cremation is cheaper, but I want to bury him. Have a spot to visit. Aliyah wants to bury him next to her mother..." Her voice gives way again, but her look is one of pleading.

Understanding the silent question, Fade feels anger. She wishes she had enough money for everything, but there's just no way. *And that doesn't even take into account trying to bond Four out.* The family always rallies to pay the 10% fee to get any family members back out of jail. It's a strategy that makes sense, considering all of the lost revenue of having them locked up. But Four's bond is really steep this time. Combining that with coming up with funeral expenses, all while pulling together rent money to give Gina and keeping the family fed, it's too much. Mama's Social Security Disability check is only $900 per month and isn't even enough to feed the small clan.

"Maybe Pro can help?" Fade ventures. "I haven't said anything about it, but he seems to want to." For some reason, the idea of asking her estranged brother for money galls her.

Mama brightens at this. "Where is he?"

As if in answer, a steady hum of a motor approaches from outside. Not the roar of the stolen Challenger, but a low steady tone. Fade stands and unbolts the door to let the returning heroes in.

Ice is the first through the door, and smiling confidently. Pro trails looking clearly unhappy.

"Where's Rae?" Fade says.

"We dropped her off." Ice withdraws a stack of bills from his pocket and pushes them toward her. "Our half!"

Pro shuts the door behind him and spots his mother on the sofa. He can immediately tell she is not as heavily medicated as yesterday and feels her eyes upon him. He pushes aside his anger at being sucked into involvement in the criminal activity and goes to her.

His voice is gentle. "Hey, Momma."

He kneels down to hug her where she sits, and she tries not to cry. She smiles as she embraces him. "My good boy. I miss you."

Ice and Fade share a glance, and Fade gives an almost imperceptible shake of her head. She counts off ten $100 bills and hands them to Ice for his involvement, hanging onto the rest. Ice nods his head, more than happy with the split.

Looking at the $3,000 in her hands, Fade speaks loudly. Much louder than needed. "A good hit, but it isn't going to cover funeral expenses. And Four is still locked up."

Ice does not hesitate but immediately pushes his share back towards her. "Hey, use mine to help. I'm straight."

She smiles at him, both happy with his generosity and that his action will put more pressure on Pro. She smacks his shoulder in camaraderie. "On the set." She looks discretely at her mother out of the corner of her eye.

Mama catches the look but hugs her second-oldest son a moment longer, unwilling to turn the moment of reconnection into begging for money. Necessity has always run deep in Mama Williams' life, though, and she pushes back from the young man. "We need help, baby. Will you help us?" Her eyes are searching, asking what kind of man her boy has turned into. "With money, I mean."

He looks sideways at the pile of cash in Fade's hand and then back to her with furrowed brows. "Of course. I got a little saved. How much do you need?"

She smiles and squeezes his shoulder but, instead of answering, looks at Fade. "You got a stick? I need to smoke."

Fade produces an Altoids tin from a pocket in her shorts and removes a lighter and a rolled marijuana joint. She hands both to her mother in a fluid and automatic response without comment or notable expression.

No stranger to marijuana, Pro's eyes still widen at his

mother handling the substance while seated between the two young girls. *She's not going to smoke it right here, is she?*

He stands quickly and offers a hand to his mother. "You wanna come outside and smoke? I'll show you my car."

"Sure, honey." Some of his alarm must show on his face because she looks defensive as she stands. She holds up the joint with one hand. "Medical."

"Yeah, I know," he tries to keep his voice the same as if she was holding a bottle of Tylenol. It feels weird, though. When he was growing up, possession of the common drug was a felony. *Is it really any different than any other medication?* He moves toward the door, unsure how he feels about it but knowing he doesn't want her to smoke in the house. The place already reeks of weed as it is.

Outside, she lights it up just the same as if it was a cigarette and takes a long drag. "Nice car, Protean." She holds the smoke in her lungs, letting her body absorb it, and when she exhales, he steps back.

Seeing her mildly offended look, he says, "Ma, I have to take drug tests." He waves his hand back and forth but utterly fails to disperse the sickly-sweet smell of the drug.

She chuckles. "A little smoke won't make you pop for anything. I thought you were a preacher, though. They drug test for that now?" She takes another drag.

"I am youth pastor, but I am also on active-duty orders in the guard. I do both. Preaching to a half-dozen teenagers doesn't pay anything, but the Army keeps the bills paid." He has never thought of his income as anything more than adequate, but back at his impoverished roots, he feels a strange need to downplay his success.

"I see that." She pinches the joint between a thumb and forefinger, motioning with it toward his sleek black Impala. "Beautiful. Must've cost a stack of cash."

Pride swells at her compliment, and he can't help but talk

about it. "Thanks. I did all the work myself. Sound system, some bolt-on upgrades under the hood, I even swapped out the suspension for all high-end parts to correct the angles from the bigger wheels."

She smiles slightly, not entirely tracking the detail of what he is describing but happy to see he is passionate about it. "You were always so smart, baby. Good at everything. That's why I named you Protean. Changeable, multifaceted, multi-talented, good at everything."

He knows this, of course, but the combination of marijuana and Xanax is relaxing her, and he lets her talk. "Phaedra too. Means 'bright.' A princess in Greek mythology. My bright princess. Protean and Phaedra, I always knew you two were going to be special..." her voice drifts off, and a faraway look enters her eye. Her head shakes slightly back and forth as she looks at the car. "But you are so *different* now."

The way she says the word makes him feel judged, measured against his twin, and perhaps somehow found lacking. He clears his throat. "I did it, Mama. I did what you said."

She looks at him with a half-lidded gaze, cool, appraising. "Did you?"

Expecting approval, her response catches him off guard. His brows knit together. "Yeah. I went to college! Got the Army to pay for it too, no student loans." His life choices spill out, evidence spread before her in an attempt to make a case he thought was self-evident. "I have a nice car, a good-paying job, health insurance. I have *respect* from my peers. I got respect at church, and it's a *white* church." He doesn't know why he said the last part, why it's relevant. As the words settle around them, he finds himself hating himself for having said it but can't explain why.

She hums thoughtfully. Her words are less articulate when she speaks, but perhaps more honest, from the mixture of drugs in her system. "Yeah, you have done a lot for yourself..." she steps forward to run her hand lightly on the fender of his shiny car.

"I have done a lot for God too," he protests. "You said I owed God a life now. I did it, right? I mean, I am teaching young people about God, trying to save more lives. I did it, right, Mama?"

"You have done a lot for *yourself*," this time, the last word has extra emphasis on it. She turns her face toward him, not judging but clearly questioning. "But for God?" Her look says she's not so sure.

"I'm a pastor!"

"What have you done for your *family*, Protean?" She jabs a quivering finger at the sidewalk. "Right HERE. Your family dying right HERE." Tears form in the corner of her eyes, and she takes an emergency puff on the last of the joint, hotboxing it desperately.

Her gaze bores into him with deep pain that tears places of him he thought were safe, but he can't look down. They cleaned the spot yesterday, but he's terrified he might see a stray brownish-red splatter, some evidence of his failure to protect his family.

She coughs as she exhales. When she speaks, she doesn't exactly blame him for Tommie's death but doesn't absolve him either. "Jesus, he says to protect your family, right? I said you owed God a life. Never said to leave your family for dead."

Pro had taken some powerful punches when he was a boxer, even been knocked out a few times. But this statement from her slams into him harder than any blow in his life. He keeps his feet, but his mind is stunned, reeling from the implication.

His mother is unable to withstand the pain of her own reproach and drops her eyes. She grinds the burned-out joint under a slippered foot and goes back inside, leaving him to his tortured thoughts.

It's not supposed to be like this. He looks skyward, frustration blooming. *I did everything right. You are supposed to handle the rest, right?* His only answer is a siren wailing in the distance. The sound turns his mind toward Isabella, and his frustration hardens to anger. *Zero loyalty! You were supposed to help us, but we on our own out here, huh?*

The siren fades, and no other reply is forthcoming. Then, unbidden, a Bible verse slowly materializes in his mind.

1 Timothy 5:8 – "If anyone does not take care of his own relatives, especially his immediate family, he has denied the faith and is worse than an unbeliever."

"But I did it. I did what you said." His voice sounds small and insignificant, and with no one left on the sidewalk but himself, he wonders who he is trying to convince. He suddenly feels eager to help, not obligated. Desperate to take care of his family.

She never even told me how much money she needed.

He turns toward his car, ready to go to the ATM and withdraw the max his bank will allow. A sound and a movement draw his attention, and his eyes focus past his Impala to a metallic-gold painted Chrysler 300 pulling into the parking lot. The windows are tinted so dark there is no way he can see inside, but his instincts scream danger.

That car doesn't belong here.

The vehicle comes almost to a complete stop before turning slowly toward him as if reading addresses and trying to figure out where to go. He is on the sidewalk, out in the open, mind still reeling from what his mother said.

The car slowly circles the small parking lot, coming right in front of him. For the first time in a very long time, Pro wishes he had a gun.

. . .

"Look at this fool slipping," Spider chortles as they slow. His sawed-off shotgun rests in his lap as he stares out from the passenger's seat. Two other gangsters in the back laugh with him.

"That our dude?" One asks. He has a pistol pressed against his door, muzzle facing outward, ready to crest the plane and start shooting in an instant if needed.

Spider raises something in his hand, pointing it at the man standing on the sidewalk. The shutter clicks as he snaps a picture with his cellphone. "Naw. 119. Right place, but this homie is different. Bigger."

The car accelerates as it heads back toward the exit. The few people who see the car duck back inside their apartments, not wanting anything to do with what the vehicle represents.

The driver laughs. "They all slippin'. No lookouts or nothing. Crips be looking soft these days."

"We should take this over," another says.

"What, a bunch of broken-down apartments? There ain't nothing here worth taking over," Spider retorts.

They pull back out onto the main street and squeal tires as the powerful sedan accelerates away from the area. "We do what Montana says. Wait for their big Homie to get out and then smoke them down."

A few minutes later, a nondescript gray sedan pulls into the gas station half a block away. It backs in between the dirty concrete building and a crumbling wooden privacy fence, well-screened but with a clear view of the entrance to Hillcrest. No one gets out of the car, and an hour later, it is still sitting there, engine running. Waiting.

CHAPTER TEN

It's tomorrow. Pro shifts uncomfortably in the recliner, and he wishes not for the first time that he had just stayed at a hotel. The stiff soreness when he moves, combined with a feeling of dread about the upcoming funeral, chases away any chance at falling back asleep, and he opens his eyes.

A quick peek into the reluctant morning light reveals nothing out of the ordinary in the parking lot, and he lets the heavy curtain settle back into place. Everyone is still asleep inside the apartment and out, but his military habits make him an early riser.

In the bathroom, he stares holes in his own reflection but is unsure what he sees. *Star of the family, or selfish prodigal son?* He shaves and splashes water on his face, trying to clear the cobwebs from a restless night. *Need a dang haircut either way.*

He lets himself out of the apartment quietly. The thought crosses his mind to go into the station, lay it all out for Isabella, work together with her to solve the problem. But, remembering her stiff, icy tone when he called her, he knows he's going to have to look elsewhere for help.

Monk.

When he starts his car, it is without his usual joyous revving of the modified motor; he keeps it to a quiet purr to avoid waking the whole neighborhood. When he pulls out of Hillcrest, he looks all around, keeping a sharp eye for the car from yesterday or any other vehicles that could belong to the Locos.

A half-block away, a gray sedan with a very sleepy driver pulls out and follows him, but he does not see it. Even if he did, he would have paid no attention to the unremarkable vehicle.

Monk's Cuts opens early, always ready to clean up your crown on the way to work. The venerable establishment is right where it has always been. A 10-foot-wide hole in the wall at a South Side strip mall, with simple blue lettering above the door so small it'd be easy to miss. Inside, four blue barber chairs are lined up, with some of the best guys in town working them.

Running the chair closest to the door is the man for who the shop is named for. Monk is an old Rollin 60s fixture and was a mentor figure for Pro through all his father's frequent stints in lockup. Pushing fifty now, the elder had managed to dial back his banging before he got killed or sent to the Pen and had gone into legitimate business for himself. His place is now a meeting place for Crips, and *the* place for street news, rumors, straight talk, and most importantly, a good haircut.

When Pro walks in, his reception is mixed.

"Pro, my man!" Monk's face brightens up, clearly happy to see a friend, not just customer. "C'mon, get up in here and let me fix that mess you got up top."

The man getting a high fade in seat two snorts dismissively. "See, perfect example." The man cutting his hair is someone Pro doesn't recognize, a heavily tattooed big-bellied guy.

Pro smiles as he heads to Monk's chair, a little uncertain about what the comment means but ready for good-natured ribbing. "Come on now, it's only been two weeks," he says, thinking of the last time he got a cut.

The man bounces a hard look off the wall of mirrors, making eye contact with Pro without turning his head. "Not talking about your nasty 'fro. I'm talking about moving away."

Pro sits down and surrenders his head position to Monk with every confidence the man will fix him up right. The older man snaps the drape to the side and then swirls it around Pro in a practiced movement that leaves a faint odor of aftershave and clipper oil floating in the air.

Client 2 carries on with the lively conversation that was apparently in full swing when Pro walked in. "Perfect example," the man repeats. "You got Mr. Williams here, comes up on the streets, gets his feet under him, goes to college, and what does he do? He *leaves!*"

Pro looks at the man in the mirror. "Do I know you?"

The second chair barber answers for his client, "Mr. Cooper here is a Fire Captain." He says the statement as if that sole fact adds weight to any claim the man makes.

"I went to school with your mother. I watched you grow up. I even went to some of your fights." The man's look is not friendly and makes Pro feel judged. "As soon as your mother said you were going to college, I knew it."

"Knew what?" Pro tries to keep his tone neutral, but he feels like he walked into the middle of a fistfight.

"Mr. Cooper is of the opinion that all of the good ones leave. With the exception of himself, of course." Monk's voice is even and thoughtful, considerate of others but reserving judgment of rightness until after full contemplation has been made. A humble man, his balanced wisdom and piercing intellect are as much a reason for the shop's ongoing success as the quality of haircuts. Never quick to judge, he takes all things into account before offering his advice.

"They do!" Cooper shifts his feet, and Pro sees black tactical boots poking out from under the drape covering the fireman. "And we will never have a robust, vibrant, self-sustaining culture because of it."

The third chair barber sits in his own chair, listening to the conversation. "Doesn't matter if we do. White man gonna take away anything good."

Cooper incorporates the third barber's comment into his own theory, "They absolutely will, and we are letting them do it. It's our fault because we are our own worst enemy."

Pro objects. "Now hang on, I'm a pastor. Nobody is taking that away from me. I am a sergeant in the Army, and they can't take that away either."

Cooper shakes his head, earning him an irritated grunt from the man who has to pause for a moment and pull the clippers away from his head. "They already have. You left. You went and got your degree, and now, where are you? Working for the white man. Not here in the community you came up in."

Starting to feel like he knows what the discussion is about, Pro is happy to engage. He took philosophy, debate, and sociology classes in college and loves a chance to bring logic to bear on a conversation. "Ok, so your premise is that any black man who does good for himself, he's going to leave, so therefore the black community can never succeed."

His use of the word premise sparks a fire in Cooper's eyes, and he warms to his subject. "Yes, and you are evidence of this. Are you back for good? Going to start a business here? Raise a family here? Join the city council, fight against the gentrification of our neighborhoods?" His look is triumphant, as if he has an unlimited supply of ammunition and has been lying in wait for a new victim to use it on. "Are you going to get us our grocery store back?"

Something resonates in the back of Pro's mind, a comment Fade said about not having a grocery store anymore. He wants to know more about that, but resentment at this man boils away that curiosity. "I'm here because my little brother is dead."

Monk's clippers, which have been buzzing steadily and efficiently by his ears, click off. "No. That was your little man?" Decades of repeated sorrow pack into his voice, "I heard about it. Real sorry about that. On the set."

Pro was expecting the fire captain to change his tune and offer his condolences, maybe mumble an apology, but to his surprise, the man blows a gasket. "On the set? Are you kidding me, Monk? Are you kidding me right now?" His haircut is done, and his barber removes the plastic shroud from around his shoulders. The Fire Captain stands up. "When does it end?"

The man's manner and negative energy, combined with his motion of rising and towering above him, make Pro want to leap up and punch the man in the face. With a massive effort, he keeps himself under control and in the chair.

Cooper is animated. "You think I don't know about your brother, Pro? I told you, I have known your mother since we were kids. I have seen this same damn cycle for thirty years, and it never changes." He raises his hands then motions with them toward Monk and Pro. "Monk, you know what I am talking about. On the *set*? Kids grow up banging and end up dead. Seen it happen like 30 times."

Pro can't take any more of what seems to be a brutally dismissive attitude toward his brother's death and pushes against the chair arms to stand up. *One to the jaw. One to the jaw will shut him up.* The desire for a logical debate has fled, but Monk is one step ahead of him. The old Crip leans casually on Pro's clavicles with both forearms, giving no indication that he is holding the former boxer in the barber chair but quite effective in doing so.

Cooper points directly at Pro's chest. "The good ones *leave*. They take all their desire and ability to do good in the community with them. The ones who stay bang the set. Bullets fly. White cops come in and tax us, bonding young Cuz back out of jail so we can shoot some more."

The younger man grits his teeth. *Too close to home.*

"I see your anger, Pro. I feel your pain. I'll be at the funeral tomorrow too!"

"Then why you coming at me like this?" Pro demands. His voice twists with pain, a high note of betrayal invading his tone despite himself.

"Because!" The man is all but yelling now, "I'll be here the day after we put your brother in the ground. I'll be here the year after that, too. I got a master's degree; I make enough money to go live with the rich white folks in Edmond. But I'll be right *here* trying to build a community."

His voice lowers as he makes a visible effort to regain control of himself. A tear glistens in his eye, the sorrow of a man who has devoted his life to fighting a battle that he is certain he will lose. "I'll be here. Where will you be?"

A lump in his throat ambushes Pro and keeps him from being able to answer.

With no counterargument left to fight against, Captain Cooper nods sadly. He digs a twenty-dollar bill out of his wallet and hands it to his barber. "Say hi to Alicia and the kids for me, Trevor."

All activity has halted with the outburst, and motion continues to stay paused as everyone in the shop watches the man walk out. He gets in a newer BMW, the only car in the parking lot nicer than Pro's Impala.

Activity resumes, with Monk turning the clippers back on

and the barber at chair four rotating the chair his client is seated in.

Barber three, still seated in his own chair, is the first to speak. "Sorry about your loss, Cuz..." after a moment, he retreats from the awkwardness of talking about the dead, "but Cooper got you, though. You can't say shit if you don't still live here."

Pro doesn't want to talk about Cooper, and he definitely doesn't want to talk about Tommie. He clears his throat. "What's this about the grocery store?"

Trevor sweeps up the hair around chair two. "Shiiiit. You didn't know? They closed down the Qwik-Mart last year."

"They didn't open a Walmart or something?"

The Qwik-Mart was a neighborhood institution, the only place within walking distance to get groceries when Pro was growing up. Many people in the neighborhood didn't have cars. Those who did tend to have barely running cars, no insurance, suspended driver's licenses, or all three. So, a lot of people walked to places. Having a place within walking distance was the only way many elderly or those without family would get fresh food.

"Nope," Monk says. "They closed it down, and now you gotta drive 15 minutes. Closest is Food Lion now."

"Anything good, white man gonna take it away," 3rd Chair doubles down on his earlier statement. "Gentrifying the city, making it to where we can't afford rent, and now we can't even have our own grocery store."

"They want us to feel like animals, that's what it is," Trevor says, "and damn if it don't feel just like that."

Monk floats a bit of additional information into the mix, "Place had been robbed three times in the past year. Bloods coming up in here."

Pro considers what everyone is saying. While it could be Bloods invading their territory, Pro knows it is just as likely kids in their own neighborhood. He also knows Monk isn't going to blame his own set for the robberies, but it amounts to the same thing regardless.

Maybe they closed it down because it kept getting robbed, and maybe they didn't. If they did, it doesn't really matter who was doing the robbing. Either way, it's clear the predominantly black community sees it as a massive insult. And it has very real consequences for people like Mama and Fade.

He looks out of the corner of his eye at his gleaming Impala in the parking lot. He has become accustomed to thinking of it as a mark of pride, proof of success. But remembering Fade's request to drive it, he now thinks about it in a new light. It's hard to imagine not being able to get to the grocery store, but when he thinks back to his child-hood, it makes perfect sense. *How many times did Mama walk it?*

The conversation turns to another topic, and Pro lets the words flow past him without engaging again. When he pays Monk and prepares to leave, the older man follows him outside under the pretense of having a cigarette.

Glad of the opportunity to speak to his longtime friend alone, Pro stands with him on the sidewalk in front of the store. "I'm staying 'till Sunday. Trying to see what I can do to help, you know."

Monk blows smoke out slowly, thoughtfully. "You said you were a pastor now?"

Pro nods. "Someday, I'd like to come back, preach to inner-city kids, you know."

Monk smiles, but it's a sad smile. "Inner-city, huh? That's some bullshit white man's term. You mean black kids."

Pro feels guilty. "Yeah, sorry."

"You been gone too long." The man takes another drag on the cigarette. "But your heart's in the right place. Always has been."

Pro is surprised by the compliment and reaches for the advice he hopes is waiting behind it. "But..."

"But you aren't doing anyone any good if you aren't here." He glances back in the shop and lowers his voice even though no one can hear them from inside. "You know how I made it? I got me some Jesus in my life."

Pro is surprised again. "I thought you still claim?" He says, referencing the Rollin 60s, "You an OG and shit!"

With the ease of years of practice, the man twists his left hand into the Rollin 60s hand sign. He gives a slight chuckle. "Oh yeah, I'm OG all right. More like O-B, Original Barber." His face turns more serious. "You gotta have some kinda moral compass out here. Otherwise, it's behind bars or six feet under. I been reading the bible a lot more these days."

Pro raises his eyebrows. "No shit?"

The older man claps him on the shoulder. "Don't look so surprised! Church is a part of us. Hell, back in slavery, God is all we had."

"When you don't even own yourself, you got nothing else but god," Pro acknowledges. "I mean, me and Trey, we grew up going to church, my momma made sure of that, but how do you square that with banging?"

Monk nods his head slowly. "How indeed? Church is on Sunday, but you're on the set 24/7. That's why I been reading my bible, really getting into it. Because God loves us, but here we are, rolling around in the gutter, killing each other."

"Exactly, we gotta get out of this life. Leave the gang behind," Pro's voice increases in volume as he talks about what has been eating him. "I want to get my whole family out of here, get them up out of this neighborhood and city! But they all are dug in, entrenched in this life. They see me as an outsider."

Monk regards him thoughtfully, trying to see if he will arrive at the same conclusion. When the younger man pauses,

Monk prods him further. "But that's not how it works, is it. Read up on it. God came down and lived *with* the lost. He went and found them where they were and helped them *where they were*."

Pro snorts. "Yeah, but he didn't start banging the streets in their gang, either." A car pulls into the parking lot and parks near his Impala, presumably Monk's next customer. He lowers his voice and speaks quickly, "Look, you know the homies, they want to go hit back."

"'Course they do," Monk says calmly, "And your half-brother Four is in jail asking the old heads to get behind it."

"He is? Where'd you hear that?"

He smiles, "I'm an OG and all that, remember?"

A man steps out of the car and starts walking toward the barbershop. Pro drops his voice to almost a whisper, "Well, how do I stop them? Stop the cycle?" His last question is also a plea, "Can you put a stop to it?"

Monk smiles and waves at the man walking toward them, greeting him loudly, "Freddie! My man." He half-turns back to Pro and whispers his reply, "I can't stop it, Pro, and neither can you unless you are here."

The new customer steps onto the sidewalk, and their private conversation is over. Monk turns to go inside but delivers a final piece of advice in a normal conversational volume, "Read up on it. He came alongside people. That's how *He* helped."

Pro walks to his car, deep in thought about Monk's words. A voice in his head tells him to get out of town, to drive straight from the funeral tomorrow back to Tulsa, to Liz, to his diversity role at what really is a rich white church.

I can't stop it, Pro, and neither can you unless you are here.

. . .

Conners chortles from the passenger seat and passes the small pair of binoculars to Isabella. "See the guy going inside?"

"Blue coveralls?"

He nods, but she can't see him because she is looking through the binoculars. The man in mention is going back inside, so she watches her ex-boyfriend walk to his car, wondering what he is up to.

"That's Reginald Earnest Montgomery," he says the lengthy name triumphantly as if she should know it and be impressed.

They are sitting across the street in the drive-through of a bank that doesn't open for another 45 minutes. Isabella's back is sore from sleeping in shifts in the cramped car, and her patience is wearing thin. She was hyper-alert all night, expecting another shooting to happen or a car full of gun-toting gangsters to go screeching out of Hillcrest on the warpath. But the only crime she has witnessed is the assault of Conners' worsening body odor on her nostrils.

The gang detective huffs slightly, displeased she gives no reaction to the name he reeled off. She wants to let it go but is worried he might be holding back something she needs to know.

"I can shut this all down," she waves her hand to indicate their current stakeout as well as his whole RICO case, "in a heartbeat. Don't treat me like a child."

He rolls his eyes. "That's 'Monk,' an OG, the real deal. Used to be tearing up these streets back when I was a Rookie. Shootings, beatings, trafficking cocaine, running hookers, you name it."

Pro starts driving to the edge of the parking lot, and she works the focus knob on the binoculars to try to read the letters above the door the man in mention just walked through. "No kidding? So, what's he do here?"

"Runs drugs and guns," he says without hesitation. "I'm sure of it, but we never can get anyone to snitch on this place. They got it set up as an active barbershop. Great cover."

She hands him back the binoculars but remains focused on the Impala across the street. "Do we follow Pro again? And why is he talking to this guy Monk?"

Conners looks around and the mostly deserted area. The light commercial zone will be slammed with traffic in two hours, but traffic is still very light right now. "He may spot us, and we already followed him here. Let him go, and we will pick him back up at Hillcrest." He puts the binoculars to his face and looks at the front of the barbershop, then at the car that most recently arrived. "We may get something better here. Maybe catch Monk leaving."

She furrows her brow as Pro leaves the area. He never looks their way, and she feels like an invader peering into his life without him knowing.

Detective Body Odor answers the second half of her earlier question. "Only reason I could think he is here is to get permission for a hit."

She is taken aback, unable to reconcile the Pro she knows with this theory. "Maybe he just got a haircut?"

He snorts. "Don't be ridiculous. Do you have any idea how many barbershops he drove past to get here?" He lowers the binoculars and looks at her. "Look, it's not like the movies, ok? The big gang leaders, they don't live in multi-million-dollar mansions with armed security. You don't go in and sit on an immaculate couch for a talk, flanked by meat-heads in suits. They don't lounge casually and mysteriously in an overstuffed chair while they ask you if their supermodel wife can get you something to drink."

He points at the nearly empty lot across the street.

"These are real people, Contreras. They have real lives, and most are poor."

She bristles at his lesson. "I know that. I grew up with them, remember?"

He dismisses her peevishness with a wave of his hand. "Right, so they get into selling drugs to make money, and that's how they recruit too. Uncle Sam won't let you get a real job until 15, 16 really, and then you are working crap hours, crap schedule, for crap money." He nods toward the barbershop. "But big Crip here, he'll give you some dope, get you running it around the 'hood for him when you are twelve, give you $100 per day. By the time you are 13 or 14, you are dealing it in middle school, making some serious cash, and if you get caught..." he slaps his wrist, indicating a light punishment.

"So, are they making a lot of money, or aren't they? You're contradicting yourself." Images of Pro's sleek car dance in front of her eyes. *The nicest car in Hillcrest, for sure.*

"Aha!" He smiles and tilts an index finger toward her, clearly glad she asked. "The problems are efficiency, scale, and security. Think about it like a business, except one where every member of that business doesn't follow the rules. Doesn't follow *most* rules," he amends before continuing. "So back in the 80's and 90's, Monk here was running strong. Cocaine was his primary market, and he was bringing in 20-grand, maybe 50 per month. Owned multiple houses, multiple cars, the whole bit. But for that kind of money, people will do you over in a heartbeat.

You got all these kids growing up being told they can get easy money. They pass somebody a small package and walk away with a $100 bill. But then they hit adulthood and start paying real bond money to get out, maybe even spend some time locked up. Meanwhile, they got two or three kids at least from living fast with multiple girlfriends, some a lot more." He laughs and shakes his head, "I knew one guy. He tells me straight up he has 14 kids from eight different mamas.

She narrows her eyes. "You are rambling."

"Huh?" His expression becomes serious again. "Where was I? Oh yeah, efficiency, scale, and security."

"The short version." She is feeling smothered by more than just his oppressive scent.

"Short version," he looks annoyed but acquiesces and makes a mental adjustment on the fly. "The short version is they need *violence* to solve all three problems."

With that, he actually stops talking and stares at the parking lot across from them. His hands reach for another energy drink, fueling both his mind and the cacophony of pungent odors in the car.

Sitting in unexpected silence, she wonders if it is a tactic to get her to ask for more information.

After an awkward minute, she gives in. With an exaggerated sigh and fake-enthralled voice, she asks, "How does violence solve their problems, Senior Detective Conners? I'm dying to know."

A tiny smile tugs his lips as his vocal cords swing back into action. "Laziness and carelessness are the building blocks of *inefficiency*, but fear cures both. If you decide to stop off at your girl's house and father kid number three instead of staying ready on the street, making them deliveries, Big Homie gonna have your ass."

He takes a swig of his energy drink. "So, you keep moving, making your moves, and making him money." His voice incorporates some street language but is discordant in an attempt to mix cultures.

She thinks about Pro's car again. She wants to believe he didn't buy it with drug money. She considers again telling Conners her Ex has reached out to give information. *There's gonna be a gang war, Isa.* She can't tell the other detective now, though, without him wondering why she didn't share the critical information sooner.

Unaware of her internal conflict, he continues with his thesis. "You can't supervise people who are miles away. Can't keep multiple layers of dealers, runners, lookouts, and sometimes cops all running in one direction. Not unless they are all motivated by greed *and* worried about getting shot. People start thinking about what Monk is going to do to them if they screw up. Suddenly, they start making decently effective decisions on their own. Imagine if McDonald's managers could shoot their employees for screwing up your order, one manager could run five stores!"

"They'd still get it wrong," Isabella mutters.

"Finally, there's security. You start running around like Monk here, 50-grand worth of cocaine hidden in the center console of your Tahoe, and people are going to want to take it. So, you roll four-deep, got a couple guys in the back, got you a *Glizzy-with-a-dick-on-it,* maybe a *Draco-with-tits-*"

She cuts him off, "Uh... sexual harassment much?" She is not serious, but he is getting into the gang language a little too much. *Just the facts ma'am,* she says in her head. She internally laughs at her own joke, but tries to keep a straight face as Conners hastens to explain.

He unholsters his Glock and points it at the floor while removing the magazine. He holds the magazine up. "You get an extended one of these," he holds a finger next to it to approximate the five-inch magazine doubling in length, "and they call it a *Richard*, or a *dick*." He inserts the very end of his standard-issue magazine into the gun handle, then wraps his bottom finger around it in a modified grip to keep most of the magazine sticking out. "Then they got it like this, and everyone can see they have more bullets for their Glizzy." He taps the Glock with his other hand to indicate the nickname is for the pistol.

Watching this demonstration and thinking about all of the awesome comments she could make, she bites her lip. "So, you are saying some men have larger magazines than others?" She manages to keep her face completely serious. Barely.

He gives her a look and rams the magazine into the gun. It makes an audible click when it seats properly. "Yep, and these guys like to have an extra-long one, makes them feel ready for anything."

She realizes her mind is drifting toward Pro's... Glock. *Get ahold of yourself, Isa.* She bites her lip and manages to resist keeping the joke going. "All right. OK. What's a Draco..." she elects not to say the last part.

He pulls out his phone. "Hang on, I'll show you." He searches the term, and when he shows her the picture, she immediately recognizes the gun.

"That's an AK-47. They really have those?"

"Yup. And see the magazine on the bottom?" He points at a ridiculous-looking double-drum configuration on the bottom.

Tits. Instead of saying the word out loud and risking more middle-school humor, she keeps her comment and facial expression professional. "Looks high-capacity."

"150 rounds." He looks deadly serious. "And that's all 7.62. I'll go right through our body armor, car doors, everything.

It's a sobering thought, and she looks back up at the barbershop with new eyes. After a minute, she attempts to recap the situation. "So, this guy Monk, he's a dangerous *Original Gangster*, probably heavily armed, running some sort of criminal enterprise."

"Yep." He nods his head as she speaks.

"And Pro comes to him a couple of days after his brother is murdered by another gang. Your theory is he is getting authorization for a hit? Why didn't this guy come with him then? Where's the Tahoe and the Draco?"

"No, it will be after the funeral. Tomorrow night at the earliest."

He sounds certain, and she arches an eyebrow. "It's tomorrow? How do you know?"

He pulls up an App on his phone and grins as he shows her a post announcing the details. "Facebook. I have a fake profile and am friends with all of them."

"Wow, dude. You need a life."

"It'll be handy for tomorrow, so we know who everyone is ahead of time."

"Tomorrow?" She is having trouble connecting the dots. "What's tomorrow?"

"The funereal, duh. We are going." He says it like it is a foregone conclusion.

She holds up her hands. "Hang on. No. We are not going to show up at Tommie's funeral and cause problems. Not happening."

Something has been bothering her this whole time, and she launches into it. "We are sitting here watching some random guy that you say is a Crip OG instead of going anywhere near the South Side Locos. We aren't investigating the homicide. We are just doing your gang investigation!"

He is unruffled by her anger. "I go to all the gang funerals; they are a wealth of intel. Everyone all in one place, throwing gang signs, hugging it out. Great place to get pictures of the gang together."

"You can't be serious! This is my Murder-One, not your RICO."

"We are doing both, and it's really all the same thing. A RICO has multiple crimes, a whole pattern in it." He spreads his hands in a placating gesture. "Look, we go to the funeral, we see the whole set there, probably Monk included. As soon as lil-G is in the ground, they are probably going to do their recon immediately. We follow them to South Side Loco territory and see what street they go down, where they roll slow, and we have it narrowed down. Then we look for a dark-colored sedan that matches our suspects' description and set up on it. When it moves, we get Patrol to stop them on some BS and get a drug dog. Dog hits, we search the car and occupants, find the gun our shooter has hastily thrown under the seat. BAM, he's a felon, of course, and goes to jail. Maybe the gun is even stolen. Got his prints all over it."

"Then we check that gun against the casings for ballistics," she says.

He snaps his fingers. "Now you are getting it. We get a search warrant for that guy's house, figuring there is a good chance he has ammo there that matches our crime scene, probable cause. We are looking for the other gun, the shotgun, because he probably doesn't carry that around on the daily."

"You make it sound easy."

He laughs. "It *is* easy." He points across the street. "Just have to follow the intel, understand the culture and gang politics. If they want to step correct, they ask the OG to approve the hit. That's step one, and your supposedly non-gang-affiliated former lover just rewarded us with that step after less than 24 hours of surveillance."

She still can't believe Pro is working on the gang's behalf but can't help but notice he is the oldest male family member not currently in jail. *Maybe it is like a chain of succession, and it is somehow up to him. Conners seems to know this culture inside and out. Maybe he's right.*

She is irritated that her instincts on Pro might have been all wrong and irritated with Conners for being right. She abruptly puts the car in gear and pulls out from under the bank awning.

"Hey! What are you doing?" He demands.

"The bank is about to open," She says, "and I need to get some real sleep."

He tries to protest more, saying the need to watch the barbershop, but she is fed up and needs to think. She has shoved Pro to the side, pushed him into the back of her memory for years. But now he is in her life again. Right in front of her eyes, whether they are open or not.

It's just work, Isa. He's a case now, that's all.

"We are going to the funeral though, though, right?" Conners is insistent, leaning half in front of her as she drives. "You have to admit we are on the right track."

She tries not to breathe. "Fine. We'll go."

Pro's going to hate me.

CHAPTER ELEVEN

Pro gives Seriah another push on the swing, his heart lightened by her delighted laughter even as the weight of responsibility presses down on him.

"Tulsa is good. I could help you. You and Mama need a fresh start." Monk's words still ring in his ears, and he feels more powerfully than ever that he needs to help his family.

Fade isn't having any of it. "Yeah? And what about Caelan? Ice isn't moving to Tulsa."

"He needs to be applying to colleges. I could hook him up with a good lady in admissions at OSU."

She snorts. "Not everyone is you, Pro. Ice hasn't really gone to school for two years now." She shakes her head sadly, her thoughts encompassing herself as well as their younger brother. "Wouldn't it be nice if everyone could get an education, land a great job with health insurance?"

"They can!" His passion on the subject boils to the fore, "This is America; you just have to reach out and take it!"

She looks bitter. "You know I tried, right?" She stops the swings and tells her girls to go play on the slide. When the girls are out of earshot, she continues, "Once Seriah was out of diapers, I tried to leave them with Momma, got a job at Sonic, was looking at night school classes."

"You did?" He never knew any of this, but something in her tone flattens his surge of hope before it can get fully started.

She turns fully toward him, hands on hips. "Look around you, Pro. Mom is an addict. Tommie and Aliyah's dad, he worked her over good, and now she just can't deal with anything."

"I thought maybe she was getting worse," he admits.

Phaedra looks down, shuffling her feet in the wooden chips at their feet. Anger and resignation tinge her voice, "Two days. Two days of working 8 hours to support my babies, head filled with ideas of getting a Pell grant, looking at geneticist degree tracks." She looks him in the eye, wanting him to see the naked truth. "I came home and found my two-year-old playing outside unattended, five feet from used heroin needles, Momma passed out on the couch, Selena eating a plate of Ketchup because she was hungry and hadn't eaten all day."

"Jeez..." he searches for something to say. "Ice, Aliyah, they couldn't help?"

She gets angrier. "They're doing their own thing. Aliyah is a good kid. She's in school like she is supposed to. Now Ice, he's all about the gang."

"I see that," Pro tries to connect with her, to find an ally in the effort to save his younger brother, "We gotta get him out of the gang before it's too late, Fade."

"You're an idiot, Pro."

"C'mon, you can't believe that's a good path for him! Look at Dad!" Their father has been in and out of prison, locked up for most of their lives.

Look at Tommie, dead before his life even started.

"A good path?" She snorts. "There's no good paths around

here, Pro." She watches her girls going down the slide a short distance away, obviously weighing something in her mind, trying to decide whether to talk to him about it.

What can I say to convince you? His mind races for the answer. He feels desperate to get her to leave the South Side, to save her even if it is too late for Ice.

She turns to him, her face serious. "I want you to jump me into the gang. Put me on the set."

"What?" His mouth drops open in disbelief. "Hell, no, I'm not going to put you on the set!"

She crosses her arms and stares directly at him. "Yes, you are."

He shakes his head, battling his surprise at her request as well as visions of what that would entail. "No. No. You are out of your mind."

"Rae's on it."

"Rae's a whore. She probably enjoyed getting put on." The words slide out quickly as if they were already in the front of his brain, surprising him.

"I'm not talking like that. I said *jumped-in*. Four would never put me on because I am his sister, obviously."

Gang membership can only be obtained one of three ways, familied-in, jumped-in, or sexed-in. Technically they were both eligible to get quoted directly by their father, who was a long-time gang member, but that method only carried as much credibility as the person quoting you could give. These days their dad wasn't around, and they had no other senior family members to speak for them.

Most people who earned membership did so by the sacred gang ritual of getting 'jumped-in.' Pro could still remember his jump-in on his 14th birthday. He had cake and ice cream, opened a few presents with his family, then later that night, Damarion and several older teen boys who were already gang members took him in an alley and beat him up. *Sixty seconds,*

Pro. Sixty seconds to be on Sixties, to be on the set, to be a man. You were allowed to fight back, of course, but 4-on-1 isn't much of a fight, and they were all bigger than him. You weren't supposed to win though, just prove that you were tough enough to take it, show that you were willing to endure fear and pain for the gang.

Looking at his pretty twin sister, standing with her arms crossed. Thinking about the girl he had protected since he could walk being subjected to that, his mind rebelled against the thought.

Of course, the third option was even more unthinkable. Female gang members were rare but not unheard of, and a girl like Rae could earn her place among the ranks by having sex with multiple gang members at once, usually all of them. Violence was often included in this initiation as well, and while Pro had never witnessed one, he knew they were supposed to be far worse than a jump-in. Despite his words, the idea of Rae, or anyone, enjoying such a thing was utterly unthinkable.

He shakes his head to chase the ugly visions from it. "No. No, none of that is going to happen. You need to be up out of here, not trying to get further into the gang." She stares at him, fully expecting this resistance but resolute in her request. He continues to try to convince her, drawing from his own negative experience in the gang, "You want to be a good mom, is that it? First thing they gonna ask you is to get behind Ice on some moves. They strapping up to hit back." He theorizes how it is going to unfold, "Rae's gonna grab a hotbox, something nondescript this time, and she'll pull up. Ice, Jiggy, Deuce, these *kids* are gonna pile in there, feeling tough, talking 'bout how they gonna put some Locos to sleep." He pretends to pull a gun out of his own waistband and offer it to her, using a twisted falsetto voice, "Here ya go, Fade, you on Sixties now, time to Crip the fuck up!"

She sets her jaw, a silent signal that she would accept the task if asked to.

He grabs her shoulders. Wants to slap some sense into her, anything to get her to consider a different course. "They'll want you to get behind them on that drive-by. They'll want to see your arm hanging out the window pulling the trigger. When you in it, you in for *all of it*."

"I know that." She says. Her calm voice confirms that she does, that she has considered this a thousand times and made up her mind. "I know all of that. I need you to jump me in. It needs to be *now* before Four bonds out. Ice and them, they'll go along with you if you give the word."

He can't believe what he is hearing. He wants to shout but speaks low to avoid the playing girls overhearing. Each word comes out individually, with emphasis "Why. Would. You. Want. That? The gang is a trap, a one-way ticket to a bad end."

She uncrosses her arms and pushes his hands from her shoulders. "The gang is family. All you remember is how it went for you, but for me, the gang is protection. The set is the only thing keeping us up out here, Pro."

A bolt of terror flashes through him when she references his past. *Does she know?* He and Damarion had only ever told his mother. He had come home crying and throwing up, sure his life was over. She had made them both swear to never tell a soul. *You owe God a life now, Pro.*

Fade sees the look. "Yeah, I know something bad happened. Not sure what, and it doesn't matter because that's not my life." She leans on the metal post holding up the swings. "Let me tell you about my life, bro. Since you been gone, let me tell you about how I live."

Still rocked by the adrenaline from thinking she knew about his dark secret, he listens as she expounds further.

"Here's how my life works," she continues, "I can't work

anywhere because I can't trust my own mother to take care of my babies, and I sure as hell can't afford daycare. Child support?" She snorts bitterly and glances at her girls, "don't even get me started on their daddy. So, I sell drugs, Pro."

"You're kidding."

"Bro." Her voice is a reproach as if what she says should be obvious, and she will only think less of him for not believing it.

He wants to not believe her, but small cues tell him it is true. *That guy who walked up in the parking lot. Handing Momma a joint as if she controls the stash.* It also clarifies why Phaedra has some power and respect among the gang members even without being an official member. *She is probably supplying them all for protection.*

Her next statement confirms what he is thinking, "So yeah, I sell drugs. No surprise there. The real question is, how do I keep from getting ripped?"

"The gang." He realizes the truth as he answers. Getting drug-ripped, having the money and drugs associated with a large sale stolen at gunpoint is common. What are you going to do, call the police? *Yeah, 911? Someone just stole my cocaine!*

She nods. "The gang keeps people in line. The gang keeps me safe. The gang keeps some meth-head from kicking in the door to my bedroom in the middle of the night, waving a gun at my girls because he wants some dope. The gang keeps me from having to pay a cut to anyone, we keep our profits, and maybe I buy Seriah a pair of shoes when she needs them, make sure Selena has a backpack that isn't ripped when she goes to school."

"I could help with that stuff..."

She continues on, talking over his objection, "Of course, there's not enough for food, rent, clothes, taking care of Mama. The guys want to go do dumb crap. Knock over convenience stores and shit."

"That's how you get caught – or shot!" Pro protests.

"I know that, Pro," she sounds irritated. They are covering ground she has considered a thousand times already. "So, I use what influence I have, I say to Ice, 'hey my dude, instead of that, hook up with Rae, she likes you, and can put us on some good cars.' Then I say to Rae, 'Hey, I can do your documents for you, get you some fake titles and shit, double the amount you are making on these *stolos*, with less chance of getting caught.' So now cars, that's safer than robbing people."

He understands her line of thinking. *The lesser, or safer, of two evils.* "And they are insured, so it's really just some big company you are stealing from, right?" Before she can answer, he shakes his head. "It's still wrong, Fade."

She looks thoughtful. "Easy to say from up there in your ivory tower, I guess." She shrugs her shoulders, "Of course, I don't have that luxury, so it's whatever. I'm trying to keep my babies fed, keep my brothers alive and out of jail."

He thinks about Four being locked up and about little Tommie. An angry part of him wants to say, *yeah? How's that working out for you?*

He is controlled enough to not ask the question aloud, but she senses it anyway, "But there's only so much I can do. When it comes right down to it, I don't call the shots in the gang. They need me, and I need them, but I'm not running anything. It's even worse when Four is around. They all follow him." She steps close, talking earnestly, "But right now, they need a leader. If I am jumped-in, I really can start running shit, try to get them to stay out of the way."

He narrows his eyes, a little suspect of her stated intention to keep the boys out of trouble while simultaneously admitting that she is heavily involved in their illicit activities. But he has to respect both her desire to guide the group in a more sensible direction, even if still an illegal one, as well as her keen observation of the opportunity Pro's visit represents.

Could she stop a retaliatory strike, stop the cycle of drivebys? He wishes he could convince himself that she could. But, even with a better understanding of how centric to the gang operations her efforts already are, he still can't believe that would have anywhere near enough prestige to forestall the obvious response to Tommie's slaying.

"As soon as Trey - *Four,*" He corrects himself to use his brother's new nickname, "is out, he will be running things again. You know that."

She utters a curse. "Maybe I tie up some of this money we putting away for it. Maybe he doesn't get bonded out all that quick this time. Maybe I give myself some time to consolidate power." She sounds like she has been watching The Sopranos. She also sounds like she hasn't fully thought through this aspect of her plan.

Pro is frustrated. He understands where his sister is coming from, but her plan is a desperate attempt. *She wants the same thing as I do, sort of.* "It's not going to work, Fade. They will steamroll you, you will be getting in that car, becoming a part of the violence, and there's no turning back from that." He shakes his head, mentally distancing himself from any serious consideration of her request to jump her into the gang.

Anger lights in her eyes as she absorbs his rejection. "Yeah. You are right. It won't work, I know that."

More than a little surprised at her sudden capitulation, he feels a wave of relief flood over him, glad he talked her off the crazy-ledge. He starts to smile. "Well, good..."

She kicks his delusion of peaceful resolution right in the teeth, "You are right, they need someone bigger and stronger, more prestige, experience, someone who can whip them into shape, keep them in line, square off against Four if necessary.

These boys, these *children*, need someone with a strong hand who can steer them toward a better path."

He feels dread at her logic, wants to stop her from speaking. But she rolls on inexorably. The entire conversation up to this point merely laying the groundwork for what she now plans to say. *Setting the trap.*

"They need someone to guide them, to lead them, so they don't end up like Tommie!" Her voice increases in volume, her passion overpowering any concern of the girls overhearing. Anger bursts from the cracks in her steely resolve as she delivers an uppercut to his soul, "So when are *you* gonna Crip the fuck up?"

Rejecting by default her challenge for him to lead the gang, his mind races for a logical argument, a rational path from the dilapidated playground and broken chain-link fence encircling them to a place of safety. *A convincing plan to help his family get away from the city.*

She steps right up to him, chin raised in defiance a few inches below his own as she senses and rejects his idealistic plan. "Ain't nobody moving to Tulsa, Pro. Our family is all here... all except for you."

When he doesn't have a reply, she knows she has him on the ropes. She places her hands on his shoulders, squeezing slightly, then harder as her anger starts to crumble. Moisture gathers in her eyes, and she repeats herself, very softly this time, "Crip the fuck up, Pro..." her jaw starts to tremble, and the anger gives way to grief and helplessness. The pain and enormity of the last few days catch up to her. The weight of loss and responsibility slam against her like a battering ram. Her hands slide from his shoulders to encircle him, and she sags against her twin.

She tries to use the hug to hide that she is crying, but her voice is tight with emotion, "We need you. We need you here."

. . .

"And now your sister wants in the gang too? Wow, that's crazy." Liz's voice tries to sound understanding from the other end of the phone but carries obvious ignorance of the implications of what Pro is saying. She took it in stride that his family was gang-involved, accepted it so readily in fact that it was almost insulting. *Like she believes all black men are gangbangers*. But her preconceptions do not stretch as far as to readily believe girls are in the gang as well.

Back at the parking lot at Hillcrest, Pro had let Fade and her girls go ahead of him inside to have a private conversation in the car. Up till now, he had been trying to keep the details of the situation from his girlfriend. But the pressure from the family and the clear need for something to change has become too much to bear alone.

"I thought you said you weren't hood?" She pokes at him.

"It's my roots babe, it's not who I am anymore." He knows she's just trying to lighten the mood and doesn't take her jab personally. She is an intelligence officer, a Psychological Operations Officer well versed in understanding different cultures and the undercurrents that drive any war – not a bad choice to discuss the situation with, really. And while she may have grown up wealthy, one thing he has always liked about her is she was never sheltered. Her parents were very modern and believed their only child should know all about the world's cruelty.

As he hopes, she falls back on her training and experience and begins to discuss the current situation objectively, as if they are planning to take over or destabilize a foreign country. "OK. So, run me through friendly forces, enemy forces, assets, liabilities, manipulatable population, offensive and defensive postures. Let's get this thing figured out."

Glad to step outside himself and the emotional timbre of

the situation, he closes his eyes and imagines it like chess-board pieces. He had done a deployment to Mali in Africa, attached to a Special Forces A-Team with Liz and a few others. They had managed to help small pockets of unorganized villagers turn the tide against tens of thousands of armed and ruthless guerilla fighters. Working closely with Liz then had been their key to success and was when they realized how much they enjoyed being together.

Putting his Unconventional Warfare hat on, he lists the information she requested. "Friendly forces are in two eche-lons, first being family and immediate gang set, seven able-bodied, five if you discount me and Damarion -my older brother who is locked up."

"OK." He hears a piece of paper rip in the background and realizes she is taking notes.

"Second echelon is allied elements which *may* be willing to go to war with us, about 300, maybe 350 jumped-in Crips." He realizes in passing that he used the term *us* but pushes the thought aside.

She makes an approving noise, "300, well that's great, Pro. Hell, I could take over Libya with a good group of 300." She can't resist quipping further, "I feel like there is some histor-ical parallel here, something about defending a narrow pass. Guys with shields and spears being heroic. Maybe someone should make a movie."

"Think you are pretty funny, don't you?" He can hear her snickering on the other end. "Problem is, this isn't a well-disciplined group of Spartans. It is a loose alliance of people who are always willing to jump but hard to keep in check." He thinks again of the worry that Four had been shooting up the Locos without backing from the OGs. "And there are a lot of reasons why we may not be able to depend on their help."

Her voice is serious again. "Ok, not that much different

than King Leonidas' allies then. Let's focus on the inner eche-lon, the few you can depend on."

He nods, silently trying to visualize Ice, Rae, and the rest as a core group of soldiers. The analogy seems a bit of a stretch, but Liz is not wrong to start theorizing a strategy around it. He is feeling better and better about sharing the problem with her.

He continues with the report, "Enemy forces: Approximately 600 South Side Locos, regarded as the most violent gang in the city. Their entrenched territory directly borders our neighborhood, and they apparently have been exercising pretty free reign in the area."

"600? Jeez, that's most of an Infantry Battalion," she observes. "Armament?"

"They have some pretty heavy stuff. Pistols, obviously, but they are aligned with the Cartel and will have AK-47s, AR-15s. It's not outside the realm of possibility they have grenades, maybe even a rocket launcher or two."

She thinks he's joking. "Oh yeah? Rocket launchers, huh. Any tanks or attack helicopters I need to be worried about?"

"I'm serious, they really will have that stuff, but they should keep that under wraps unless we go to serious war. They aren't trying to get the FBI involved, but they have that stuff around to keep people scared."

"All right." Her tone indicates that while surprised, she has taken him at his word, and she doesn't say anything for a minute while she writes.

When she prompts him to continue, he looks around the apartment complex, "Assets... well we have one apartment under direct control, two ways in and out. An apartment *complex*, indirect control, one way in and out, not counting all the gaps in the fence. One car, I guess... mine. Probably half a dozen pistols."

"You brought your guns?" She asks sharply.

"No, no. I left them home on purpose, trying not to get in it, you know?" He wishes, not for the first time, that he had made a different decision. When he came back from overseas deployment, a stack of cash had accumulated in his account. So, of course, like every good soldier returning from war, he had immediately invested in some quality weapons. "No, we just got whatever pistols the guys have here, I am fairly sure. Nothing that will even reach across the parking lot, really."

Speaking with Liz now in a military mindset, the lack of protection makes him feel horrifically unprepared.

He feels even worse when she digs further into their defenses. "Body Armor?"

"No."

"Ballistic protection on the walls? Is it brick at least?"

"No. Vinyl siding. It won't stop anything."

Access control to the apartment complex? You said only one way in, is there a gate?"

A gate? He scoffs bitterly, "No, babe, it's not a gated community." The comparison to her hometown of Edmond is implied in his tone, but she chooses to ignore the jab.

"Early warning systems? Video cameras, alarms, anything like that?"

He shakes his head, squeezing the steering wheel in frustration. "Gina can't afford any of that. This place barely even has lights."

"Emergency egress? You said the apartment has two ways to get out?"

"Back door, but I don't know where we would go. It just leads out along the fence to the main street."

Her questions are all reasonable, but he gets more irritated and restless for action as she speaks.

Anyone could just roll up on us and pour bullets into the apartment, and right now, we couldn't really even fight back.

"Any other assets? What about the cops. Surely they are helping because of your brother?"

You are so white. He bites back the comment and revises it into something more helpful. "That's not how it works around here... my family doesn't really talk to the cops. We handle things on our own."

"Makes sense, what with all of the illegal activity and everything." Her reply is a logical challenge to the way of life he grew up in, and having revised his thinking as an adult, he immediately sees it as such.

However, he also resents the bald implication that his entire culture is criminal and takes a defensive posture. "Not just gangs, a lot of black people don't talk to the cops. We handle our own business." He grows more animated, "My grandparents went through the Tulsa Race Riots, people getting bombed by government airplanes, Liz. Your people may have forgotten, but our people still remember that!"

She absorbs his outburst and comes back with a softer tone, "I'm on your side, Pro."

"I know!" He heaves a frustrated sigh. "I know you are, Baby. Yeah, there is an investigation. They trying to put something together, but they won't get anywhere. They never do."

She wants to go into cop mode. "Well, what do they have so far?"

"They got nothing, and it'll all peter out as soon as the news stops talking about it. I have seen it like 100 times." He thinks of Isabella and chuckles awkwardly, "Even with my Ex running the case, they still will dead-end it pretty fast. Just a poor black kid, you know."

"What?" Her voice is sharp.

"Nothing. Just a coincidence. Girl I used to know happens to be a detective now."

"You said your Ex."

"A long time ago," he waves his hand and jumps back to his report, ticking off the things he has already covered, "Friendly, enemy, assets- liabilities, we are on liabilities." Without waiting for her assent, he picks up with a list of their challenges, "My mother. She is pretty out there, staying heavily medicated. Lack of legal income or financial resources -other than my own. Oh yeah, and Fade's two small girls, like seven and four years old."

She lets him get away with bailing on the conversation about Isabella and zeros in on his last statement, "There are more kids in the middle of this?" She sounds offended.

"Yeah, Babe. My sister lives here with her two daughters. It's real-life happening around here, not a war in some faraway country."

"OK." Her tone becomes businesslike again, prioritizing facts over emotions. "I have questions."

"Go."

"You mentioned these South Side Locos were coming into your territory. Don't gangs defend their territory?"

"Well, they are coming over here by Hillcrest, but really most Crips are up around like NW 63rd and Bryant area, or in Midwest City." Both areas of the city are over twenty minutes from where he currently sits in his car. "It's complicated, but in answer to your question, no one except for my brother and his set is defending this area. That's probably how the problem started."

She takes that in stride, no doubt writing it down. "OK. Your only reliable maneuver element is your Brother's *set*," She uses the unfamiliar word correctly, if a bit awkwardly, "But if I understand right, their leader, your brother Damarion is currently in jail."

"Yes."

"Which would appear to be a problem and a major reduction in force capability and leadership, but also represents a short-term opportunity for important change."

His eyes narrow as he follows the sentence, and his answer is unsure, "Uh...yes?" *Where are you going with this, Liz?*

"Yes. An opportunity." She says it with confidence, telling him, not asking him. She is his commanding officer now, done collecting information from the field operative and now rendering decisions. "And you missed a friendly element."

"I did?"

"You said her name. Gina. If you know the landlord of the apartment complex, she is an ally because she has a shared interest in not having the place shot up."

Well spotted, Elizabeth. He is again glad he decided to open up to her about the situation, trusted her enough to bring her in on the problem.

She starts issuing him a scheme of maneuver, a battle plan for improving his tenuous situation. "First, go engage this Gina. She likely lacks resources but does have the criticality of desire to upgrade the security of the complex."

"True, but I could help with that."

"Exactly, and it would be an efficient use of resources."

"Maybe she could install a gate..." he starts thinking out loud, but Liz cuts him off, like any commander less interested in the details than the big picture.

"You're on it. Then you have to engage your second eche-lon, find out if those several hundred will stand with you or at least stay usefully neutral."

"I was hoping they would broker peace, actually. I already reached out to one OG," Pro says.

"Peace in the Middle East, huh? Come on, Pro, you are smarter than that."

"The cycle has to stop," he protests.

"Of course. And you are just the man to stop gang violence forever." She does not say it with malice or derision, just factually highlights the absurdity of his goal. "Let's not kid ourselves. From everything you have told me, you don't have any more chance of bringing about peace on the South Side than America has of winning the war in Afghanistan."

He sets his jaw. "It's not like that. We just gotta keep the hotheads, the YGs under control."

"Yep. Just like every other maturing generation of men in every warlike society in the whole entirety of history." She dismisses his argument entirely and moves on. "What you need to do is win, and win decisively, and the first step of that is an active and effective defense of your base, not sticking your head in the sand and pretending nothing bad will happen, much less an assault on a 600-man army!"

He feels like he is getting reprimanded for lack of strategic vision by a superior officer. *Which is exactly what is happening.* He falls in line, "I'll go talk to Gina. Then the OGs."

"And I'd think about ballistic blankets on inside walls."

He remembers the heavy black Kevlar blankets they used in Africa as ad-hoc defenses inside civilian structures. "That's a good idea." He is itching to swing into action and starts to think about ending the lengthy call. "Thanks, babe. I love you."

"Oh, one other thing."

"Yeah, what?"

Her voice is clear and instructive, an order that must be obeyed, "Walk away."

"What?" He isn't sure he heard her correctly.

"Go to your brother's funeral tomorrow, then get in your car and drive straight back to me. Do not pass Go, do not collect $200. Drive straight back home, rip off my clothes, cry on my shoulder, buy some more speakers for your car, buy some more guns if you want, spend a bunch of time at the Gym-"

"What? I thought you said talk to Gina!"

She keeps right on, "Go teach a couple sermons at your church, tell those kids all about Jesus if that's your thing. Study your bible. Hell, I'll give you a blowjob while you read it out loud to me."

"Liz!"

"You pay your respects and then get your ass straight back here. Forget all about that little war down there and come back to *our* life."

The allegiance and solidarity he had felt a few minutes ago have been ripped to shreds, and he is left reeling. "But you said-"

She interrupts him, her voice thick with emotion. "You want to fight a war? I told you how to do that. You want to live that life, die that life, go right ahead. You do your thing. But I love you, Protean Williams. If you want to live *this* life, with *me,* then stop getting sucked into that losing battle. Come back to me."

He understands now. An essential technique in PsyOps interrogation is compartmentalization, whether you are the one asking the questions or the poor bastard making up the answers. For the whole conversation, she had compartmentalized his problem outside herself, taken herself and her desires entirely out of the equation to drive toward an objectively optimal solution. But military officer or not, she was still human, and the problem with compartmentalization is you are lying to yourself as much as the other person. He silently berates himself for not taking her feelings and desires into account.

"I'm sorry." It sounds woefully inadequate, leaving his lips. He tries to bolster it, "I'm really sorry I just have been so-"

"It's fine," she says it with the voice that all women use to let you know it is anything but *fine,* then her tone softens to pleading. "Just come home, Pro."

She hangs up.

Pro sags in his seat in the ensuing silence, feeling battered and lost. He feels stretched thin, one foot on two different continents that are drifting apart. He knew this life, this *problem,* was always here waiting to drag him back in. Monk's voice echoes in his memory, a common saying. *The Streets always take back their own.*

A powerful magnetic force pulls him back toward Liz, to Tulsa, to his life. He pulls his bible from the glove box, tries to weld faith in God to that magnetic pull, tries to make himself believe it will be enough to overcome the quicksand he is slipping into.

The Streets always take back their own.

His phone buzzes. A text from Liz *"Stop screwing around with that mess and come home. You have better things to screw."*

The accompanying picture makes him chuckle. *Them Streets need to chill. I've got places to be.*

He looks around the parking lot, considering some of the upgrades tactical-Liz had offered up.

I'll just talk to Gina tomorrow, spend a few days fortifying this place, then I am out of here.

He knows' he can't fix this whole world any more than he fixed Mali but feels an inescapable need to at least try to help. *It's just like those villagers. Give them a few advantages, try to tip the scales, then I'll get back to my life with Liz.*

He envisions it like a military deployment, a quick one. A short trip to a dangerous area, where you try to help the disadvantaged natives, then you return to your own family in the States, safe and sound.

He nods, finding it easier to think about it like that. Compartmentalization.

CHAPTER TWELVE

A funereal is never a good event, but a funeral for a child is terrible.

The normal defense against loss is rationalization. For an elderly deceased, it is a simple and optimistic view of an inevitable but theoretically positive change in circumstance. *Grandpa is a better place now. Old Mrs. Sorenson was in a lot of pain, but she isn't hurting anymore.*

For younger adults, it is a comparison between their lives and that of others of their age. *He died doing what he loved, you know?* Or, *your daddy was a wonderful man; he did more good in 35 years than most do in a lifetime.* Of course, there are variations on the fallback, *Only the good die young, and that's a fact. God must have wanted him home early; he was too good for this world.*

These tried-and-true tropes have been passed down from generation, often with a chance to observe them second or third-hand first. At that time, you don't really believe them, but you nod along comfortingly. Later in life, when you are directly affected by a loved one's death, these excuses come quickly to your rescue when your mind spirals in torment.

But the death of a child is plain terrible. Little people are a living representation of hope, unrealized potential, of innocence. Children are the best of humanity, and no matter the cause, their death wreaks havoc. Not just on their family but on our entire internal theory of justice. When they die, a piece of our soul dies with them.

In Matthew 19:14, Jesus said, *"Let the little ones come to me."*
But why did he have to go so soon, God?

It's this thought that weighs on Pro as he sits in the Baptist church's front row. Flanked by his family, with Jiggy, Deuce, and other gang members in the row immediately behind. Relatives, both close and distant, crowd the pews around them, united in grief and doubt.

The five stages of loss are Denial, Bargaining, Anger, Depression, and Acceptance, and nearly everyone in the building cycles through the first three without getting anywhere near Acceptance. One man does enter who is already very much in the acceptance stage, but his white skin is like a beacon, and his face lacks the requisite sorrow for admittance. He is turned around by a couple of large ushers before he can even get fully in the sanctuary.

So Conners waits in the car. But while the ushers were busy glaring him out of the building, Isabella manages to slip in unnoticed. She keeps her head down under a large black hat, the dark tan of her skin not drawing as much attention.

Someone has lit candles on the walls, and there are little paper brochures with Tommie's smiling second-grade school photo on them. Pro wants to use the candles to burn the little folded papers but instead sits motionless. Fade and Ice are immediately next to him, faces stony. Seriah and Selena are on the other side of their mother, both looking forlorn and unsure what to do, what to feel.

Mama is on the other side of Ice, and Aliyah holds tight to her, crying steadily on a crumpled paper image of her little brother.

Compartmentalization. Pro reminds himself to breathe and reaches over to squeeze Fade's hand as the slideshow starts.

Terrible.

Pro is really glad he didn't know Tommie any better. He feels an enormous weight of guilt for having the thought, but it's there, nonetheless. That distance allows him to skip right past denial and bargaining. Still, anger and depression bash his soul back and forth like the fists of a heavyweight boxer.

I should have been here. I could have prevented all of this.

WHACK.

NO! Four did this! These idiots need to quit this life!

A cute picture of little Tommie blowing out three candles on a birthday cake comes on the screen. Fade's stony face cracks and tears form and run down her cheeks. A low keening starts in her throat, and the sound is more heartbreaking than the picture.

Still looking forward, Pro puts an arm around his twin. Selena cues on her mother, letting loose her own pent-up grief over the loss of an uncle near her own age, "Noooooo!" The strength of emotion emanating from his sister and niece hits Pro like a vicious hook to the belly.

WHACK.

He wants to put an arm around Ice too for support, but the younger man remains motionless, somehow living up to his nickname.

It will be Calean next. You can't stop it.

A little boy riding a bike. Probably five years old. A hammer blow to Pro's skull.

WHACK.

Expressions of grief and disbelief start to rumble through the church as Mama's family starts getting vocal about the tragedy. Deuce, Jiggy, and other Rollin 60's in the second-row pew, cycle between bargaining and anger, muttering curses and talking about what comes next. "...Put them Locos down... they done fucked up... on the set."

In the back of the church, Isabella feels dizzy. Her heart leaps to the screen, wanting to share in the grief for the boy. The first couple of pictures are especially hard, as she recognizes the boy she briefly knew. The closed casket was one thing, but these pictures... *Who thought this was a good idea? It's terrible.*

But she has a job to do and tries to ignore the slideshow. She looks around, trying to identify gang members. Some are easy, and she tries to remember everything Conners told her to look for. *They may be wearing special shirts. They'll have the kid's face on them, maybe a nickname, and light blue lettering.* He had explained the shirts were basically mandatory at the funeral for an older gang member, but he wasn't sure if they would have them made for a kid. In any case, it was hard to tell with everyone facing forward and sitting down. A lot of people seemed to be wearing black suits and dresses, just like any funeral.

There are a lot of flat-brimmed hats, though. She angles the front of her own hat toward each of them, hoping the camera hidden in it captures what they need. Conners voice again, *Look for Seattle Mariners emblems.* She pulls an image of the stylized 'S' to mind. *They use that to represent Rollin 60s.*

As she moves her head slowly around, she spots a collection of men and women on the left side of the church about halfway back. At first glance, they seem to be mostly in all black, but she realizes there are accents of blue on every single one of them. There is also clearly a central figure in the group, a smaller man in an expensive suit. Other than one woman in the group sniffling slightly, there is no animated crying or visible grief in that group. *Curious.* She lets the camera stay on the section and gets lucky a moment later. The man in the middle turns his head to glance back and make eye contact with the massive ushers guarding the door, his movement giving her a full-face profile for the camera.

She sees motion up in the second row, two bigger men getting agitated.

The picture is of the 4th of July, of an eight-year-old Tommie playing with a sparkler. The boy's face is aglow with joy in the reflection of the firework. In the shadows at the edge of the picture, the face of a big, smiling, white teenager is visible, his youthful expression as happy as Tommie's as he vicariously enjoys the child's excitement.

Seeing the image is too much for Jiggy, and the connection he felt with the kid crashes into him like a wrecking ball. He wasn't ready for that picture. It stuns him with grief and brings a double helping of tears to his eyes. The sound of a grown man crying is not a thing anyone wants to hear. Terrible.

Deuce, his own eyes moist, grabs his friend with a hand on either side of his head. He leans into his friend, forehead to forehead, in a willing communion of pain as he whispers, "*I got u, bro.*"

After too many years in the foster system, the gang is the only family Jiggy claims. Tommie was the younger brother he never had. The support now offered by Deuce is a stark reminder of the strength of that bond, and his grief rapidly twists into white-hot rage at any who would attack his family.

His voice is a tortured whisper. "*Motherf-*" A loud mechanical noise mingles with his words as the grieving youngster racks the slide on his .45 semi-auto. "*We gonna get 'em!*"

Deuce immediately releases his friend's head and half rises from the pew as his hands seek the weapon in his own waistband. "*On the Set-*"

At the unmistakable sound behind him of a gun being readied for action, Pro's head whips around in alarm. Looking down, he sees the large handgun. He immediately bounces the most intense look imaginable back up to the youngster's face.

"Put that shit away!" He hisses in a loud whisper.

From her vantage point in the back of the church, Isabella sees Pro turn and glare at the two men causing the commotion. She doesn't really want the camera to film him. To identify him as part of this gang. She had intended to *accidentally* forget to aim it at his face throughout the event. But the damage is done; she is already looking in that direction when he looks back, already locked in on the exact spot.

His face is framed between the other two, who are slightly turned toward each other, and she thinks she sees the glint of metal between them. *Is that a gun?*

Up in front, the force of Pro's will overcomes the brief escalation toward a show of force, and the younger men tuck their guns back out of sight.

"Right after. We rollin'," Jiggy whispers.

Ice turns his head slightly, totally aware of what is happening but trying to avoid breaking decorum. He mumble-whispers a resolute, "On the set," out of the corner of his mouth without changing his expression.

The slideshow mercifully ends. As the pastor walks to the podium, everyone quiets down with both habitual respect for the man of God and the natural hush of collective expectation.

"We are gathered here today to share our sadness, but also to share in hope." The church's elder statesman begins in a clear voice to make a case for God's grace. To outline the promise of a silver lining in even the darkest of times.

Hope? Pro feels his vision swim when the pastor's words hit him. *This doesn't feel like hope.*

The preacher looks at Mama Williams with compassion. His heart clearly breaking for a woman who has steadily attended his congregation since she was a small girl. A daughter of God, already broken by a hard life, now beset by fresh tragedy.

"Sister Rose," His gaze sweeps the front row in what is meant to be a comforting embrace before rising to address the entire crowd, "Williams family, and all of us gathered here today..."

The screen behind the man slowly pixelates, then resolves into the same picture on the brochures in their hands. The final peak of young Tommie's life. The end of his potential. The finality of the image is a clenched fist to Pro's jaw.

SMACK.

The man on the stage struggles valiantly on, trying to make sense of the tragedy for all of them. Leading his flock. The wise and gentle shepherd. *Is this future-me?* Pro's mind wanders as he envisions himself conducting the same orchestra of death in the future. Sees himself standing in front of a grieving family, explaining how everything will be okay, *you know, 'cause God.*

God says to follow the law. Says those who live by the sword die by the sword. But Tommie just rode bikes and played with fireworks, and he still died.

Pro believes in God, but he's not buying any of the crap that the preacher is selling about how this is all part of God's 'greater plan.' *This Pastor is just trying to give us an excuse to accept this.* Pro realizes he doesn't want a reason; he wants the truth. He wants a course of action. He finds himself hating the man at the podium for offering excuses for God, hating everyone in the pews for wanting to believe the logic.

Silently, he appeals directly to heaven, *what do I do?*

Instead of an answer from on high, more words emanate from the sanctuary speakers, "We will see young Tommie again, I *promise* we will, and that day will be a joyous day. Can I get an Amen?"

A smattering of 'Amen' filters up from the faithful, and the chorus feels like a stinging betrayal to Pro. It's the ropes of the ring at his back, trapping him in place, keeping him from dodging the hard rain of guilt.

THUD. He can't breathe. Can't move.

He hates the congregation intensely for so readily accepting the excuse. He wonders if the more distant relatives are already wondering where they are going to eat dinner later. Maybe hoping they can get back on the freeway before rush-hour traffic. *They don't care.*

He thinks about his decision to stick around for a few days and help where he could and then wash his hands and run away back to Tulsa. A wave of self-hatred hits him, pushes him over the edge, into the fourth stage of loss, depression.

"Can I get an AMEN?" The pastor repeats it, drawing on a time-honored tradition of whipping the congregation into a frenzy. While far more muted than a regular Sunday, the response nonetheless comes back as a more powerful rumble than before.

It is less like a blow this time. Not the sting of anger, but a paralyzing chokehold of depression. *You are a traitor, Pro. They are all in agreement. They know they will be shoulder-to-shoulder in this life tomorrow, and you will be gone again.* He knows there may be a few outliers from out of town, but really his hatred should be rightfully aimed solely at himself. *You are the one who is running away. Again.*

The pastor calls the congregation to their feet for a final hymn. They obediently stand together, faces raised toward heaven. Even with eyes closed or blurred by tears, they are unified by their belief that there really is a silver lining.

It's a beautiful thing, a hopeful note. But to Pro, it feels... terrible.

Everyone stands except for Pro. He is frozen by despair, scarcely able to breathe. The sudden wave of hopelessness holds him down like a wrestler on a mat. *You aren't one of them, Pro. You see the truth now. You don't belong here. Stop trying to pretend you are here to help and just run home.*

Fade tugs on him to stand with her, but her voice rings in his head and holds him down. *Ain't no one going to college or moving to Tulsa, Pro.*

He imagines his sister disparaging his plans to talk to Gina, throw a few punches in their fight before bowing out. *Just stop, Pro. Go live that white life and leave us alone.*

A part of him wants to give up, stay on that pew forever.

Murderer.

The weight of the old accusation slams down on him, pinning him to the bench. He has built so many walls to keep that word away from his soul, but in his weakened state, that ancient guilt begins to pummel him relentlessly.

Fade is pulling up steadily on him now, and without looking, Ice also reaches an arm down and hooks it under his armpit to help him rise. A hand slaps his shoulder and a low voice from behind him, probably Deuce, offers support, "Come on, we got you, bro."

They think I am broken with sadness. The thought of looking weak is almost too much to bear. But their support snaps him out of his tumble into depression. They are not treating him like an outsider, like the traitor he feels to be, but like family.

He really is broken by sadness, more layers than any of them know, but he allows them to draw him to his feet. The guilt, doubt, and grief still slam against him but surrounded by family, he straightens to his full height.

Standing several inches above most of them, he suddenly feels closer to God, able to breathe. A fierce relief mixes with his other emotions, and he suddenly realizes he is crying. He is desperately afraid that his existence is chained to death but reaches for the hope that there is also *life*.

His mother's words come back to him stronger than ever before. But they seem to mean something different now.

You owe God a life now, Pro.

He has always taken that to mean his own life, to make something good of himself. Now he wonders if he is meant to *protect life* instead, the lives of his family.

When the cue is given for the family to file up past the closed casket, he moves as one with them. He feels closer to them now than any time he can remember and feels a fierce allegiance. He holds Fade's arm, pretending he is supporting her but really drawing strength from her presence at his side. He wields his twin like a shield against depression and loneliness, holds onto her bond like a lifeline.

When they stop in front of the casket, Mama collapses against it. He puts a hand on her back to comfort her and finds himself staring over her wailing head at the crucifix on the wall, at Jesus on a cross. The crucified Christ stares holes in him.

Murderer. The thought returns that he is an impostor, preaching to rich kids in a different town while his family suffers here.

Stronger now, he rejects the accusation. With one hand resting on his mother and the other linked in solidarity with his sister, he holds onto the promise of God's grace. *I repented of that! I am not that man anymore. I'm redeemed, a believer!*

The eyes on the statue bore into him harder than ever, and the verse from 1st Timothy hits him like an uppercut to the jaw, *"If anyone does not take care of his own family..."*

His vision tunnels as the guilt and self-doubt all come pounding back in. His head reels and he feels his legs turn to jelly. He barely has the presence of mind to lean toward the casket before everything goes black.

. . .

I sabella slides into the driver's seat of her department-issued sedan, eyes moist. "Let's get out of here."

Conners is in the back seat where the window tint is impenetrable and quickly reaches a hand forward to stop her from putting a key in the ignition. "Hold up. Don't start it."

People are streaming out of the church's wide double doors fifty yards away, and she feels a powerful need to be gone. "Come on," she urges him, "someone is going to recognize me, and all hell will break loose."

He withdraws his hand, and she hears a camera shutter clicking in rapid-fire. "There you are... now just look up for me..."

Feeling conspicuous sitting in the parking lot, she tips her head against the steering wheel as if she is crying. She looks out of the corner of her eye at who her partner is snapping pictures of. She recognizes the distinctive group of people who were sitting halfway back on the left side. "Who are they?"

"That's who we are after right there. S-Loc and his inner circle, all OGs and close family." The shutter clicks repeatedly, and he directs his comment to the subject he is photographing, "C'mon look *up*, you little prick."

The man keeps his head down, hat pulled low, as he slides into a large black sedan close to the door. His associates pile into his car and two more beside it, and the entire entourage exits the parking lot.

"OK. We can go now." Conners clambers over the center armrest to get into the passenger seat, his backside getting *way* closer to her face than she would have ever wanted. She leans back as far as she can against his door, idly wondering if punching him the balls would get her fired.

Oblivious to his own offensiveness, the man settles heavily into the front seat and starts previewing pictures on the back of his camera with a frown. "Sonofabitch. Never looked up."

She starts the car and quickly drives to the parking lot exit before Pro and his family can come out and spot her. "I think I might have got him inside."

Her partner looks up at her face with interest, then at the place where the camera is concealed in her large hat. "Really?"

"If it's the guy I am thinking, then yeah, he turned for a second." She gets a break in traffic and jets across both lanes to turn left, heading back toward the station.

"Who else did you get? You get a good shot of those little gang bangers, the kid's immediate family? Your guy Pro?"

She thinks about Pro turning to interact with the other young men, the flash of metal. "Uh, I'm not sure. Why is it so important to prove this guy S-Loc was there? It was just a funeral."

"*Associates In Fact.*" He states it like she should know the implication while obviously aware she doesn't.

This asshole. Likes to show off what he knows. She envisions herself turning toward him, with doe eyes of an attractive young detective. Wide-eyed with wonder as she asks, *What, oh wise and handsome gang detective, are Associates in Fact?*

Resenting the thought, she elects instead to ignore him until he coughs it up without being asked. Her emotions are still reeling from the funereal, and she knows she needs some time to adjust. However, she also welcomes the distraction talking about the case provides.

Oblivious to her internal struggle, he holds forth. "*Associates In Fact* is an important element for a RICO case. I must show several things," he ticks off items on his fingers, "A group with a membership, admittance process, and identifiable organizational structure. Two or more crimes, two or more times, committed in concert with each other." He editorializes his own list, "They got that in spades."

Her phone buzzes and she drives with one hand while checking the text message. *Tony.*

Her eyes on the phone, she multitasks, engaging just enough with Conners to keep him talking. "Just any crimes? So, we can just pull them over twice in the same car together?"

He shakes his head. "No, they have to come from a list of predicate crimes. Kidnapping, shooting, dealing drugs, stealing cars, armed robbery... it's like two whole pages of what the crimes can be, but basically all of the heavier stuff. Trust me, we have all that well-documented. They all have extensive criminal records."

"How was it. Are you OK?" Emotions swirl as she feels Tony's love reaching toward her through the simple words.

"I'm ok." She balances the phone in one hand, using her thumb to get letters in one at a time between glances at the road. She looks back at Conners to show she is engaged, just in time to see his eyes bulge.

"Red. IT'S RED!" He pushes against the dash with both hands, eyes fixed on an intersection fast approaching.

She breaks hard, keeping her face neutral as if that was her plan all along. Playing it cool, she picks up the conversation where he left off. "So... extensive criminal records. Why aren't they already locked up?"

He snorts. "You know the deal. They get snatched up on a weapons charge or whatever, 7th felony in three years. A liberal judge gives them a five-year suspended sentence and pops them right back out on the street." He taps the fingers he had extended for the list repeatedly on the dash. "Unless we can tie them together as a criminal organization."

He holds up the hand again and again ticks off the elements for the case. "A group with an identifiable structure, with goals, predicate crimes that further those goals, and

Associates In Fact who support by action or inaction the crimes which further those goals."

She is silent, wondering how Pro would fit into the picture in Conners' head. Trying to figure out if there is any way she can keep him out of it.

Another buzz. *"You sure? Was he there?"*

She hates that Tony is so intuitive and bites her lip.

Conners takes her silence to be embarrassed incomprehension and explains further. "Think about it like a movie. The production company is the *organization*. Producing the next big hit movie is the *goal*. Everyone who helps make the movie, everyone would be on the credits at the end, there's your *Associates In Fact*."

She tunes into the implication. *Damn, Conners could make that... everyone.*

His next statement confirms her fears. "Now, instead of making a movie, imagine the *goal* is to use fear and intimidation to help the gang more easily and profitably rob people, shoot rivals, steal cars, deal drugs, and evade the police." He waves behind them in the general direction of the church they just left. "Everyone who helps make *that* movie, whether they are the star actor or the guy holding the lights, they all get to be in our RICO."

"Too bad they don't just roll the credits for us," she quips to show she understands the analogy. *I am partnered with the least sensitive person on the planet.*

He nods, pleased she got it. "Yep. Would make it easy, huh? And that's exactly what we need to do for the Judge, get a long list of people, list all of the crimes they have committed in one document. We describe their extensive gang organization, paint a picture of what their goals look like, and then show all of our pictures of these *Associates In Fact* being together."

"We roll the credits for the judge, and you get a stack of warrants to serve," she summarizes.

He snaps his fingers. "Bam. You got it. It's mostly just a lot of groundwork and getting photos of everyone together for the jury." He drums his fingers lightly on the large camera in his lap, "Especially of OGs like S-Loc."

Another message pops up, *"Are you investigating him?"*

She types, *"Tryin' not to,"* then deletes it and writes, *"Kinda."* She deletes that too.

She drives on in silence for a moment, trying to analyze her thoughts. She clears her throat and voices something that has been bothering her. "You aren't even investigating the homicide. This is a gang investigation for you."

He looks up, a denial on his lips. However, when he sees how certain she is, he just smiles slyly. "That's what I said, right? I said I'd help you with the homicide, but I wanted the RICO."

Irritation builds at the base of her skull. "You aren't helping with anything, just burning up my critical window after the shooting, taking pictures of career criminals you have probably known about for years."

He has the good grace to not deny her accusation. Instead, launches a counterattack, making a case for his method, "Yeah, these guys are killing each other. Yeah, we got another Murder one, and oh damn, if it isn't a kid this time. Thing is, they have been and will be doing this until we stop them. And you don't stop them by catching a single shooter and putting him behind bars. We both know this homicide is a long shot anyway."

He gazes, unfocused, out over the hood of the car, his eyes taking on a distinct cynical look. "Only way to stop it is to lock up the whole gang at once, and the only way to do that is a RICO. That's how they brought down the Mafia. It's why they invented these laws in the first place."

"Shouldn't you be off the case?" Tony's message makes her wince.

Conners turns back to her, eyes serious. "You want justice for that little kid in the closed casket? You want to make these streets safer so families can go to church without worrying about bullets flying? We got 92,000 people on the South Side, living in fear. You want to make an impact in that community?"

His questions drill into her, the weight of his conviction like a strong arm thrusting a spear repeatedly. He leans toward her, eyes awakening as the fire of long-disappointed zeal burns through the heavy ash of cynicism.

Feeling uncomfortable with his closer proximity and passion of belief, she realizes he is waiting for her answer. "Yes?" It comes out like a question mark, so she clears her throat and firms her brow before trying again with a lower and more confident voice, "Yes. Hell yeah, I do."

He sits back, satisfied he made his point. "Well, Captain said we had whatever hours we need on this thing, so let's go. Two cases at once. Don't think about it as not pursuing the Locos. We will get to them too. They need it, trust me. But right now, we got the Crips right in our crosshairs. We take them out on the way to the Locos, then get the guys who killed little Tommie, and trust me, the South Side starts calming down."

She thinks about Pro. *He's probably not involved.* The mental determination doesn't change what she knows, though. *Even the guy holding the lights... Conners is going to put him on the movie credits for sure.*

She still hasn't answered Tony's last question, and now it is joined by another, *"What are you going to do?"*

The seasoned investigator has narrowed his eyes, gauging her reaction to his last statement. He starts to try to read her thoughts. "Unless... unless you are more worried about keeping your old flame out of trouble than putting murders in prison."

"Of course not!" She objects on instinct but is immediately aware that such a direct denial only made her internal conflict more apparent.

"Mmmhmm. Not too late to get you pulled off the case, to let the Captain know you have ulterior motives in this one..." He lets the threat hang in the air.

She looks at him, shocked.

He shrugs mildly. "Just so we understand each other." He smiles slightly to soften the proposed betrayal. "Here's how I see it: I am a good gang investigator who is using my knowledge to help you solve this homicide. While so doing, I accidentally stumbled on all the elements I need for an excellent RICO case. You are laser-focused on justice for Tommie -not trying to protect a gang member you have literally been in bed with- and are willing to pursue any and all options to connect the dots, to get that justice."

Her face reddens. She wants to throat-punch the arrogant man, but she knows he has her outmaneuvered. She frowns and quickly swallows to make sure she can produce a manly, confident reply. "Yeah. Of course. That's how I see it, too, obviously."

He nods and sits back, satisfied with the exchange.

Frustrated, she looks at her phone again, silently reaching toward Tony for support. His last question still stares back at her, unanswered. *What are you going to do?*

The subterfuge still doesn't sit right with Isabella, but she can't go to the Captain now and get Conners pulled from the case. He will just throw her under the bus, and when the Captain hears she used to date a family member, she will be off the case and could even get hit with an internal investigation for hiding her connection.

I could just call Pro, get a message to him that he needs to leave town. The problem is that merely delivering a warning like that could put Conners' RICO at risk, as well as cast serious doubt on the impartiality of her own investigation. She feels like Internal Affairs is lurking in the back seat of her sedan, getting ready to pounce. No matter which way she twists, the jaws of the trap grind tighter.

She finally answers Tony. *"Don't worry. It's fine."*

She hits send, and the words feel as much reassurance to herself as her husband. *I can be objective. It's just a case.*

She tells herself actions have consequences. *Pro chose this life. They all did.*

CHAPTER THIRTEEN

Pro clutches the keys to his car tightly in his hand as he walks as if the tighter he squeezes them, the less chance there is Ice will steal his car.

We are doing this, Pro. You either with us or against us. When the family got back to the apartment, emotion was at a fever pitch, and Ice, Jiggy, and Deuce were dead set on rolling out immediately to strike back at the Locos. *You don't have the balls to come? Fine, just let us use your car. Report it stolen in an hour or two.*

He walks quickly, fully aware the boys may try to steal the car even without the keys. They were beyond logic, and he feels like he is sitting on a powder keg. *If I don't show them something big and quick, they are going to blow up.*

He walks between the two rows of solemn garden gnomes that line the sidewalk going to Gina's apartment. *Got her own set right here*. He chuckles inwardly at the thought of a gang of porcelain figurines.

When she answers the door, it is through a crack with the security chain still engaged. "What you want?"

"Ma'am, it's me, Pro." He feels flustered at her lack of

recognition. It doesn't seem that long ago, she gave him a tongue lashing for childhood fights in the parking lot.

Her eyes regard him suspiciously, estimating the truth of what he says. Without betraying whether she believes him or not, she repeats her question, "What do you want?"

"Just to talk for a few minutes? I have some ideas of how we could increase security around here." He feels awkward talking to her through the crack in the door with his back positioned toward the parking lot. Vulnerable. "Could I maybe come in?"

Ignoring his last question, she addresses his stated purpose. "We? You gotta mouse in your pocket?" She gives a little derisive snort at her own joke. "Or maybe a stack of cash? Security cost a lot of money."

He sighs. *And here comes the bargaining.* He tries not to be racist, but he can't help but feel the little Asian landlord is a cliché tightwad. He doesn't have time to waste maneuvering over a few dollars, though, and offers an olive branch to speed the process along. "I do have some money, Gina, as a matter of fact. C'mon, you've known me since I was a kid. Are you going to let me come inside or what?"

Apparently, 'money' was the secret password. The diminutive woman lets him in, then closes and locks the door behind him.

He stands awkwardly in a crowded but very neatly organized living room. Shelves and cabinets full of curios line the wall. A single sitting chair is positioned opposite an impossibly small and old television. A large picture of a middle-aged Asian man in a suit dominates one wall, hanging in a gilded frame with an array of candles on a shelf below it.

"You all grown up now." She states it as fact, a brief and unnecessary observation of the old seeing a younger person take the first step on the inevitable path of aging. She sees him looking at the picture, and a mixture of love and bitterness rules her voice. "My husband."

He remembers the man vaguely. An amiable figure who always seemed to be in the background of his childhood. *Picking up spilled trash. Carrying a ladder. A bucket of paint.* He hadn't realize that her husband had died, but her tone combined with the shrine and the man's absence warns him not to inquire further.

Without volunteering anything further about her deceased mate or offering a place for Pro to sit, she gets straight to business, "What idea you have? How much money you got?"

His thoughts had been geared more toward a general discussion than a factual itemization, and he finds himself at a loss. "Well, maybe a gate? You know, so people don't drive right up in here and shoot us up?"

She laughs. A sharp bark that lacks any joy. "A gate? You got 15,000 dollar?" She invades his personal space and starts patting his pockets as if looking for a roll of cash. "You maybe buy me a private jet too? I can fly back to China. Visit my family any day I want."

He steps back, moving his arms around to fend off her hands but stopping just short of actually swatting the money-seeking appendages. "Gina, stop." He thinks about his savings. *Maybe $3,000? And I'm not trying to spend all of it.*

She stops poking at him but raises her finger like she has a brilliant idea. "Oh, I know. Maybe *we*," she motions the two of them, like they are a team, "should get security camera, hmm?"

He furrows his brow, trying to take the small, animated woman at face value. "Well yeah, that would be a good idea too..." *But we really need to control access.*

"A couple thousand dollar for that." She holds out her hand for him to place the money in, a slight smile playing at her lips. When he doesn't put anything in her hand, she uses her other hand to tap her palm. "Right here, Mr. Williams. You put money for camera right here."

"Gina, I'm not going to just give you cash."

She keeps her hand out and slaps the other hand against it repeatedly in a light tapping motion. Each time it connects, she bounces it back into the air and snaps her fingers as she opens the hand, miming releasing dollar bills into the air. "You put it right here in my hand, and we can watch it disappear together!" Her tone is jovial, like they are sharing a joke. "Water heater broken in three units right now, POOF. Small electric fire in 127, Fire Marshall say no one can live in it, POOF. AC out in 221, $3,000 to fix, I give them half rent instead, POOF. Half my units are empty. The other half won't pay. People move in, and they stop paying."

He gets her point, but she is far from done. "Water leaking in two units. Plumber wants $150 just to come look at it, POOF. Taxes, POOF." She laughs, again without joy. "The roof. Oh my god, the roof. POOF, POOF, POOF!" The snapping fingers have been getting closer to him, and the last poof almost goes up his nose.

When he does not react to her theatrics, she steps back. Head shaking, she moves to sit in the solitary chair. "Security," the word comes out like a bitter curse as she sits down. "My husband and I, we thought *this*," she waves her hand generally to indicate the apartment complex, "we thought this was security. Retirement. We go to America, spend all of our savings, own property."

She closes her eyes, suddenly weary, exuding helplessness, disappointment, and loneliness. "My Han worked himself to death trying to give me security. Now I am stuck here, watching it fall to pieces around me, trapped. Going broke."

He opens his mouth, trying to think about what words should come out of it.

Her eyes come back open, and she stares at him without malice. "Security? I'm trapped here, alone. In hell. Those bastards can shoot me. I don't care."

"Gina," he protests.

She waxes theatrical again, "Security? Naw, just shoot me. Come on, do it." She leans back in her chair and closes her eyes again, motioning with an index finger toward her forehead. "Right here. I'm ready."

He rolls his eyes. "Look, I can help. Maybe we could do a simple gate? What about if I went half on the cost?" He's begging, and he knows it but thinking about the revenge-seeking teenagers back in his apartment, he knows he has to come back with something hopeful. *She's probably exaggerating a bit on prices. Maybe we could get something done for $6,000.*

She opens her eyes again but holds her tongue for a moment as she regards him. Her face is serious now, all theatrics gone. After a moment, she speaks, and her voice is soft this time, "I'm sorry about Tommie."

The statement hangs in the air. Something about the way she said it gives him a new realization. Some of her bitterness comes from knowing a child died on her watch, on her property, and she was helpless to prevent it.

"Me too." Finding an ally in guilt, another party who wishes they had done more, he steps forward. "We have to do better. We *can* do better."

"I have no money to go half." She says it as fact, not bargaining or complaining. "I don't even have enough money to pay the water bill. If the Simmons don't pay their rent by Friday, water is getting shut off to this whole place."

He believes her, and his mind races for another solution. Liz's inquiry into their available assets returns to him. He tries to think about the best possible, not most ideal, option. *You gotta fight with the army you have, not the one you wish you had.*

Gina is still watching him, perhaps despite her professed

readiness to die, hopeful that he will come up with a viable plan.

He thinks about base defense in Mali and how they used ultra-simple and improvised methods to create defenses. *Like a truck parked sideways to block the entrance.*

"What if I could rig up something simple, at least temporary? Something to keep the Locos from rolling up in here."

"Something free?" She sounds dubious.

"Free for you at least," he equivocates. "I have an idea, but I have to look at it first to see if it will work. "If I can rig up something effective to keep them out, do I have your permission?"

"Just at the fence, nothing attached to the building, right?"

Visions of attaching something to the building evaporate, and he waves his hand reassuringly, "Yeah, just at or around the fence, I promise."

They talk a little more, and she gives conditional permission to make the alterations he has in mind. When he leaves her apartment, he feels upbeat and thinks the small woman may even have gained a little hope.

All that changes when he steps back inside Mama's apartment.

I n all times, in all places, and with all people, war preparation always looks the same. There is the readying of equipment -sharpening a sword or double-checking a magazine is fully loaded.

Readying of the mind -prayer, meditation, pep-talks from leadership, reminders to self and others of purpose, of *rightness of action.*

People don't go to war certain that they are in the wrong. Rather, opponents on opposite sides of a conflict both ride out to battle with confidence in their hearts that *they* are in the right. People who doubt their purpose stay home.

"Gonna put them Locos to sleep, on Crip!" Deuce is leaning his forehead against Jiggy's in the same way as at the funereal, sharing pain but now also sharing purpose. One hand is wrapped around his fellow gang member's neck, pulling his lighter-skinned brother in tightly. The other hand is wrapped equally tightly around the grip of his favored weapon, a .22 caliber semi-auto with an extended magazine: a *Deuce-Deuce, probably the source of his nickname.*

Ice has two guns laid out on the table, his Glock pistol, and an ancient breach-action single-shot shotgun. He lines up three shotgun shells and puts one in the bird gun before snapping the action shut with a loud click. The sound and feel of loading the shotgun flow into the teenager, through his hands and up his cervical spine, lending confidence when it reaches his brain. He nods silently, morale elevated by the feeling of power the gun provides. He takes aim at the back patio and makes a silent exploding motion with his lips as he pretends to pull the trigger.

Historically, but not exclusively, the lot of women in war has been waiting, wailing, weeping, and wishing. Waiting for the men to return, crying when they don't, and wishing that wars didn't exist. However, there have been notable examples of women who joined in the fighting, fierce tigresses every bit as fearsome in battle as their male counterparts. Hollywood would have you believe that being more flexible, faster, or some other gender-associated nonsense gives a woman the same power to wage war as a man. The truth is it's the power of the mind, the singularity of purpose, the willingness to give battle that gives all people the ability to voluntarily place themselves in danger.

Rae is wearing that mantle when Pro steps inside. She wears it naturally and without guile, the aura of readiness resting comfortably on her shoulders. She holds her weapon of choice against her lips while she sits on the couch.

She has a Draco? What Pro first thinks is a fully automatic AK-47 is quickly revised to its semi-automatic cousin when she stands to meet him. *An SKS.* The Chinese weapon is cheap and plentiful, and with the thirty-round magazine hanging off the bottom, a serious piece of hardware to be rolling out with. Her look as she turns her face toward him is far more dangerous than the battle rifle she holds, though. No anger, no fear, but *eagerness*.

Eagerness for war among our youth is more deadly than an atomic bomb in the hands of a terrorist. Pro can't remember who said those words. But seeing this girl's smoldering expression as she cradles the rifle, the lustful hunger for battle in her eyes as they turn toward him, her nostrils flaring in a heated smile, he gets it.

Fade looks to be the only one in the room not headed for a shootout at the OK Corral. She stands against the closed door to her bedroom, making sure her girls do not come out. Her arms are crossed, and she wears a difficult-to-read look. Pro's lightning-quick assessment slows for an extra fraction of a second on his twin, as she is the only unknown quantity. The younger people, the gang members itching for revenge, sure of their own invincibility, are a known variable that he was aware would need to be dealt with. But his sister has both surprised and confounded him since he came home. *Jump me in Pro, put me on the set.*

He can't read her expression, but that in itself is telling when everyone else is sharpening their spears. *She's against this.* It's a snap judgment, without much to go on, but he's sure of it. He hopes he is right because critical fractions of a second are ticking down. Now is the time for action, and everything depends on him being right.

He smiles broadly at Rae and steps directly toward her. "Nice piece, lemme see it?"

She starts to think 'no,' would probably have said 'no' or at least done 'no,' but he gives her no time to respond. His left hand snaps out in a lightning-quick jab, closing on the center of the weapon. He snatches it from her grasp before her hands can even tighten to resist.

"Hey-" She starts to protest, but he is in motion, speed and surprise his only advantages.

With the tigress' teeth now in his hands, he moves straight through her in the narrow living room, using his forward momentum to shoulder-bash her off her feet and back onto the couch she just rose from. His eyes are only on one thing, or rather four things, *guns*. Each of the standing boys has one in hand, and Ice has two.

Deuce and Jiggy are moving apart, heads beginning to turn toward him. They are between him and Ice, who is still aiming the shotgun toward the back porch.

Hands. Neither boy has registered what is happening yet, but they are both holding handguns. There is no chance he can disarm them both simultaneously, and while he holds the more dangerous rifle, he has no intention of shooting anyone.

He steps toward the pair, sees their hands begin to tighten on their pistols, their brains starting to think about whether they should raise them, and takes the biggest gamble of his life. He pushes the safety into the 'on' position with his thumb and tosses the SKS to Fade, muzzle pointed to the left so if it still manages to go off, it will fire harmlessly out the front of the apartment.

The boys' eyes follow the weapon as it floats through the air, helpless against the distraction of the lofted assault rifle. Pro is counting on this exact thing but cannot join them in their fascination. He uses their momentary distraction to step forward in a boxer's stance and deliver a one-two punch.

His left fist is first, streaking in a bone-snapping jab across his body to connect with the face of the man on his right, Deuce. He projects the punch a good eight inches through the teenager's unprotected jaw, and it makes a sickening sound.

His left fist retracts from years of practice, like a bungee-jumper at the end of a rope, zipping back to a chambered position at his shoulder. Even as it starts to retract, his other fist is already moving forward in a powerful right cross toward Jiggy's face.

The blows are so quick the second boy does not have time for conscious thought, but animal instincts and street-honed reflexes do afford him the barest of moments to flinch. The train has already left the station, with no chance of redirection. Pro's hand misses the youngster's chin and smashes into his eye instead.

Deuce drops like he was pole-axed, falling backward with straight legs, all muscle control gone. From the way he falls, Pro knows from experience in the ring he won't be getting back up soon. Amazingly, Jiggy survives Pro's jackhammer right hand, remaining conscious but crashing back against the wall next to Fade. He drops his gun as his hands move instinctively to his injured face, and the pistol bounces off the cracked linoleum floor, then skitters over toward the dishwasher.

That'll have to do. Pro nimbly darts forward, closing on Ice as his younger brother turns in alarm. *If that shotgun gets all the way around...* Pro doesn't have time to finish the thought as he throws his body toward the side of the swinging barrel. He gets his side up against the steel to stop the arc and smashes viciously down with his right forearm on the radial bone in Ice's forearm. There is a chance the gun could go off, and Pro prays the thin sheetrock of the wall between the kitchen and Mama's bedroom will be enough to slow down the birdshot.

His maneuver works perfectly, though, and the blow smashes the radial nerve against the bone, sending a numbing jolt through the young gangster's arm. Instead of his finger tightening on the trigger, Ice's grasp loosens. Pro manages to trap the shotgun against his side and twist it away.

Ice's face contorts with pain and anger, and his left hand darts toward the table to retrieve his Glock pistol.

"No-" Pro shoves the shotgun away from them, pushing it to the other end of the kitchen table so he can free up his left hand. It slides to a stop and balances precariously just out of their reach.

"-Gethefuck offmee," Ice growls a curse as he tries to bring the pistol to bear on Pro.

Pro's right hand wraps around the gun's action, trying to push the pistol away, but the younger man has both hands on the gun now and his shoulders squarely behind it. Pro's left hand is coming, moving to join the fight to control the weapon, but it is too slow.

I'm gonna get shot.

His right elbow is already pre-tensioned, his one arm straining against both of his brother's. In a sudden release, he relaxes the fingers of his right hand, allowing him to keep some lateral pressure against the side of the gun while his elbow shoots forward like a pent-up spring. The unpadded bone of his elbow accelerates across the narrow gap before Ice can react and connects with his temple.

CRACK.

The boy's eyes swim as the blow rocks his brain, but while the strength behind the gun's motion lessens, he retains his grip on it.

BOOOM!

The sound of the gun going off is deafening in the small kitchen, and Pro feels something tug at his shirt. His left fist is already swinging, a vicious and efficient hook that catches a dazed Ice right at the tip of his chin.

The next sound is a loud clatter as the gun falls from suddenly limp hands and cartwheels unceremoniously from the edge of the table to the floor. Miraculously, or perhaps thanks to Glock's internal safety mechanism, the weapon does not fire again as it falls.

"WHAT THE HELL?" Jiggy pushes against the wall with one hand, the other pressed against his rapidly swelling eye. His words are obviously loud, but they are muted by the ringing in Pro's ears.

"Sit." Pro gasps for air. "Down."

Not listening, Jiggy looks at where his gun came to rest over by the dishwasher and instinctively moves as if to retrieve it.

"Nope." Pro stands from where he was half-crouched over an unconscious Ice, coming to his full height to block the enraged teenager from reaching the pistol. "SIT." He grabs Jiggy by the shoulders and manhandles him toward a kitchen chair across from Ice. The back of the kid's knees hit the chair, and he half-complies as Pro forces him into a seated position.

"WHAT THE FUCK?" The boy is still confused, but his yell also carries a distinct note of wounded betrayal.

Deuce stirs on the floor, not conscious enough yet to moan, but arms starting to twitch. Pro moves quickly, collecting all three of the youngsters' handguns, then the shotgun he had wrestled from Ice. As he does, he becomes conscious of a stinging and throbbing in his left side. *Shit.*

He tries to control his breathing, to regain control of his racing heartbeat. His hearing starts to come back, and he realizes Rae is screaming at Fade, trying to pull her SKS out of his twin's grasp. His instinctual thought is to bounce forward and drill her with a right cross as well. *Solving problems with fists Pro? So much better than bullets.*

He feels like a barbarian. He feels the betrayal that Jiggy is complaining about. He feels guilt for the frustrated and embarrassed tears the boy is trying to hide at being viciously and easily beaten.

He moves toward his sister and makes eye contact with her. She has her arms locked around the rifle in a figure-eight, desperately trying to keep the weapon from the furious girl as Pro moves to intercede.

Instead of punching the feisty female gang member, he steps directly behind her and snakes a forearm around her neck in a chokehold. Her hands move from the SKS toward his forearm, but she is too late. He locks his right hand into the crook of his left elbow and uses his left hand to push gently forward on the back of her head, forcing the blood vessels in her neck against the 'V' his right arm creates.

"Go to sleep," he commands her quietly.

She tries to say something but can't, and the expertly applied wrestling hold begins its effect almost immediately. As the blood to her brain slows dramatically, she starts to go limp.

"Motherf-" Jiggy tries to get up from the chair, a misguided sense of chivalry incensed at seeing the girl choked out in front of him.

Arms still at work on Rae's sagging figure, Pro balances on his left leg, and sidekicks Jiggy in the chest, sending the poor kid crashing back into his chair. "SIT."

Pro looks at Fade around Rae's head, keenly aware that he is completely tied up and she still holds the assault rifle. Her lips press together thoughtfully, watching him choke out her friend but not moving to stop him.

Her look is one of agreement, a silent justification for his violence. *It had to be done.* At least that's what he hopes she is thinking. She doesn't shoot him, at least, so that's something.

Less than ten seconds later, Pro feels Rae's full weight sag in his arms as she goes completely unconscious. He releases the pressure on her neck and maneuvers her, heels dragging, to another kitchen chair.

Seeing Jiggy's accusing stare, he feels compelled to reassure him. "She's fine. Just hit the reset button, that's all."

As if to confirm this statement, she starts to jerk and gasp for air as he sits her in the chair, and he slaps her back with a cupped hand to stimulate her lungs. She looks around confused, and he leaves her there. He moves to prop a moaning Deuce in a seated position against the counter. With that done, he turns toward Fade.

He is about to ask her for the rifle, eager to have all the guns under his control, but something in her expression tells him she has no plans to give it up. Her face is resolute, just like when she said, *jump me in, Pro.* He knows at that moment that whatever happens, she will not be sidelined. *She is in this fight, and as of right now, she is on my side.*

Pretending like he had no intention of taking the gun from her, he places a hand on her shoulder. "Thanks," he says simply.

She nods once, acknowledging that she accepts his gratitude for not turning the gun on him and at the same time indicating she still stands with him.

"Cover them?"

She looks unhappy with the request and does not turn the gun on the sleeping beauties at the table as he asks. She does turn her body slightly toward the kitchen table, though, holding the gun crossways across it like a guard, not pointed at anyone in particular but ready to enforce order.

"Stay in there, Honey!" Fade's words are directed at the bedroom door beside her. Pro becomes more keenly aware of her position and decisions during the flurry of fighting, all hinged on trying to keep her daughters safe.

The defeated warriors have all gained some degree of consciousness now, and he moves to lean against the counter. He positions himself so all their guns except for the SKS are stacked neatly behind him.

Their eyes follow him, a mixture of hatred and embarrassment on their faces, but no one speaks.

Finally got them quiet. The only thing they respect is strength.

"Buncha straight Gs, aren't ya. *Killas.*" He speaks the slang he grew up with, throwing their language in their faces along with their defeat. He holds up Ice's Glock. "Lil' Homie got a Glizzie, gonna go pop them *Ops.*" He uses the slang for *opposition* while hitting the button to release the magazine. He lets the magazine bounce on the counter as he racks the slide to eject the round from the chamber. He tosses the unloaded weapon back on the counter. "Now you ain't gonna be poppin' *shit.*"

Ice scowls at him and nods toward Pro's left side. "Popped you already."

Pro refuses to look down at the throbbing spot. "*Shit.* I was banging when you were in diapers. Had worse wounds on my eyeball." He waxes poetic, staring them each down as he wields boastful words like a machine gun. "You think I ain't be ducking lead in the Army? I been putting bitches to sleep on the *regular*, gunning homies down *anywhere.*" He moves his hands like a rapper to punctuate his words.

"Shiiit," Deuce glares from his seat on the floor.

Pro reads their expressions. *They don't quite believe me, but they don't entirely disbelieve me either.* It's a start.

Rae sneers. "You a traitor in the Army too? You an *Op* there too, or just here with your *family.*" The last word becomes a poisonous twist, an accusation of the worst sort.

The boys rumble their agreement with her question. Ice

subtly pushes knuckles toward her, a motion of solidarity with her sentiment.

Pro sighs inwardly. *Kicking their asses was one thing, but this battle is far from over.* Winning over their minds will be much more challenging. He switches away from street slang, starts trying to make his case. "I saved you. You should be thanking me. You all think these guns make you tough? You think the Locos aren't ready for all that?"

They want to say yes, of course. Their pride and pumped-up self-assessment want to scream yes, but their recent defeat puts a damper on that perception. No one is willing to speak up, so he continues. "I just stomped the lot of you, and I didn't even have a gun. The Locos have *hundreds* of guns. Hundreds of Gs too, just looking to make a rep by putting you down."

He points in the direction of the parking lot, the uncomfortable memory of the car slow-rolling the other day lending weight to his words. "Hell, I'm pretty sure they already scoping, looking to catch you slipping outside."

"Ain't nobody slipping here," Ice asserts, "we *stay* ready."

Pro laughs a mirthless bark of derision. "Oh yeah, I see that. How's your face?" He motions toward his own temple and jaw as if pointing to the injuries he knows Ice must be feeling.

His younger brother's features remain a mask, but his eyes glow with hatred by way of response.

"That's why we have to hit back," Rae takes point, arguing with him. "If they already looking for it, we have to hit first, or they are just gonna roll us." The boys again nod with her, rumbling agreement.

This is all they know. This is the truth they have been taught. Pro knows the mentality, he grew up steeped in it. The only way he can see outside it is from having experienced different environments, *different warzones.* He tries to think about how to convince them like his Youth Group at church, how to make them see the error of their ways, but all he can think of is how to explain it like a warrior, not a preacher.

He goes with that. "There's a lot of ways to fight a war. You are stuck in this back-and-forth raiding strategy. Uncivilized warfare, like Indians."

This draws a low whistle from Jiggy. "Whelll, look who moved up and went all racist? I'm half Choctaw-"

Oklahoma has many people of Native American descent, and Pro winces slightly at the misstep but refuses to let his analogy get derailed. "Point is, at some point, you have to move into a more strategic approach, which always involves a defensible base."

"A castle." Fade follows the conversation with interest, not committing to either side, and is quick to grasp where he is going.

He nods to her, glad to have her understanding, if not overt support. "Exactly. We can't kill enough Locos to keep them from rolling up in here wanting revenge."

"They can't kill enough of us either," Deuce says. "Last homie standing, last gun blasting."

Pro ignores the bellicose comment and continues outlining his idea. "I just talked to Gina, and she gave me permission to start beefing up security here. This place only has one way in and out. We can make it a lot like a castle," he nods at Fade as he uses the word, "pretty easily."

"You keep on using this word, *'we,'*" Ice says as he massages his jaw. "There is no *we*. You an Op."

"You're a retard," Fade snorts at Ice, "let him talk." She looks back at Pro, her vocal support offered while her face silently pleads, *please have an actual plan, Pro.*

"Ops don't save your asses. Ops don't' spend their life savings to get a gate put up. Ops don't use their cars to operate as guard shacks, and Ops don't put their lives on hold to get you set up safer. Ops don't help you make good decisions when your Big Homie is locked up, don't help you stay out of the way long enough to live another day."

He looks around the kitchen table, pausing to make sure his next words are heard. "Family does that." He looks at Ice specifically. "There is a *we*, and it's called family."

He has their attention now; at least none of them are vocal about their doubts. "All of us," he moves his hand in a circle, motioning to include everyone in the room, "are a family. I am here to help my family, and I'll put that *on the set.*" Swearing on the gang is the highest order of commitment in their minds, and he gives it that same importance in his own to connect with them.

He begins to lay out some of his security ideas, illustrating how they can turn Hillcrest Apartments into Hillcrest Castle. There are a lot of derisive remarks, but there is also a spark of interest. Fade gets involved, talking about a way to get her clients in and out, a back door.

Pro keeps the guns behind him while building up the concept in their minds of castle doctrine vs. raider tactics. Principled defense vs. generating protection through fear. He's not sure how much they are buying into it. *But at least I stopped the drive-by. For now, anyway.*

It's a dubious victory, but an important one. Steering his family from self-destructive to productive will entail changing their minds, their whole outlook on life. He can't do that all at once, of that he is certain, but changing their actions, stopping them from doing the next thing they were going to do to destroy themselves, is a start.

Gotta start somewhere.

He has brought them to heel for now. Pro feels like he has succeeded for the moment, but his victory only gives birth to a far more significant problem. What comes next?

CHAPTER FOURTEEN

Damarion leans his head against the concrete-block wall next to the stainless-steel wall phone. He jams a finger in his left ear and tries to concentrate on the voice emitting from the cheap earpiece.

"He did what?"

Ice talks haltingly, trying to get the message across without saying anything incriminating on the recorded line. "Pro. He stopped us. I mean, we were gonna roll out and shit."

"You tryna step without me?" Four slaps his hand against the wall in frustration. "I *told* you, no one moves till I am out. I got the OGs behind me now." The last part is a lie, or at best a *future* truth, but Four knows that political power is one of his few cards to play right now.

"We working on that bond, bro, but $15,000..." Ice trails off. They both know the gang isn't going to be able to put up that kind of cash anytime soon.

"How much you got? My pussy-ass public defender says he's getting my bond reduced."

"They gonna OR you?" *Order Released* is a magic phrase all

criminals and their families are familiar with. If a Judge says to let you back out of jail while you await your next court date, then you hit the streets immediately. And in America's overcrowded jail system, it is far more common than most people think. The funny twist is they usually wait to see if you can pay bond first because as soon as you screw up again or miss a court date, the County will get to keep that money.

The older brother laughs. "Naw, my dude. Not on this stack of bullshit charges they got me on. They pilling it on, trying to get me to plead. DA offering two and eight right now."

Damarion has seven total charges on three different pending felony cases. His latest shenanigans are just the most recent additions to the pile. Criminal cases often take two years to make it to trial, and trials are expensive, so the State uses a different approach. They repeatedly let offenders back out of jail on 'pre-trial release.' One of two outcomes is assured. Ideally, the criminal learns their lesson, stays out of trouble, and eventually pleads to a suspended sentence - no jail time. Or, they keep committing crimes and getting caught until they have to take a plea deal for minimal prison time. Four is in the latter group and having already been in prison, has old time hanging over his head plus the fresh charges.

"You gonna take it?" Ice's voice is worried. He is grown up enough to know it is a real possibility. Two years inside and eight on probation is a walk in the park next to the long years Four could face on another conviction. Good behavior inside, and Four could be back on the street in 18 months instead of a jury putting him away for twenty-plus if he fights it. A smart man would be taking that plea, and quickly.

"Hell no!" Four sees it differently, and lays it out for his younger brother. "He says he can get my bond down to $3,000, talking to the judge about how I grew up disadvantaged and shit. Y'all get that together, and I am gonna be fresh out and ready to *roll*. We gonna bust on those Locos so hard they *stay* gone."

"Hey, watch what you say—"

Four talks over the younger Williams, "They aren't listening to this shit." He looks over his shoulder at the long line of inmates waiting impatiently to use the phone. "Like a million calls per day outta here. Ain't nobody got time for all that." He leans back on the wall. "You got me on three grand?"

"We are close. Rae is bringing some good stuff in. Maybe another week?"

Four senses something hidden in Ice's speech and goes after it, "What's the problem then? Pro?"

"He's talking about fortifying... like defending a castle," Ice distances himself from the strategy, "I think it's dumb, but Fade and them are behind it."

Four swears. "Why you let him say anything? He doesn't run shit. He been gone!"

Ice pauses, too embarrassed to detail the whipping Pro gave them or admit that his older brother still has all their guns locked in the trunk of his Impala.

Four swears again. "Bond me out. Just get me outta here, and I will straighten that pussy out. We CRIPS. We don't hide. We go hard."

"I went hard on your momma last night." When he whirls to find the voice, he sees a bunch of hard faces smirking. A few nodding heads of men who probably didn't make the comment but would happily take credit for it.

His eyes narrow, but the next guy in line just stares coldly back at him. "Hurry up, *Big Crip*." The man's tone contains no disrespect, as that would necessitate fighting. Still, even Four is wise enough to know his gang membership is unimpressive to the guys waiting to call home.

Oblivious to what is going on in the jail, Ice talks about the money. "You sure $3,000?"

"That's what he said. He sounded sure." Four thinks about his other brother. "Pro doesn't know *shit*. Just hold him off till I get out, and I'll handle up on him." He hits upon an idea. "He talking to anyone? Tell Rae to get all up on him," he smirks suggestively, "she'll keep him busy."

This last suggestion, casually made by Four, drives a wedge between him and his smitten younger brother. Rae is none-too-stingy with her favors, and Four makes no secret that he enjoys this particular gang benefit. But Ice still fancies himself her boyfriend.

"He has a girlfriend in Tulsa," Ice says stiffly.

"HURRY UP." The impatience in the line of inmates is now palpable.

"Well, hell, why doesn't he go back to her then?"

"I don't know. He wants to help."

Four swears again, the language of the furiously helpless. "Gotta go. Get that three, OK?"

Ice insists he will and hangs up. He looks around in the narrow space between the back of the apartment and the wooden fence. He feels trapped between the structures. And trapped between his two older brothers.

"What the heck are they doing?" Isabella peers through binoculars at the apartment complex a half-block away.

Conners stirs slightly, the only indication that he has woken in the reclined passenger seat. He had no problem going straight to sleep when she took over watching duties an hour ago. After a moment, with his eyes still closed, he marshals enough sarcasm to speak, "I don't know, committing crimes? Why don't you give me your best guess as to which ones, since I am sleeping, and you are watching."

She ignores his sarcasm, shifting the focus knob to try to make the flurry of activity clearer. "I am not sure..."

"*Was* sleeping," he corrects himself, then sighs and pulls the lever to raise his seat fully upright. When he sees what she is talking about, his irritation is replaced by puzzlement. "What the hell?"

"That's what I'm saying." She hands him the binoculars. "Are they making some sort of armored car to do a drive-by in? Is that a thing?"

He furrows his brow as he peers through the device, leaning forward in his seat to rest his elbows on the dashboard as if being an extra foot closer might help him make sense of what he sees. "Not that I ever heard of, but who knows with these monkeys."

"You are a fricking racist pig, you know that?" She wonders what slurs he applies to her behind her back. *They got me with this fence-hopping split-tail, guys. Softest wetback I have ever been in the car with.*

He takes her criticism in stride. "All cops are racist. Everybody knows that." His statement is curious. It's as if he resents the implication and disagrees with it but has long since given up trying to convince people otherwise and now accepts the mantle with poor grace.

She does not have an answer, and he does not expect one. After a minute of further study of the activity, he renders his first useful observation, "Well, that pile of crap isn't driving anywhere."

She stares at where he is looking, feeling helpless to see without using the binocular's magnification. "Yeah?"

"He nods his head slightly. "Mhhm. Got two bald tires and two donuts and smokes like it's on fire when they start it."

Even with her naked eyesight, she can see they have the vehicle crossways to the apartment entrance. "Do you think it broke down right there?"

"No. They are getting it more stuck, all jackknifed in there, not trying to get it out..." his voice trails off, and he mumbles to himself, "what in the Sam hell..."

"It looked like they had attached a sheet of metal to one side?"

He grunts in grudging agreement, "Yeah. I thought plywood at first, but you are right. I think they bolted it right to the side of the van." As he speaks, he sees that they have gotten the vehicle completely sideways in the narrow space. No sooner have they managed this dubious accomplishment than a minivan with a mismatched fender and hood arrives at the complex. "Fricking *idiots*. Unbelievable."

"What's happening?" Isabella asks impatiently.

He chuckles and shakes his head, then hands her the binoculars. "Take a look at this."

There has never been anyone more purposeful in the history of humankind than a single mom in a minivan. A mom's day is a finely balanced work of art. *Drop off Maria at daycare at 7, then Jason at school at 7:15...* This particular driver has just labored for two hours at the coin-operated laundromat and driven twenty minutes to the closest grocery store to supply the clan. She now has just enough time to drop off her dubious plunder before heading to work her shift at the Waffle House. And that's before Johanna calls in sick again, and she ends up staying for a double shift.

When the binoculars reach Isabella's eyes, it looks like the up-armored contraption is about to get rammed by the minivan.

. . .

"Out of the way! Oh my god, what the hell are you doing!" The horn is a week squawk, but the irate woman applies it in a long blast that makes up for lack of loudness with annoying insistence.

Ice looks pissed, and his hand moves toward his empty waistband. He moves threateningly toward the woman, but Pro puts a hand on his shoulder. "Let me."

Ice glowers at the woman but lets Pro move past him to deal with her.

"Hi, Mrs.?" Pro tries to disarm the woman with a broad smile as he approaches her window.

She isn't having it. "Are you guys crazy? You are blocking the only entrance!"

He keeps the smile fixed on her but lets his face turn more serious. "We are working with Gina to make the place safer. Trying to keep people from being able to drive up in here…"

"Doing a great job of that!" She does not mean it as a compliment. "How am I supposed to get in? I live here."

"So do we—"

"*That's* the problem." She jabs her finger at the other gang members trying to maneuver the odd vehicle up over the curb. "No one's shooting at me up in here. It's you Crips out here banging and causing problems. You get out of Hillcrest, and it'll die down."

He is a little surprised by the woman's bravery and directness in calling them out. *Yeah? And where is my family supposed to live? They have to live somewhere.*

He wants to keep the diplomatic smile, but his face reverts to a more challenging expression. "Oh, you all angels, huh? You never had anyone in your family Crippin'?" He jerks his head back toward Ice. "Never had a younger brother who wanted to roll like that, couldn't convince him otherwise?"

Her look becomes guarded, and he knows he has struck a nerve. The pressure to join gangs, the rap culture glorifying it, and the perception of easy money when you have nothing is like a siren call to the youth in the area. Some grow out of it as they got older, some go to prison, some…

She squeezes her lips together and shakes her head to dismiss something tearing at the edges of her memory. Her eyes have taken on a haunted look, and she clears her throat and looks down. "I'm sorry about Tommie. Good kid." She chokes up, thinking about her own son Jason.

"We don't want that to happen again." Pro sees Ice starting his way, ready to threaten the woman, and keeps his voice low, speaking quickly. "I'm trying to keep them out of it, you know. Defend our home instead of keeping the cycle going. Protect you all."

Ice arrives at her passenger window and leans against it with a dark scowl meant to add weight to whatever Pro is saying to her. His right hand is tucked up under his long shirt as if grasping the handle of a pistol.

She makes a point of looking at Pro instead of the teenager, doing an admirable job of keeping her nerve. "OK, but I still have to get in." She waves at the parking lot. "We all do."

"I'll get you in. I have a plan," he assures her. "Just give me a minute. Help me, help you."

He pushes up from her window and looks at Ice as he moves away, "I told you I had it, bro. She's good."

Ice puts some swagger in his step as he follows his older brother, choosing to believe he had been of assistance in Pro's diplomacy.

A grating sound makes them both wince as they reach their project vehicle, a dilapidated 1995 Astro van. "Stop!" Pro holds his hands out to Jiggy. The teenager is revving the motor, trying to get the beater to climb the curb.

Pro jogs toward the van. "You are gonna tear out the clutch!" He turns his head to Ice, "See if you can find us some boards or bricks or something. We have to make a ramp." He motions for the other gang member to exit the driver seat, "Get out of there. You never drove a stick before?"

Deuce smirks at Jiggy's embarrassment. "He never drove anything before. Crip needs glasses. Can't see shit."

This revelation strikes Pro as odd. A 17-year-old in America needing glasses doesn't seem to add up, but the expression on Jiggy's face says it's true. *And I have been here for several days without realizing it.* It is an unexpected reminder that you don't know what people are going through, what hidden battles and disadvantages they fight until you come alongside them and really try to help.

His thoughts are interrupted by a shorter and more respectful but no less impatient honk from the minivan still half in the street. With all apparent progress halted, any faith the woman had in Pro's methodology is quickly evaporating.

He steps past the exiting teenager and levers into the seat of the old work van. It smells like cigarettes and a couple of decades of hard labor, and the engine runs rough, barely sustaining an idle. The license plates expired two years ago, and the pile of scrap probably hadn't been covered by insurance for at least three, but at $700, it had been the right price and close at hand.

The reluctant gears grind slightly as he surges forward instead of trying to back over the curb. The brakes barely slow the vehicle as he quickly reaches the curb on the opposite side of the apartment entrance, and he winces as the front wheels come to a jarring stop against the concrete.

He tears down the plastic serving as a side window, pulling the material away from the faded duct tape holding it in place. Revving the engine and leaning out, he gauges the distance to the other curb. He wonders if he can hop it with enough momentum or if the impact will tear the back axle out from under the cheaply made van.

The right side of the vehicle being weighed down by 320 lbs. of steel probably tips the odds in favor of breaking, so he decides he better wait. "Hurry up, bro," he urges Ice.

$700 in cash helped out old Joe who's painting and carpentry days and usage of the van were both slipping into the past with his advanced years. A questionable road trip in their unlicensed van had yielded an enormous steel plate from the local plant and an assortment of hardware from Home Depot. Their adventure had been punctuated by no less than three stops to add air to a badly leaking front tire, but they had made it back safely.

Another exasperated honk comes from the street. Pro leans forward to see around the steel, waving in what he hopes is an encouraging gesture. *Patience. We'll get it.*

He had spent a little over $500 on the improvised armor piece. The plate was 4 feet tall by 8 feet long and ¼ of an inch thick, and it took all of his and the other gang members' ingenuity and strength to get it bolted onto the side of the van. After much swearing and head-scratching, he had made another trip to Home Depot in his Impala. He had returned with a shiny new cordless drill and saw set, as well as an assortment of abrasive saw blades and heavy-duty drill bits. The collection of additional supplies had cost him another $320, and his bank account was starting to feel pretty thin.

He had seriously underestimated how hard it would be to drill through that much steel, let alone cut slots in it to see out the passenger window, but late last night, they had put the finishing touches on his inspiration. The result looked like something out of Mad Max but was very similar to what he had seen used in actual war zones. ¼" of steel would stop all but rifle fire and looked even tougher than it was. In theory, bolting it to the van made it a cinch to roll out of the way when a resident needed to get into the parking lot.

Finally, Ice runs up with some wood scraps, pieces from some discarded furniture that he had smashed into suitable chunks.

"Yeah, that's it, stack it at the curb," Pro yells out the van window.

When the pieces are in place, he revs the motor again and feathers the aging clutch. The contraption surges backward and gains momentum. With a bump and precarious sway, it mounts the curb and rolls neatly onto the gravel area between the fence and the apartment building wall.

And the people rejoice. Pro smiles as the gang members pump their hands and grin at the accomplishment. The minivan finally can access the parking lot, and as it surges past, the woman's irritation appears to have at least some measure of acceptance mixed in.

Pro feels jubilant. His side hurts from the bullet graze he had taken in the fight, his back and shoulders ache from last night's labors, and half of his hard-earned saving is gone, but they have a workable gate! *Now we can close the castle at night, keep the Locos out.* $1,500 seems like a small price to pay for something that might have saved Tommie a week ago, and he is happy to have spent it.

I could have done this a year ago, probably something better than this even. He shakes himself, trying to fend off guilt. *You didn't know they needed it.* His defense is technically true, but only because he didn't ask, didn't try to know. *Just like you didn't know Jiggy can't drive a car for lack of a pair of glasses. They need help, Pro. Help you can give.*

He had been trying to do good on his own, thought he had been on the right path, but now Monk's words come back to him. *He came alongside people and helped them. That's what Jesus did.*

Ice comes up to the window of the van, shaking his head but also smiling. "You crazy, bro. On Crip, I never seen anything like this."

Pro smiles at his brother and the other boys. He imagines they are fishermen, their nets now full of fish he helped them catch with a new idea, kind of like in the bible. He wonders if Jesus ever built a gate for a village that needed it.

Probably not. And you're no Jesus either.

It still feels good, though.

Like taking care of family.

CHAPTER FIFTEEN

"Yay! I miss you so much!" An unusually girlish delight invades Liz's voice, making him feel even more guilty.

"I miss you too, babe."

"You got everything handled with your family?"

"Wellllll..." He tries to think of how to word it.

She senses his hesitation, and her tone hardens. "Well, *what*? Are you coming home, or aren't you?"

Shields up, Pro. Safe behind the wheel of his Impala on the outskirts of Tulsa, he finds himself ducking his head instinctively. *Locos aren't the only ones out for blood.* "Well, I need to get some stuff to bring down there... you know."

"Some *stuff*?" She is incredulous. "No, Pro, I don't know. Please tell me what *stuff* you need to get."

Guns, obviously. Saying that will go over like a fart in church, so he backpedals. "Just clothes, I didn't bring enough." It sounds stupid when he says it.

"Clothes? So you are going back and need more *clothes*?" Her voice hits a high note, one that carries a warning. "Something nice, so you can reconnect with your ex? How about all of them? In fact, I'll just pack up all of your stuff. Make it easy for you."

"Liz." He tries to protest, but the line goes dead. She doesn't answer when he calls back, and his dread grows with every mile.

When he gets to their apartment, he half expects to find all his personal belongings stacked on the curb. What he finds is even worse. Liz curled up on the couch in yoga pants and one of his old hoodies, an empty bowl of ice cream, and a framed picture of them on the coffee table in front of her.

"Hey babe," he says from the doorway, trying to feel her out.

She stares straight forward with smeared mascara and reddened eyes. Trembling lips keep her from speaking. Guilt smashes into him. He moves quickly to her side, sitting on the couch and pulling her into his arms.

"Aw, c'mere girl."

She lets him hold her but is passive in his embrace.

"Nothing is going to keep me from you," He tries to reassure her.

She clears her throat and points to something on the table. "That came for you."

He notices the manila envelope for the first time. "What—"

"It's your packet. Your Commander brought it by personally."

He puts the pieces together. "For Ranger School?"

One of his dreams, since he joined the Army, was to go to Ranger School. It was a rite of passage to prove he had what it takes to hang with the toughest in the ranks. Roster spots for National Guardsmen are sparse, and the prestige from passing the school would be a significant coup. A lifetime accomplishment.

She relapses into silence again. Refusing to comment or congratulate him on the acceptance package.

Trying to use it as neutral ground, he attempts to build a conversation around the topic. "Took three tries, but I finally got a slot. Awesome!" He sees that it is open and reaches for it. "What dates did they give me."

She remains stiff as he moves his arms from her toward the packet. "Two weeks."

"What?"

Withdrawing the cover letter from the packet, he sees she is right. They got him in on a standby slot, but on very short notice. Flipping through the packet, he sees that he needs to get a thorough physical and make several other pre-qualifying preparations. His momentary surge of excitement crashes into the day-to-day urgency of events back home, leaving him feeling stretched thinner than ever.

Back in OKC, you mean. This is home. He mentally corrects himself.

Clearing his throat, he slowly places the packet on the coffee table. "You knew?"

She still hasn't looked at his face. "It came the day after you left..." her voice tightens, "I was going to take leave, hoping we could spend some time together before you go."

Of course. I'm an idiot. Pro silently berates himself as he becomes aware of her viewpoint. Ranger School is 61 days of hell, more if you get hurt or fail a phase, and communication with your loved ones is limited to sparse letters. *No wonder she has wanted me home so badly.*

The situation is clear in his mind now that he has all the pieces. *She has been planning an emergency vacation so we can be together, and I am off playing hero with my family.*

He places the thick stack of papers on the table in front

of them and reaches for her hand. When their palms meet, her fingers interlace with his and grip him tightly. Neither of them says anything, her choked with emotion and him trying to figure out how to balance everything.

I am just now getting the gang to a place where they just might not get killed. He thinks about his well-equipped semi-automatic AR-15 rifle in the upstairs closet. *Some decent weapons, and they should be able to make the Locos think twice about pulling up on Hillcrest.* His brain's strategic part grabs ahold of the variables like favorite toys, lining them all up to pour over.

He had been planning on telling Liz that he would stay with his family for another week. *Two really, if I'm honest.* Just enough time to "get the family settled," AKA fend of the Locos until Four got out of jail. But now, he needs to spend the better part of a week getting his physical and other tasks done, leaving precious little time to spend with her before he drops off the face of the earth for a few months.

He's not good with analyzing his own emotions, much less other people, but Liz's feelings are pretty obvious this time around. *You can't blame her, Pro. Give your girl some time. She deserves it.* Thankfully, she didn't pack up his belongings like she threatened. But every ounce of relationship intuition he possesses tells him that outcome could easily change if he ditches her for his family again -and then leaves for two months.

"I could pass," He offers the solution without conviction, "wait for another slot to open up."

"You're going." She says it as a statement they both know to be accurate, and he doesn't argue with her. She continues, her voice stronger now that she is talking about something she is familiar with, "You know it will help you with promotion and will set you up to apply for SF."

With the Army as a shared experience, they have spent long hours talking about their respective career paths. Their dream is to get into a Special Forces unit, her as an Intelligence Attaché and him as an A-Team member. Ranger School is his next step on that path, a primarily male-only opportunity she is jealous of.

Words tumble from his lips in a confused jumble of truth, hope, and lies. "I am loaning my brother some of my gear." He uses the word as a substitute for 'guns,' moving quickly past it. "I just need to take them some stuff, and I'll come right back, I swear."

Plus, maybe a day to train them on tactics to react to a raid or drive-by. He knows it is far from enough time. A week would be more accurate, a month even better.

"Some *gear,* huh?" Her tone makes it clear she knows exactly what he is trying not to say.

He rushes on, ignoring her comment. "A day, maybe two at the most, and I'll be right back here." He puts one arm around her shoulders and gives her a squeeze. "Find us a hotel, a resort someplace quiet. I'll meet you there, and we can have some time together."

"Bullshit."

"No, really. I have helped set them up down there, just have to do a few last things, and I am all yours."

She finally looks at him, an accusation written across her features. "A few last things? What *things,* Pro?"

"You know," words fail him, and he feels his face getting warm, "fixing doors and stuff, making the place safer."

"*Fixing doors?*" She pushes away from him, her face a mask of incredulity. "You are so full of shit, Pro!"

"Liz, come on-"

"NO!" She jumps up, towering over him and jabbing a finger toward his face. "I will not come on. I will not watch you go down there and get yourself killed in some gang shoot out, trying to be a hero."

"It's not like that!" He feels defensive, like she is calling his family a statistic.

"Yeah? Tell me. What's it like, Pro?"

He surges to his feet. "It's people, Liz, it's family- my family."

She looks hurt. "Yeah? And what are we?" She snatches the picture of them off the coffee table, her sudden motion knocking the bowl and spoon to the floor. She pushes the picture toward his face, the two of them smiling together on a beach. Young lovers far from home, far from their different childhoods, free to be together.

She shakes the picture in front of him. "Are we family, Pro? Or am I the wrong-"

He doesn't let her finish the thought. "YES!" He grabs the picture and holds one edge of it, taking equal ownership of the memory. "Yes, we're family too." He means it, says it as a fierce declaration, pouring all his passion for her into his words.

Something about his look breaks through her doubt, and she softens subtly. He sees her face changing, feels the tide shifting, and wraps his arms around her in a powerful embrace.

His arms encircle her, and it feels right. Feels important. Worthy of protecting. Vague thoughts of a ring steal unbidden into his mind.

She closes her eyes and hugs him back, loosely at first, then tighter as the moment lengthens.

"One day." Her words are a gift —a peace offering to bind them together.

"One day?" He echoes her, but in a tone less sure, his mind racing in an automatic calculation of all the things he planned to do.

She squeezes him, pulling his ear close to her lips and emphasizing the words as she repeats them. "One. Day. I'll get us a hotel, something nice. I'll send you the address." She pushes back from him, holding him at arms' length so she can read his response. "You do what you need to do, Protean Williams, but I swear to God if you leave me hanging..."

"One day." He nods confidently, putting aside all other thoughts so he can infuse his words with certainty this time. He knows if he screws it up, his stuff really will be on the curb when he comes back.

Searching his face, she appears satisfied. "And then you come back to your life here, to *us*."

D riving back, his trunk is stuffed full, his AR-15 and several other guns crowded in alongside the gang's previously confiscated weapons. His mind is even more heavily laden.

If a man had only one day, what could he do? And would the difference he made in that one day be worth doing?

It seems impossible. Part of him feels he should just turn around and go straight back to Liz. But he sees Jiggy squinting over the steering wheel. He sees Fade selling drugs to support her children, sees bullet holes in the siding, blood on the sidewalk. He sees war and them living in it.

You can't fight a war in one day, Pro.

His common sense agrees with the assessment, but a Bible story he recently taught his Sunday School students comes to mind.

In the story, Joshua, a mighty man of God, was leading his army in battle. Against all odds prevailing against a horde of Amorites, routing the enemy. Joshua saw that they were winning the fight and that God Himself was helping by hurling massive hailstones to kill the evil Amorites. Still, their enemies were so vast in number that they simply didn't have enough time left in the day to kill them. So, Joshua prayed a singular prayer, a bold one:

"Sun, stand still at Gibeon, And moon, in the Valley of Aijalon." (Joshua 10:12.)

According to the Bible passage, God granted Joshua's extraordinary request. The sun and moon stood still for around 24 hours, long enough for Joshua and his army to achieve a crushing triumph.

What can a man do in one day if God is on his side? In the story, the Israelites were Joshua's tribe, his set, his family, and his prayers and leadership brought them victory.

Pro wants to believe like Joshua. He wants to pray that he will have enough time to protect his family and have his wish be granted. He wants to feel his cause is just.

He thinks of the small family gang in his Mama's kitchen, a bunch of kids trying to come up tough.

It's family... but is it right?

He turns up his music as he exits the freeway on the South Side, and Ludacris fills his ears.

*Get back, M******! you don't know me like that*

He rolls his shoulders and adjusts the Glock tucked in his belt.

Yeek yeek woop woop! I ain't playing around!
Make one false move, I'll take ya down.

He rolls the windows down, and he and the music hit the streets of his neighborhood together. He feels eager to be rid of his trunkful of weapons.

I sabella jerks awake when her bed accelerates forward unexpectedly. She tries to collect herself and sit up, an effort impeded by the front end of the unmarked car bouncing hard and then swerving sharply as Conners pulls out onto the street.

"What are you doing?" She demands.

"Got him." His eyes are fixed like a laser beam on the black Impala in the center lane.

"Is that-"

"Yep, middle of the night, and he's back. Time for a little talk." Conners accelerates up behind Pro's car and reaches for the switch to activate their car's discrete emergency lights.

Isabella's heart sinks. They had tracked Pro to the edge of city limits when he left. She had felt victorious when her prediction of him leaving town and her insistence that he wasn't in the gang had been proven right.

A bar of red and blue lights is discretely mounted inside the vehicle, mostly hidden behind the windshield. When Conners flicks the switch, they flash to life and begin their dance across the inside of the glass. The brake lights on the car in front of them stab on immediately. But just as quickly, they go back off again, and her heart sinks even further.

Conners grins. "He gonna run?" He sounds hopeful, and he steers with a knee, putting on his seatbelt with one hand and reaching for the radio mic with the other.

"No way, he's too smart." She hopes the words are true as they leave her lips. The Impala rolls steadily in front of them, neither slowing nor speeding up. *Come on, Pro.*

Conners is bringing the mic to his lips, "Victor 75, City, Traffic."

A detective coming up on the net to make a traffic stop is rare, and Dispatch takes a second to answer. Isabella's heart pounds, knowing every cop in the area will be tilting their head toward the radio, trying to figure out what's about to go down.

All hell is about to break loose. She thinks about her son, about wanting to go home to him. Unbidden, the thought comes of her telling her son his father died in a high-speed chase, crashed out in a ball of fire.

STOP IT.

"Go ahead, Victor 75?" The dispatcher's voice is a giant question mark. They may as well have said, "What in the sam hell are you doing out there, detective?"

He keys the mic, his lips parting to call out their position, to say they have an uncooperative subject, but just then, a turn signal comes on in front of them.

"59th and Grant, black Impala. Start me a Back." His request for a backing officer is all he has time for, and he swerves to follow Pro's track as he pulls into a nearby gas station. He drops the mic and unfastens his seatbelt, again steering with his knees to free his hand up to work the door handle.

Seeing him prepare to jump out quickly, Isabella feels irritated. "He's not ditching. He was just looking for a good spot to pull over."

Conners ignores her. All his focus is on the dark windows of the vehicle ahead. When their speed drops to a crawl, he slams the transmission in park, kicks his door open, and is out and moving.

Isabella gets out, too but moves slower. She feels behind the power curve and helpless, wanting very much for Pro to be clean but scared something big is about to go down.

The dome lights come on in the car, and Pro is visible in the driver's seat, alone. *Thank God.* She realizes she was half-expecting to see a car full of gang members armed to the teeth.

Conners moves quickly to the driver's window, giving Pro little time to get organized or pull something. He slows at the last second, adopting a casual body posture and tone as he reaches the open driver's window. "Hey, how are you doing tonight?"

Isabella eases up to the passenger window and sees a confused and irritated Pro trying to act polite.

"I'm fine, Officer." He makes a show of looking at Conners' lack of police uniform. "*Are* you an Officer? Why was I pulled over?"

Pro clearly wants to be respectful but struggles with the deeply ingrained distrust of police he grew up with. The feeling that he will always be persecuted, perhaps even more so if he does well for himself.

Conners pulls his detective badge from inside his shirt and lets it hang from a chain. "Detective. Gang Unit. And I'm sure you recognize me, so stop screwing around."

Recognition dawns on Pro's face, and with it, anger. "You're the one-"

"Looking into the gang violence that got your brother killed, yes."

From her vantage point, Isabella sees Pro's powerful shoulder muscles tense. His involuntary response to Conners' casual mention of the boy's murder clearly signals that he wants to punch the detective in the face. *Hell, I kind of want to punch him in the face too.*

With visible effort, Pro controls his response. He speaks through clenched teeth, "Why are you pulling me over, *Detective.*"

Conners smiles like a snake. "Noise violation. City ordinance states if your music is audible from 50 feet away, you are in violation, and I could hear it clearly as you drove by."

At this, Pro's iron control cracks, and he slams his hands against the steering wheel, then squeezes it like he is choking the man outside his window. "My music! Are you kidding me?"

"Naw, Crip, I swear, on the set." Conners mocks a serious tone and holds out his two fingers and a thumb with one hand for Neighborhood Crips, then twists two fingers of his other hand into the sign for South Side.

"I ain't even on that shit anymore, dawg!" Pro agitation

231

ramps up, and he rocks back and forth between the steering wheel and his seat.

Isabella feels things are spinning out of control and makes her presence known for the first time. "Pro. We are here to help."

Hearing her voice behind him, he whirls to see her at the passenger window. Realizing he was outflanked and didn't know it, his discomfort and irritation both climb higher. "What the hell? Isa, what is this shit?"

His question includes not just the traffic stop but her life choices, and she knows it. A feeling of betrayal rides his words and stabs deeper into her than she expects. She battles the guilt with reasoning she has used for years. *You left Pro. I met a good man and made a life. A good life for our son.* She wants to blurt the words out, but it is hardly the time and place.

Conners doesn't like being ignored and clears his throat. "Hey, Cuz, over here."

Pro pivots back to him, every fiber of his being screaming to jump out and start smashing fists into the irritating detective.

"Here's the deal. You got a little baby gang war kicking up here, and I'm not having it."

"No, we don't!"

Conners shakes his head, waving his hand dismissively at Pro's objection. "Not asking ya. I'm telling ya."

"I'm clamping down on that shit," Pro's eagerness to be on the right side of the problem is a misstep, and he realizes it a second too late.

The detective's eyes gleam. "How you gonna clamp down on anything? I thought you said you weren't in the gang."

"There's no gang!" Pro puts all the conviction he can muster into the claim.

Conners laughs. A genuine sound of amusement rising from his belly and spilling out through his lungs. He pretends to wipe tears from his eyes. "This is why I love this job. Next, you are going to tell me there is nothing illegal in the car."

"There isn't!"

Conners grins wolfishly and winks at Isabella over the top of the car. He leans in close to Pro's face, eyes searching past him to the interior of the vehicle, nose sniffing deeply. "Oh, good! Then you won't mind if I just check real quick?"

Isabella sees Pro freeze almost imperceptibly. He immediately begins moving his hands dismissively in exaggerated, overly casual gestures. "What? That's not necessary, is it?" He tries to joke, "What are you looking for? Gonna see if I got my loud music hiding in the center console?"

He's hiding something. She senses it. And suddenly feels afraid for him. *C'mon, Pro. You were supposed to stay gone.* A part of her is still drawn to the striking figure in the driver's seat, perhaps wishing life had taken some different turns. *You chose your life, Isa. And he chose his.*

Conners continues to work him, and Pro slides further into the legal pit the detective is expertly digging under him. Seeing the smiling face of her diabolical partner and the clear frustration on the features of her former lover, the logical side of her brain wrestles for control of her emotions.

More flashing lights approach, and Conners looks at the police cruiser who answered his radio call. "Ooops! You took too long, big Crip. It's a party now."

"C'mon, man. I didn't do nothing!" Pro squeezes the steering wheel like he wants to break it.

"Lemme go talk to this officer, see if he has a K9 to sniff out your drugs." Without waiting for a reply, a cheerful Conners turns on his heel and walks off.

Isabella is still perched at the passenger window, and Pro swings his face toward her. His expression is earnest, giving her a chance to distance herself from Conners' actions. "Isa, what is with this guy? You know me. I'm not doing anything. I sure as hell don't have any drugs."

Her reply is delayed by doubt. Doubt about what he really is or isn't doing. Doubt about what to tell him. Doubt about her decision to keep Brock from him. He is leaning toward her, and she fights an impulse to reach out and touch his face.

He misreads her doubt as anger and pleads desperately with her. "I'm sorry, Isa. So sorry for everything, I swear."

Tell that to your son. The words almost escape her lips. Red and blue lights flash around her, and any thoughts she had of including Pro in Brock's life seem less likely than ever.

She tries to get her mind on the task at hand. "Why are you back?"

"I'm just trying to help them for a few days. One day really." He smiles nervously. "Any more than that, and my girlfriend is gonna be pissed."

"Your girlfriend?" Even though she is married to someone else, the word feels like another betrayal.

His expression falters at her response, and a shadow of something comes across his eyes.

More desperate than ever to keep an emotional distance between them, she rushes on. Words tumble from her lips in a low, secretive rush, "He's after your gang, Pro. Talking about a RICO."

His eyes sharpen. "A what?"

He didn't deny there is a gang. The realization makes her feel dirty, wrong both to share information with him *and* be party to the trap he is in. She tries to choose words to warn him without giving too much away. "You have to get out of here. Whatever you have going on with your family has to stop."

Pro glances in his side-view mirror and sees Conners walking back toward him with the uniformed cop in tow. Knowing he only has seconds, he watches the approaching pair while hissing to her out of the corner of his mouth, "I'm trying to stop them from hitting back. Trying to help." He pulls his eyes from the mirror to her in a last desperate entreaty, "My family are killed out here. I'm just trying to save them. Are you?"

Conners is about to arrive, and she speaks loudly in her best interrogator tone, "What do you have in the vehicle, Mr. Williams? Everything will go easier if you just tell us." Her head is still inside the car, just two feet from Pro, and she shakes it almost imperceptibly. *Please don't tell us, Pro.*

He reads her expression, the slight shake of her head, and appears to understand. His eyes dart, perhaps inadvertently, to the trunk, and she knows her worst fears are in play. She whispers two words to him and hopes it is enough.

Conners reaches the driver's side window again and tries to play off what he thinks are her efforts. "Yep, cooperation goes a long way. You let us take a quick peek through your car, and we'll have you on your way. If you have nothing illegal, you have nothing to worry about."

Next to Conners, the uniformed cop pulls on a pair of black rubber gloves and pushes a button on the body camera attached to the front of his uniform. A little red light illuminates on the device, indicating it is recording, and he looks back up, ready for business.

Pro uses a respectful tone. "Sir, I have driven a long way and am almost home. I don't really want to go through all of that."

The cop looks at the car, not Pro, and chuckles dryly. "I bet you don't." He starts peering in the back window, and Isabella moves around the car to position herself between him and the trunk.

Conners acts unconcerned. "Well, we have a drug dog on the way, which I am sure will hit on your car anyway. If that happens, we will take it apart piece by piece until we find out why..." he lets the threat hang in the air between them.

"What's your," Pro glances at Isabella, then uses the words she gave him, "probable cause?"

Conners scowls. "What, are you a fricking lawyer now?"

The cop stops what he is doing and looks at Conners with raised eyebrows. "You *do* have PC for the search, right? I'm not trying to get IA on my ass again."

The detective splutters. Stalling, he tries to play it off and looks to Isabella for help. "He make any statements against interest while you were talking, Contreras?"

She steps around the cop and turns, making sure both she and Conners are in front of the blinking body camera. She speaks clearly and loudly, "No. Nothing. We have no probable cause for a search."

Conners makes a disgusted sound next to her. The cop nods his head once and sighs, frustration creeping in as he realizes where this is going.

"You'll let us take a quick look, though, right?" Conners isn't ready to give up yet and smiles at Pro in what he hopes is a friendly fashion. "You know, to avoid the drug dog?"

"I don't have any drugs in this car!" Pro's voice rings clearly.

Cops get lied to every day and know what it sounds like. They also know what the truth sounds like, and at Pro's declaration, the uniformed veteran promptly strips off the rubber gloves. "Can't extend a traffic stop for a drug dog anyway. *Denny Vs. Rodriquez, 2015.*"

"I knew that." Conners looks even more pissed at the cop for quoting the infamous case decision than at Pro for not consenting to a search.

"Mm-hmmm." The cop sounds very much like he thinks Conners didn't. He claps the detective on the shoulder, "Maybe Gang Unit doesn't have to worry about case law, but the rest of us do." The last part of his sentence is said directly to the camera recording on his chest. He pushes a button to stop the recording, then promptly gives the offending device the middle finger.

All three of them stare at the cop for an awkward moment. Ignoring the lot of them, he abruptly turns to leave. Isabella can feel the bitterness rolling off the man. *Burn out much?*

Pro looks at the back of the retreating police officer, then back up to Conners and breaks the silence. "Uh, can I go now?"

Conners grinds out, "Let's go," to Isa, then turns on his heel and stalks toward her unmarked car. Suddenly she and Pro are alone, and she is right outside his window. He looks up, relief spreading across his strong features.

"Thanks."

She opens her mouth, but the words get tangled in her throat. There is too much to say, and her hesitation costs her the chance to say any of it.

"Coming?" Conners has turned to stare at her, hands on hips, clearly pissed.

"Yeah." Her reply is loud, and she starts walking toward her partner immediately. But she hisses a warning to Pro as she leaves, "Get away from here."

When they get back in her unmarked car, Isabella concentrates on not shaking with emotion.

"What was that?" Conners looks intently at her.

Taking a steadying breath, she flips the emergency lights off and watches Pro pull out of the small parking lot. "What was what?"

He doesn't reply for a second, instead taking a moment to observe her watching the Impala leave, trying to read her expression. When he does speak, it is quiet and in an even tone. Not openly accusatory, but a voice she immediately recognizes as investigative.

"Whose side are you on, Contreras?"

CHAPTER SIXTEEN

The smell of fear mixed with stale sweat rolls into Hillcrest.

I need a shower. Pro tries to rein in his emotions and calm his nerves after the unexpected encounter. His guns were legal, but he had to assume that those he had confiscated from the gang were stolen. He could have been looking at a prison sentence just for having them in his trunk.

When he sees the gate is out of place, his irritation heightens. The armored vehicle is drawn back along the fence and abandoned, with no guard in sight.

"C'mon, guys." He mentally tells himself to be patient. Reminds himself he is working with undisciplined teenagers, not hardened Army soldiers. However, his defense plan's complete breakdown after he was gone less than a day is both highly irritating and a stark reminder of how much the family needs his leadership.

Another of the few remaining streetlights keeping the parking lot illuminated has burnt out in the last 24 hours, but the deepening darkness feels welcoming, not threatening.

Duck and weave, Pro. He pulls the car in a wide arc to back up to the door directly in front of 119. The shadows are deeper than ever there now, and he feels fortunate.

"Thank you, Jesus..." *for helping me get these guns into the house without being seen.* It feels inappropriate to finish the prayer out loud. He tries again. Keeps it simple, "Thank you, Lord, for your protection."

He kills the motor, takes a breath, and lets it out. He needs a moment to collect himself and rolls down the window to let in the night air. It is early evening, and the normal sounds of the apartment complex blend together and float through the atmosphere to reach his ears.

A loud TV, a couple arguing... someone having a drunken rant. *Probably Dale, all by himself.* The thought is surprisingly endearing, and he grins in the darkness. Laughter flows through the thin walls of a unit across from him, and he imagines a family enjoying a moment together.

His senses continue to attune in the darkness, and movement on a second-floor balcony catches his eye. Adrenaline wants to surge, but he realizes it is just a couple teenagers making out in the dark. The cramped apartments don't offer much privacy, but the dimly lit porch provides a protective embrace around the young lovers.

His pulse lessens, and the adrenaline starts to be replaced by a new feeling. It feels like home.

He staggers into the apartment, unbalanced by the heavily loaded duffle bag. Seriah and Selena are ensconced beneath a fuzzy blanket depicting Frozen characters, eyes glued to the YouTube antics of JoJo Siwa. When they see him, the girls both jump up and rush him.

"Uncle Pro!" Their arms wrap around him simultaneously. Their diminutive height makes their embrace the equivalent of a good open-field tackle.

"Hey!" He teeters precariously, laughing and putting his free arm around their shoulders.

"What did you bring us?" Seriah eyes the duffle bag like he is Santa Claus, and she expects a new bike.

Fade appears from the bedroom and smiles at him. "Yeah, what'd you bring us?" Her eyebrows are up, and her tone playful. For a moment, she is a child again, hopeful, excited about what her brother might have brought her.

Images through his mind, little presents, and trinkets he used to bring home from the nighttime raids he and Damarion would go on. Her favorite was a thick tangle of Mardi Gras beads he took off someone's rearview mirror when she was about 11. She was old enough to know they were just plastic baubles but wore them to school for a week.

Their twin bond is reviving, and she intuits that he is waxing thoughtful. The playful expression on hers stays warm but turns more purposeful. She moves closer and expertly disentangles the little girls so he can regain his balance. She hugs him with one arm and prods the bag with her other. "What, *did* you bring us."

He coughs and looks pointedly at the girls. "Hardware. For the family business." Realizing there will be no presents forthcoming, the little girls' short attention span pulls them back to the bigger-than-life teenager bouncing around on the TV.

Fade nods toward her bedroom, and Pro follows her into it.

Pro lowers the small arsenal to the bed and looks in the direction of the kitchen. "Where are the boys?"

"They went to get food," she says.

He blinks. "Food? And none of them could stay and guard the gate?"

"Yeah. We need food." She crosses her arms. "And I tried to say about the gate, but they wanted to roll deep, just in case."

Pro snorts. "They three deep to get snacks, but no one left here to hold down the fort?"

"I'm here." She hesitates, and he immediately knows there is something she isn't telling him. He reaches down to unzip the bag, revealing a jumble of guns with his prized AR-15 assault rifle crowning the assortment. He starts opening individual gun cases, showing her exactly what he brought.

All of the guns he had taken from the younger gang members are there, including Rae's SKS assault rifle. Her eyes widen as she takes in the new additions. He removes a black pistol-grip riot shotgun, two Glock pistols, a bolt-action rifle with a powerful scope, and a massive .50 caliber Desert Eagle handgun. Several hundred rounds of ammunition in boxes and a plethora of extra magazines crowd around the guns.

He pulls his AR from its case with practiced hands, flipping on the holographic projection sight and extending the stock. He retracts the bolt and lets it fly forward, loading a round in the chamber of the weapon. The action creates a distinctive mechanical noise. His thumb immediately and expertly follows the sound by rotating the safety lever to 'safe.'

"Dayyyymmm." She moves protectively between him and the door. "You trying to start a war?"

"We already in a war, and I am here to help."

"OK." She bites her lip, considering.

"So, don't tell me them YGs are just 'getting food.'"

She takes this in stride and nods slowly. She reaches toward the bag and selects the heavy shotgun. While pulling it out, she looks in the direction of the living room. She maneuvers the gun's business end to be facing away from where her girls are sitting with effort. She looks up at him in a mixture of defiance and allegiance.

He reads her look and actions to mean that she chooses a position of power alongside him and nods his approval. He doesn't speak, leaving the ball in her court while he battles conflicting emotions and ideals. Liz seems far away in that moment, like a glowing treasure at the end of a long tunnel, and he reminds himself he must get back to her.

Fade makes up her mind and speaks. "If you are with it, I'm with you. Ice took a half-pound of tree to make a drop. $1,200. They went mobile on bikes."

He nods wordlessly, accepting the revelation for what it is, bringing him into her inner circle. It also makes sense that the boys would abandon the gate for this big of a sale. *Still can't leave us unguarded, though.*

Her eyes dart toward a red leather bag nearby, her purse, and she continues, "I been saving, doing real good with what we have coming in."

"To bond out Trey?"

"Four?" She shakes her head and lowers her voice, "Nope. Not with you here. He can chill while we do some building out here."

He is surprised by this but, thinking about her desire to get jumped-in, to increase her control of the gang, realizes he shouldn't be. He feels stretched, one hand reaching back through the tunnel, trying to touch Liz's fingertips. The other hand wrapped around the handgrip of the semi-automatic rifle in his hands.

With an ally, someone she can tell her plans to who might approve, she is eager to lay out her vision. "We need a car. Four's dumb ass got ours impounded, but for like $3,000, I can get something decent. Something that can fly under the radar for drops and shit and be good for getting food. Hard to feed the family with what Ice can carry on the handlebars." She eyes him, "Of course, if you are here now, we can use yours for stuff like going to the store, but I wouldn't want to put you in a bad spot like doing deliveries."

I can't stay, Fade. He thinks it by reflex but finds himself doubting his own thoughts. He has always felt a brothers-in-arms kinship with Liz because they wore the same uniform. But standing face to face with his sister, guns drawn and pointed diagonally at the floor, hands prepared to do what is necessary to protect the family, the same feeling pounds in his chest with even stronger conviction.

"I think that's a good idea," he hears himself agreeing with her.

"Once we have a reliable car, the next thing is to expand." She waves vaguely at the wall next to her. "Gina said I can get 117 cheap because the water is messed up. It's off right now, but we could get that whole apartment for $250 per month, and then we got a place for business." She inclines her head towards the girls in the living room. "Else, it's only a matter of time till they start seeing stuff."

He looks pointedly at the guns in their hands and then at her purse as if expecting a pound of cocaine to tumble out of it. Her face heats at the implication that the girls have already seen way too much.

Before she can get defensive, he moves to support her plan. "Extra space would be key. Ice and them could hold it down, come over here for showers and the bathroom."

"Exactly." She smirks. "They are teenage boys. Don't take showers anyway." Her smile fades back to business. "With the gate for protection and an extra apartment for space, we can get a couple more people in here. Rae could move in more permanently, making her moves more efficient and her a more stable ally."

"You actually think the gate is a good idea?" He feels she might be buttering him up. "You guys dropped that shit the second I was gone."

She looks apologetic. "Yeah, I do, actually. I think it's brilliant, but we need numbers. I can't send Ice out solo with a half-rack of medical grade. He'll get ripped for sure."

He knows she's right and can't fault her for sending three on a deal that big. Ripping off a drug dealer, usually at gunpoint, can happen for any amount of substance, but above a quarter-pound, $600 worth of product, the odds tended to skyrocket.

"So, you're thinking one for the gate, three for big moves, Rae for cars, you holding down the crib." He thinks about it like a military camp, all the duties and responsibilities necessary for daily operations. "Really, you need to be posted up *here*. You need some muscle running 117 while you stay looking clean in the background. One to go with Rae, two would be even better really, with another car obviously." He adds the numbers up in his head and narrows his eyes.

She's ambitious. He thinks of his position in the army. He measures her visions of organizing the gangs against his plans of going to Ranger School, holding down a youth pastor gig, getting serious with a rich girlfriend. *She's ambitious, like me.*

She sees him doing the math and moves her head up and down firmly. "Yes, it is. And we can do it. *We* could have quite the deal going here. Real stability, serious protection."

"You got recruits in mind?" He can't help but engage in the strategizing. Liz can handle herself; he knows that. But his sister is gearing up to bite off the mother of all mouthfuls.

"A couple. Kids we went to school with that are still out there like that. Rae knows a couple 60s who are ready to bang but are trippin' with their set. Ice has a couple kids who want in but aren't quoted yet."

He shakes his head, suddenly nervous. "Kids. You're talking all kids." He thinks of his youth group and feels sick.

"C'mon, Pro," her tone is scornful, "you grew up here. There's no kids here." She shifts the shotgun in her hands. The steady weight of the weapon is becoming a noticeable burden, but she is still unwilling to put down the power it represents. "The 60s are straight G's. They been putting in work. The others, we can bring them up quick."

He notices that she used the word *we* again, and something clicks into place. He should have seen it before. He realizes he *did* see it but had been too focused on the mechanics to fully think about it. "You need me."

She freezes up. Her features display a war between the openness with which she has been speaking and the defensive mask she usually wears. She wants to speak, but her lips remain squeezed together.

He speaks for her, "You need me to be the muscle in 117. You need me to bring these young kids up smart. Ice and Rae would be running them as crash dummies. Four too if he gets out."

Her eyes say he's right, but she lets him continue to do the talking. "You can't do this without me. Those boys, even Rae, they are gonna always treat you like second class because you aren't on the set."

"Unless you jump me in," she reminds him.

"I'm not doing that!" His fingers tighten on his rifle, and the sharpness of the trigger guard bites into his flesh.

She relinquishes her weapon, carefully placing the shotgun on the bed with the muzzle pointed away from the living room. With her hands empty, she moves very close to him in the tight confines of the bedroom. She places a hand on either of his shoulders and looks him in the eyes. "Then you have to stay."

"Fade..." he can't endure the eye contact and looks to the side, "I can't."

She expects this and reaches up with one hand to gently force his face back toward her. "You can. You can do one. Or the other. Or both."

He wants her to be wrong. He wants her to leave the

shotgun on the bed and the drugs in her purse. He wants her to get her girls and get in the Impala.

She is relentless. She stands on her tiptoes. She moves her face close to his as if they would kiss, but not for that purpose. "You can, and if you love me, you will."

He wants to tell her she is ridiculous, but the words won't come.

"I only need one. You owe me one, Pro. Choose."

You owe God a life, Pro. "Fade-"

A hand goes to the back of his neck, cupping it angrily. Her eyes stop being gentle, and a fierceness blazes in them, the heat of her emotion filling the inches between them. "Do it! Beat the hell out of me, Pro, give me my sixty seconds. Give me a chance to prove myself, so I can take care of my family."

"No!"

The angry hand is joined by another, pulling her even closer but then softening into an embrace. The fire in her eyes disappears, replaced by something even more intense, the deep longing for the twin connection they have always had. "Then *stay*. Stay with me, Pro."

Instinctively he puts his arms around his sister, a fierce embrace made awkward by the hard metal of his rifle trapped between them. His world tilts. The long, dark tunnel lengthens, as does the silence between them while he tries to find his answer.

"No. We are going now." Montana's eyes flash dangerously.

Carlos, 22, balances a semi tire and glances around the automotive shop. "I gotta get this truck done before morning, or it's my ass."

Spider leans out the window of an SUV with tinted

windows, tapping his shotgun loudly against the door. "El Cachorro, get in. Those dumb putas fucked up. We got shit to do."

The mechanic looks hesitant. "Man, I just got this job. My Probation guy is gonna lock me up again if I walk off."

The Loco gang leader steps toward Carlos, the metal of his pistol glinting in the darkness. "We gonna settle them for good. If you're *with* us, you're coming." He holds the gun in his right hand, muzzle pointed at the ground, but with a finger tightening on the trigger.

Carlos tries to conceal his nervousness about the gun, keeping his face neutral while absorbing the unspoken threat. The only way out of the Locos is to be dead, so he is *with* them, no question. He squares his shoulders and his jaw, letting the tire fall. "Let's go."

As they drive to their next pickup, Montana works his phone furiously, threatening, yelling, and spitting bile at whoever is on the other end. "Well, get his ass outta bed then!"

Spider tries to light a small glass pipe with white crystalline powder in it, cupping his lighter's flame against the wind coming through his open window.

Carlos shakes Spider's shoulder, further interrupting his efforts. "Hey, my shit's at home."

They take a hard turn, and Spider crashes against the side of the vehicle, knocking the newly-lit pipe away from his lips. He twists in his seat to direct a pointed gaze and the barrel of his gun at the younger man. "You slippin, Esse." He pretends to pull the trigger, making the weapon recoil in his hands. "Gonna be dead."

"My boss isn't playing around, man. He said if I bring it a gun to work, I'm *gone*."

Montana tunes into the exchange and curses, pulling the phone down long enough to jerk his thumb towards the voluminous back of the vehicle. "We got plenty of shit, man, just grab something."

The mechanic feels much bolder when he sees the kind of hardware the gang leader has brought for the occasion. "Oh snap, we going in heavy."

"Fuckin-a, we are." Spider rocks in his seat, the methamphetamine hitting his lungs amplifying both his energy and penchant for violence. He points the sawed-off shotgun out the window, miming shooting at buildings as they speed past. "Getcha some, getcha some."

A pair of headlights swing in behind them, and Montana nods, still talking into his phone. "Boom, I see you. Just stay with us."

The gang leader hangs up the phone and calls another number. "Put Espinosa on." His face twists with rage at whatever the person on the other end says. "Fuck that. It's everybody. We rolling NOW." He looks around the vehicle, and at the street they are flying down. "Yeah. On 59th now. Get your shit and get out here, or I will be in that ass!"

He is nearly screaming into the phone by the end of his call.

"Those three coming?" Spider may be high, but his eyes narrow in a calculating manner.

Montana's eyes bulge, but he doesn't look up. "They better." He squeezes the phone like he is trying to kill it, then relaxes and dials another number. "It's now. Les' go."

"What?" His face turns red. "WELL, HOW DRUNK IS HE?"

Carlos looks a question at Montana when he ends the call and immediately wishes he hadn't. The agitated leader reacts badly to the younger man and shakes with rage. "Motherf-" His hand thrusts out the window, and the end of his sentence is obliterated by the roar of his pistol.

Carlos sits back, eyes lidded, not daring to confront the other man even with the AK-47 he now firmly clutches.

Another vehicle joins them, and Montana takes a long breath. "Don't matter. We got enough." He looks at Spider. "We got plenty for these baby Gs."

His right-hand man sticks out his tongue, grinning maniacally. "Yahhh. Les' GO!"

"Not a bitch. Left. Standing" Montana motions with his heavy .45 pistol, punctuating each syllable with a rise and fall of the barrel, "Not. One."

R ae bursts into the apartment. "Bringin' that heat, on the Set!"

Confusion blooms on Fade's face as she moves into the living room. "Rae?"

Pro follows his twin, forgetting for the moment he is still holding the rifle.

Rae, resplendent in a neon green tube top and store-bought long cherry-red curly hair, starts twerking in front of the television. She expertly shakes and rolls her hips like a stripper, one hand on her thigh and the other holding a pair of keys up like a prize.

"What the hell? You supposed to warn me when you get a hotbox!" Fade is put off both by Rae's antics and her unannounced arrival with a stolen vehicle.

Ice stands nearby, grinning at everything Rae has going on. "No need this time," He gives a laugh and a hoot and rapidly flips his hand toward the girl in a show of approval, "My homie got em' good. Ain't nobody calling *this* one in to the cops."

Pro feels something building, something bad. He starts to move to the front door to see the car in mention. "What do you mean?"

His movement catches Rae's eye, and she turns toward him. She smiles when she sees the assault rifle he is holding.

Her eyes are lit with excitement and probably a few illegal substances. "Oooooh, I knew you had a big gun hidden somewhere." She alters her suggestive dance, scooting her backside across the narrow space to get in his way. "You wanna come take a ride with me?" Her eyebrows take on a suggestive arch, "In my new whip?"

She may as well have said take a ride on *me*. He sees it plainly. But too many things are happening at once for him to even begin to feel turned on by her.

"You going out with that?" Jiggy, standing near the door, nods toward Pro's rifle, eyeing it with jealousy but also wise enough to know it should probably stay inside.

"Shit." Realizing his beeline for the door was a bad idea, Pro feels trapped in the small space between Rae's heat-seeking hips and two small wide-eyed girls on the couch. He feels a growing urgency to see what is outside, what Rae is crowing so loudly about.

Fade ignores Rae and her hype-man Ice and looks past them to try to get answers out of the calmest member of the group, "Deuce, You guys make the drop all right?" Her eyes are intense, 'where's my $1,200' kind of intense.

"He has it," the gang member says loudly, pointing his finger down at the top of Ice's bobbing head.

"Has what?" A bit unsteady on her feet from weed and Xanax, Ma emerged from her bedroom. Even the extremely introverted Aliyah has moved into the kitchen to see what is going on. Mama's eyes land on Pro. "Why you got that big heater, baby?"

Running out of patience in the chaos, Pro does the only thing he can. He cradles his rifle in one hand and puts the other on the only part of Rae he has access to. She tries to back further into his hand, but he ignores her, slipping past to reach the curtains behind the couch.

When he sees what is out there, the maelstrom of sound around him becomes muted, and his heart skips a beat. A dark-colored Oldsmobile 88, fancy paint job, undersized wheels. *A beaner car.* For the briefest of moments, he is terrified, thinking the South Side Locos are parked neatly a few feet from the window, ready to gun his family down. As quickly as he deflects that irrational jab of fear, another follows it, and this fist smashes into him like a solid right cross. *Oh shit.*

He whirls back toward the room, wanting to speak but for a moment completely unable. He feels like he is outside of himself, maybe outside of the room, looking down at a chaotic but happy family.

Fade has managed to get ahold of Ice, and he is none too discretely slipping a roll of cash to her. Rae is still dancing while watching Ice and Fade, especially Fade, when she takes the money to her bedroom. Deuce flops down on the couch and puts an arm around the girls, pretending he likes Jojo Siwa too with a serious face that makes the girls giggle. Jiggy moves into the kitchen, seeking something to eat like any teenage boy, completely at home with his family. Ma is smiling, happy. The kids are happy, a much-needed uplift after the darkness of the past week. Even Aliyah is smiling faintly, looking like she has maybe forgotten about her little brother for the moment.

He wishes he could step away at that moment, leave them happy and melt away with this picture in his mind.

You could probably still make it, Pro. The voice of cold logic, of self-preservation, is there in the back of his mind. *Go now. Save Yourself.*

A gunshot echoes in his mind, darkness, flashing light, HONK, HONK, HONK. Death. *You owe God a life, Pro.*

His childhood memory invades the living room, and he hears gunshots, lots of them. He sees holes in people, blood, faces of the little girls turning from laughing to screaming. Rae's seductive curves shattered. Ice's young shoulders, full of potential, smashed to pieces. Fade's determination all for nothing, blown away by machine-gun fire that rips apart the world she had been desperately holding together without him. Deuce and Jiggy, lying still in death, forever part of the family they found. *His family, all dead.*

He knows he can't leave. The tunnel is collapsing, the light from it too far away to see now. His life with Liz feels like it is dying, bleeding out like the man he once murdered. *Maybe my life is the one I owe.*

An icy sadness flows from the thought and down his spine. As it spreads through him, it blends with a new feeling, rage.

He finds his voice, a booming, commanding voice that cuts through the noise. Time is short, and he attacks the culprit first, "RAE! You stole a *Loco* ride?" He steps toward her, destroying her playfulness with a withering glare. "You. Fucking. Idiot!"

She stops dancing and sticks out her chin in defiance. "Caught 'em slipping at a gas station. They left the keys in it and running."

Ice steps to the defense of his girl. "She got balls bigger than you, man. Swooped right in there and snagged that shit."

"Idiots." Pro includes Ice in the comment as he towers over both. Deuce and Jiggy come to their feet, and Fade emerges from the bedroom with an alarmed expression. He is facing down all of them at once, but his growing rage keeps him roaring forward. "They are coming, coming for blood now, you know that, right?"

The boys look like maybe they hadn't thought it all the

way through. Fade seems to immediately understand and moves protectively toward her girls.

Ice is meeker but still tries to stick with Rae, "They don't know who took it. They don't know we have it."

Surprisingly, Rae appears unfazed and agrees with Pro. "Probably are." She looks at his gun. "But we're Crips, and we stay ready." She looks around at the boys, making sure to make eye contact with each. "Right? Ain't nobody gonna roll us. We be the ones *Rollin*." She starts stacking hand signs, throwing an 'N' rapidly followed by a stylized 'R' and six fingers. As she does so, she turns half toward the other gang members, inciting them to join her but keeping her front toward Pro.

Perhaps by reflex at first, but then by chosen solidarity, all three boys join her with spoken word and gang signs. "On the Set," Ice stands at her shoulder, backing her play.

She did this on purpose. The suspicion has barely struck him before she confirms it.

"They comin' all right, and we'll be right here." She crosses her arms. "What about you? Are you with it?"

In general, he knew the Locos would be coming, but his fear is sharpened further by how sure she seems that it is imminent. His mind starts racing, but he doesn't have time to figure out how she knows.

"Guess you better give us back our straps." She looks at the rifle he is holding, then back at his face, her eyes suddenly very cold and hard. "Unless you want to fight this war all by yourself."

"You *bitch!*" The words are the only thing he can hit her with as he bulls past them toward Fade's room. There is no time. He yells over his shoulder as he grabs the bag, "how long, Rae?"

Ice's face lights up when he sees his old guns plus the new additions. "Shiiiit, I told you he was with it, Rae."

Pro drops the bag on the kitchen table next to a wide-eyed Aliyah and starts handing out hardware. He hands Rae her SKS assault rifle and demands an answer, "How much time?"

She takes her gun back, and to her credit, looks scared, maybe even a little ashamed for the first time. "Hell, I don't know, probably soon." The boys behind her can't see her eyes, but Pro can, and they tell him she is lying through her teeth. *She knows.*

The weight of her weapon should make her feel more comfortable, but instead, it just makes the upcoming battle suddenly seem real to her. A sudden desire for self-preservation engulfs her, and with her back still to the boys, she decides to tip her hand. She uses one hand to withdraw her iPhone out of her pocket just a little, so Pro can see it.

No. TWO iPhones. Pro understands immediately. iPhones are trackable with an app when they are stolen. She must have found one in the vehicle, and like an idiot, kept it. *Or maybe she thought she wanted what is coming.*

It doesn't matter now, and Pro kicks into high gear. "They think we'll all be holed up inside. We gotta get out there, NOW." Shoving guns into the youngsters' hands, he knows they may have only a moment before they are in the fight of their lives. He issues orders with each weapon.

He hands the scoped rifle to Jiggy. "Follow the fence up the back and post up in the bushes so you can see cross-ways to the gate. When they hit the gate, they are gonna spread out to try to find their way around it, so you should have some good shots." The young man is physically huge but suddenly seems small and scared. Pro shoves a box of twenty extra bullets for the large caliber weapon into Jiggy's front pocket and quickly demonstrates how to operate the bolt-action rifle and turn off the safety. "It's hot now. Just stay in the bushes, lay down flat. You'll be stable, and they'll never see you. He claps the other man on the shoulder. "You got this. Go."

He gives Deuce the Desert Eagle. "Your twenty-two is no good. This hand cannon will punch through car doors. You get up by the gate, up close, but lay flat down by the fence. Flat on your stomach out of sight." The kid grabs the gun firmly and heads for the door, trying to look tough. Almost too late, Pro thinks of something. "WAIT! You will be in Jiggy's line of fire. Don't go to the fence, post up in the closest alcove to the gate, but stay out of sight unless they bust through. If they do, blast 'em from the side as they go by, then in the back."

With a nod, the boy is gone. Pro shoves Ice's two guns back toward him. "Get that van back in place, then get out of it. Get back around a corner where you got something solid. Actually, get behind that big metal dumpster in the parking lot. It'll stop bullets. You know the one?" Receiving a nod, Pro takes a brief moment to grip his younger brother's hand. "Keep your head down, G."

As the 17-year-old bolts for the door, Pro calls a final warning after him. "Don't stay at the gate!" He knows the heavy metal on the side of the van might seem like safety, but he fully expects the makeshift barrier to be destroyed in the coming battle.

"Shouldn't we call the police? Aliyah, backed into a corner of the kitchen, speaks up in a small voice.

Ma chides her from the door to her bedroom. "Hush, child. Police ain't gonna do nothing. We on our own out here."

Fade closes the door to her bedroom and takes a position outside it looking grim. "I got them under the bed," meaning the girls. The riot shotgun is back in her hands, and her expression says she will make her stand right there to keep her girls safe.

Pro nods and tries to reassure her. "I'm trying to stop them before they get close, but they may be rolling 10 or 20 deep. If one slips through…"

She racks the slide on the shotgun, showing she is more than ready to deal with the problem.

"I should stay back too." Rae's face is drained of color. "I could be by the front door."

Pro shakes his head. "That won't work. You would be shooting right toward us by the gate." He shoves a pistol into a clip holster and secures it at his side, then grabs all three extra magazines for his rifle and shoves them in his back pockets. "I need you up with me. We have the best rate-of-fire weapons and will be on the second-floor landings with cross coverage on the gate from either side."

He starts to move toward the door, but Rae doesn't follow. He looks back, and when she doesn't move, shifts his gaze accusingly toward her pocket. "C'mon, you did this!"

"I should guard the back door." She edges further from him.

"Rae! We'll lay down on the second-floor balconies. They're made of concrete, we'll be fine!"

She shakes her head. "I'll protect the back door. We got no one on it." She glances at Ma and Aliyah for support.

We are out of time. He imagines a flood of heavily armed gang members overwhelming their meager defenses while he stands and argues. Heading to where he knows the battle will be fiercest, he also doesn't want to rely on someone getting cold feet. Cursing, he surges toward the front door.

CHAPTER SEVENTEEN

Montana's driver slows to around 15mph as they reach the apartment complex. And the other cars slow behind him.

"NO, bro, keep your speed up, man," the gang leader instructs, "get in the middle lane and turn in quick-like. Don't slow down. We go right in. Blitz them down."

Spider bounces excitedly in his seat. "Quick, yeah. Locos gonna play quick, motherfuckers gonna pay quick."

Adrenaline is thick in the air as they cross the last half-block. The west edge of the complex flashes by, and the driver swings to the middle to make the turn the way Montana instructed.

"**H**ERE THEY COME!" Pro forces a high volume of air from his lungs past his vocal cords, yelling as loud as he can like he is back in the Army in hopes that the spread-out gang can hear him. "GET READY!"

From his second-floor vantage point, the line of three approaching vehicles is unmistakable in the sparse traffic. His suspicion is further confirmed when they curve in a long arc to pour into the apartment entrance. Because of the high fence, from their approach, they couldn't see the Mad Max gate he had built until it was too late. The van was set back just a bit, recessed in the narrow area between the buildings, their only defense against being immediately overrun.

If they had been going slow, they would have turned and nosed up to the armored vehicle without enough speed to do much to it. But the way they swerve in quickly, one right after another, should have guaranteed their momentum alone would smash the gate out of the way.

This is precisely why Pro had done what he had to do.

The lead low-rider is a 90s Chevy suburban truck with turquoise paint, a battlewagon that could easily have plowed the gate out of the way at the speed it was going. From Pro's vantage point, the turn occurs in slow motion. Playing follow-the-leader, the vehicles swerve to the center of the wide 4-lane road, briefly riding the center turn lane before swaying sharply as they bank into Hillcrest.

The space between the front of the Chevy and the suddenly insignificant-seeming armored van evaporates, and Pro flops belly down on the concrete landing. He shoulders the AR-15 and puts the red dot of the holographic sight on the front windshield of the Chevy. A street light penetrates the dark interior of the vehicle for a brief moment, and he clearly sees a man outlined through the windshield. The man is holding an AK-47.

His finger tightens automatically

He hesitates. *I can't believe this is happening.*

BANG!

The quiet night shatters as the Chevy slams into the barricade at speed. The impact smashes the improvised armor into the van's body, crumpling the thinner metal behind it. Glass explodes in all directions like grenade fragments. The van heaves toward the parking lot like it got hit with an uppercut. A motion immediately arrested by the shiny bumper of Pro's immaculate Impala.

In a desperate move to reinforce the gate, Pro had backed his car right up to the side of the van, cranked the wheels all the way to one side, and set the parking brake. Now his heart leaps with both joy and agony as he sees the effect of his choice. The momentum of the 5,000lb suburban crashing into the sideways van pushes it back like a battering ram, crumpling the back of the Impala like an accordion.

At the speed they hit, it *might* have been sufficient to clear the wreckage of both cars, enough to squeeze past in the narrow space. But as the Impala surges forward from the impact, the turned front wheels cause it to jerk sharply to the right and crash into the building across from Pro.

The suburban slows from the impact, almost coming to a full stop before itself being impacted from behind by first one, then a second vehicle, neither of which have time to react.

The shockwave of twisted metal, flying glass, brick, vinyl siding, and wood pelts Pro as his pride and joy gets sandwiched between consecutive hits of tons of steel and the immovable building.

From his vantage point, he has a front-row seat to the destruction. *My car!*

Tires rupture below, car horns go into emergency mode, and he sees Liz leaned over him in bed, a playful smile on her face. He's supposed to be in a hotel with her, not here. He feels his relationship with her being smashed, just like his car. *I had a great girl.*

His gun feels cold in his hands, and he imagines himself holding it, gesturing how he used it in a sermon to his youth group kids. *"And then I gunned them G's down, just like..." Just like what, Pro?* A good biblical reference eludes him in the thin slice of time the thought occupies. Probably something Old Testament. It doesn't matter; he knows that part of his life is over now.

The damage is slowing below, the vehicles finally coming to rest directly below him. His kill zone worked. He thinks about his Army training on ambushes, realizing he has put what he knew into practice without conscious thought. *So much for Ranger School.* He will be lucky to avoid court-martial now. *Kill zone.* The people who wrought his destruction are in it, piling out of their vehicles, bloody and battered. Pissed and armed to the teeth.

His car is smashed beyond recognition, its alarm blaring from the wall it's now embedded in. His carefully constructed *good life* destroyed along with it. Rage floods in, and his well-cultivated iron control turns to molten steel. He rotates the safety switch on his AR-15 from 'Safe' to 'Fire.'

HONK.

POW. POW. The sound reverberates in the semi-enclosed space of the landing Pro lies on. The sound of his rifle much louder than the cacophony of honking vehicles below. The first pair of controlled shots goes straight into the chest of the first man out of the suburban.

The first hit staggers the man, and he drops the shotgun he is holding. When the second impact strikes him an instant later, he drops abruptly. He makes no effort to catch himself, just hits the ground and becomes part of it.

HONK.

"What the hell!" Contreras sits bolt upright, pulling her gun before she is even fully awake.

Conners is beside her, his eyes riveted in on something down the block as he brings the radio mic to his mouth. "Victor 75, City. Uh, we got a problem!"

Jiggy lies flat on his belly, the discomfort of the sharp branches around him forgotten. He shakes uncontrollably as he tries to get the sights to settle on the figures swarming 100 yards away. In full fight-or-flight mode, the adrenaline makes his vision tunnel, makes it impossible to focus on detail even with the help of the 4x scope he is looking through.

BOOOOOOM. The high-caliber hunting rifle pushes back against his shoulder, bruising his collarbone as it launches a 210-grain piece of lead in the general direction of the attacking force. He has no idea if he hit anything and whimpers as he yanks on the bolt in a panic to reload the rifle. A mewling sound escapes his nervous vocal cords, and his bladder weakens. He feels helpless, ineffectual. He wants to run.

HONK.

On his third attempt, Montana manages to kick the bent suburban door open. Cradling the AK-47, he rolls out, staying low. He crawls toward the rear of the Suburban, looking for something solid to get behind. A critical glance at Spider's prone form gives him a guess at where the bullets are coming from.

"Driver's side." He says it to himself, then louder, yelling to try to be heard over the honking horns and gunfire, "DRI-VER'S SIDE! Put him down!"

He comes to a crouch at the rear of the suburban, motioning for more people to join him. One of his heavy hitters gets on one knee beside him just in time to be blasted in the face by plastic shrapnel from an exploding taillight.

HONK.

"Shit!" The man drops his gun and hunches over. He's not seriously hurt but is suddenly very concerned with protecting his eyes and making sure they are still intact.

Montana looks at the taillight and a long, jagged furrow that extends from the shattered light across the metal tail-gate. *From right to left.* Confused, he slowly looks to his right, to the long empty space along the front of the apartments.

No one is there, but the bullet came from that direction. He suddenly feels completely vulnerable.

"Spread out!" He doesn't know where safety lies, but as more bullets impact around him, and he hears someone cry out in pain, he knows they need to move.

Pushing the AK-47 in front of him, he leaps to his feet and bolts toward the nearest building. As he runs, he fires the weapon for the first time, spraying a burst of powerful projectiles toward the closest building.

Pro reminds himself to breathe. His nerves are ragged, but training has prepared him for this. He focuses on moving air in and out of his lungs. He moves the red dot from the man who just fell toward the next available target.

POW. POW.

Another pair of controlled shots, streaks from the muzzle of his gun, and a guy who was raising a pistol toward him... stops. They are pouring out like angry ants, though, faster than he can take aim, and he wonders if he's the only one shooting.

A couple dart from the back of the wrecked suburban toward his building; one has a raised AK-47, and fire flashes from its muzzle. Shifting to try to get an angle on them, he rushes his first shot. It goes wide, and he tries to control rising panic as he takes an extra split second on his follow-up shot. The rifle bucks again, and the second of the two sprinting men goes down in an uncontrolled dive.

Out of time. Pro rolls to a knee and pivots toward the stairwell. The downside of his excellent vantage point is that he is vulnerable to being overrun. He thought he would be able to stay there longer, but without Rae setting up for crossfire, the attackers can hide against the wall below him. There just isn't enough fire coming from the rest of the gang to keep the Locos pinned down. *C'mon guys, a little help here.* Bullets impact the wall next to him before he can make a break for the stair-well and ducks back.

"They're shooting." Rae stands in the middle of the living room with wide eyes.

Fade peeks out the curtains into the parking lot, her shotgun resting across her shoulders. "You think?" Her voice is sarcastic, but only slightly so. Most of her effort is focused on what is happening outside instead of the other girl.

They are in the far back corner of the apartment complex, so the battle is around 200 yards away. It is killing her to not be able to see what is happening. All she can see is flashes against the siding of the buildings. Every interior light in the apartment complex was turned off in rapid succession, every apartment trying to avoid being a target. The screeching tires and first several crashing noises were loud, but now a constant staccato of gunfire is even louder. Her mind jumps to the last time she heard those sounds.

Tommie. Her fingers tighten on the pistol grip of the riot shotgun. She presses her face against the window. She wants to run and join the battle, but her desire to protect her daughters in the bedroom is even stronger.

She strains her eyes, trying to somehow see the battle through the walls. "He needs our help out there."

Rae grips her SKS tightly. "I'm, uh, gonna guard the back."

Fade, intent on the battle raging just out of sight, doesn't reply.

Rae takes a quiet step backward, then another. She pauses again, watching Fade for a second, then reaches back and slowly turns the knob to the bedroom door. When the door swings open and Fade still hasn't looked back, Rae makes her move.

Her eyes scan the small bedroom. *Gotta be here somewhere.*

The nearby gunshots combine with a sharp point of guilt, both pressing into her, telling her to hurry. Her gaze stops on the large red purse sitting on Phaedra's dresser, and her heart leaps. *That has to be it; she was only gone a second.* Fending off any thoughts but her own desperate need to escape, to have money to survive, she begins rifling through the purse and finds the $1,200 Fade stashed earlier. Her hand feels a lump in an interior pocket, and when she sees what is hidden inside, her eyes widen. A new thought enters her mind —a game-changer. *I'm sorry, girl.*

Ice moves from a crouching position to standing behind the large steel dumpster, irritated he can't get a shot. The angle is such that he can see the front of Pro's car, embedded in the side of a building, but he can't quite see any people without exposing himself.

He curses under his breath, caught between wanting to add the weight of his pistol to the lopsided gunfight but remembering Pro's instruction to take cover behind his current protective barrier.

The constant, discordant honking of the multiple car alarms of crashed vehicles is unexpected and grating on his nerves even worse than the gunfire. He hears heavy automatic fire, a sound he heard once when Four took them out in the country to practice. *Shit, someone's got a Draco.* He looks at the quarter-inch-thick steel next to his face, wondering if the sour-smelling trash barrier will be enough to stop that kind of firepower. *Probably not.*

Deuce is pissed. The spot he chose seemed all well and good until cars started crashing into buildings. When Pro's Impala impacted 10 feet away from him, self-preservation had become his only goal.

"Sorry." He isn't sure if the young couple whose bedroom he is in heard him. Either way, they lie flat on the floor without replying, devoting all their attention to trying to crawl under the bed for protection. He shakes his head at the futility of what they are attempting. Moments before, he had kicked their window in to get inside, desperate to escape the chaos of crashing vehicles. Now, he feels disgusted by the relative safety they share.

He shakes his head at the man crawling along the ground next to his girl instead of trying to protect her. "Bro. Man UP." *How you gonna live in Hillcrest and not have a strap?*

HONK. BUH-BUH-BUH-BUH.

Another Loco crumples, and Montana screams in a fury. His eyes blaze, and he lets the assault rifle blaze with them. He empties a 30-round magazine in the direction of the landing, taking satisfaction in the little pieces of wood, siding, and concrete that are kicked into the air wherever his bullets strike.

The bolt slams back as the assault rifle runs dry, and he spins back behind the corner of the building. He reaches toward his back pocket for another loaded magazine, and out of the corner of his eye, he sees a couple of his guys huddling nearby. "Let's GO! Put some lead on these guys!" He jabs the barrel of his rifle toward the landing where all the shooting is coming from.

He starts to turn back to fire some more but then sees his guys haven't moved. Enraged, he reverses the direction of his twist, bringing the muzzle of his freshly-loaded weapon downward in a sweeping arc toward them.

A curse bubbles toward his lips, but the pair of men get the message and break into action.

"We are with you, bro!" They crowd toward him, guns raised and firing in the general direction he indicated.

He nods and turns back toward the fight. Firing and moving, pushing forward like a madman. He hugs the building as he enters the gap, laying down suppressive fire to keep the ledge guy's head down. When they see him cross the space, two more gang members get a dose of bravery and bolt toward him, joining the pack.

Deuce hears the shooting outside increase to an almost constant stream of sound. He knows Pro is going to work on the Locos, but there's a lot more than one gun going at once.

He looks at the guy huddling with his girlfriend under the bed. The dude is crying now, literally holding his hands to his ears and crying.

"Shiiit." A burst of heavy automatic gunfire outside rakes his nerves, but Deuce makes his decision. He would rather be beside Pro, fighting to the end, than waiting to get gunned down beside these two.

Maybe we're all gonna die, but at least I'll do it with a gun in my hand.

He racks the slide on the Desert Eagle pistol and feels dumb when an unspent bullet ejects. *It was already loaded.* Silently berating himself, he takes a breath and moves back to the window. He peeks an eye cautiously around the shattered window frame, knowing the apartment's thin siding will not stop a Draco but still feeling safer behind the wall.

He sees a man with an AK-47 running toward the stairs leading up to Pro's position. Pro is visible above, trying to position himself to cover the stairwell but having to duck back to avoid bullets still coming at him from the cars.

He's pinned down. Deuce pokes the barrel of his large pistol through the window and squeezes off a couple of shots. The angle is poor, though, and he doesn't hit anything. He takes another peek and what he sees gives him an icy stab of fear.

The man with the AK seems to have realized Pro is above him. Deuce sees him motioning with his hands to the other guys that they need to go up the stairs. Two join him, and all three cram shoulder-to-shoulder to start slowly going up the stairs. Their guns are raised, ready to mow down Pro as soon as they crest the landing. Two more guard the bottom of the stairwell, looking for someone to shoot.

Deuce pulls his barrel back through the window, his bravery from a moment before replaced by caution. "I can't get a good shot." He says it to Pro, but with his ears still ringing from his last effort isn't even sure he heard himself.

He feels helpless and glances back at the two under the bed again.

Gonna die.

Jiggy talks himself through it out loud. "Twist up. Back. Forward. Twist down." He has the hang of the bolt-action rifle now and feels safer by the minute in his concealed position. He silently thanks Pro for thinking of such a good location as he takes aim again. About a half dozen gangsters are using the two vehicles still in the street for cover as they maintain a withering barrage of fire. They are shooting upward at an angle toward the apartments. While Jiggy can't tell from his position what they are aiming at, he can tell from their gesturing and how they are all looking in one place, they must be focusing fire to try to bring down one of his gang.

BOOOOOM.

Ow. The rifle bruises his shoulder again, and he wonders if he is doing something wrong with it. *Who would ever use one of these for fun?* The scope settles down after the shot, and he sees that one of the guys is down on the ground behind the furthest car. Several others have turned away from the gun battle and are hunched behind the car now. They are looking at their downed comrade instead of shooting.

He works the bolt, smoother than before, and mentally prepares to be kicked in the shoulder again. In the distance, sirens wail.

Pieces of siding spatter against Pro's face, and he scoots by reflex further back into the corner, trying to get away from the hiss of bullets passing inches from his head. *Out of space.* He can't hold the gun to his shoulder anymore. Raising it that high will expose both it and his arms to gunfire from below. He lays it in his lap, pointing it toward the top of the stairwell but keeping it low enough to not get shot by the guys at the cars.

They are coming. He knows it instinctively. He hasn't heard the rapid-fire belch of the AK-47 for the last minute or so. He has to assume the reason is the owner is coming up the stairs to root him out of his elevated position. *I'm on the ropes here.*

He can't use the red dot sight from the awkward angle and instead maneuvers the weapon's muzzle with his feet. He tries to position it for an effective point-blank shot whenever his enemy appears. He knows it probably won't be enough.

Ludacris flows through his head, and he tells himself it doesn't matter. If it's the last thing he does, he's gonna put these Locos down.

Sorry, Liz.

Ice feels like the gunfire is slowing, and none of it seems to be headed his way. He darts from behind the dumpster, sprinting for all he's worth to a corner of the apartment building closer to the action. *I'm coming, bro. On the Set.*

His momentum slams him into the corner of the building when he reaches it, but he ignores the pain and pops his Glock around the corner, looking for an enemy. There are plenty to pick from.

POP. POP. POP. POP.

Deuce can't see Ice, but he sees one of the two Locos at the bottom of the stairs get hit. The guy just drops, face forward, gun still in his hands. His head looks wrong somehow. The other takes one look at his buddy, eyes wide, and then bolts back toward the cars. He fires back blindly with his pistol as he runs, trying to cover his retreat.

Deuce, sensing his chance, takes aim at the running man's back but then thinks better of it. He steps back through the window, pressing against the twisted frame of the building for protection. Peering out and up, he strains to get the angle he needs on the three on the stairs.

They are almost to the top, and he has to half-crouch painfully to get the sights of his pistol to line up with them. The heavy chunk of metal wobbles in his hands, and he squeezes his fingers tightly to try to steady it.

C'mon, Crip, they are almost to the top. Sweat drips into his left eye, and he squeezes it shut. *Gotta be now!* The tips of their guns are now almost at the top of the stairwell. Their upper bodies are starting to disappear behind the landing.

BAAM... BAAM... BAAM.

The gun kicks up and back with every shot, but he takes the time to let it settle back each time before firing again. He makes each shot count, and it pays off.

Almost there... Montana's finger tightens on the trigger of his AK, and he gets ready to empty every bullet he has left into whoever is at the top of the stairs.

Annoyingly, he is knocked off balance in the tight space when the Loco next to him suddenly lurches sideways and goes down screaming.

Montana's foot is already on the next step, already drawing him up onto it, but he can't help but glance down at the man. His leg is destroyed. Splintered bone and bits of bloody flesh spatter against the wall behind him, the remnants of the damaged limb twisting unnaturally as the man folds over backward and starts tumbling down the stairs.

Trying to avoid becoming entangled with the flailing man, Montana's other companion surges forward, taking the last two steps at once. His decision costs him his life.

Hearing the scream in the stairwell, Pro has two thoughts, one right after the other. The first is that his instincts were dead on, and death was indeed coming up the stairs for him. The second is, *the gang is still in it. They are fighting.* Fatalism gives way to hope, and his hand tightens on the handgrip of his rifle just in time for the first attacker to appear.

POW.

He gets off one shot with the gun in his lap and hits the man at the very top of his shoulder, stopping his forward momentum. Then instinct takes over, and Pro is bringing the weapon to his shoulder, getting the red dot into his field of vision, standing up. If he thought about it, he might have hoped the guys on the ground would stop shooting at the landing for fear of hitting their fellow gang members.

He doesn't have time to think about anything, though. The red dot enters his line of sight, and he immediately shoots the man in the neck at near point-blank range, ripping his life out and spraying it all over the hand railing.

Before he can even fully understand he won that battle, the next person appears, and Pro twists desperately sideways to avoid the muzzle of an automatic weapon. Flashes of fire erupt in the small space, and Pro feels his gun twist violently in his hands.

The combination of Pro's sudden maneuver and the bodies of the other two bouncing against Montana proves critical. The Loco's burst of automatic fire strikes the barrel of Pro's turning rifle instead of his unprotected chest, and the weapon is ripped violently from Pro's grasp.

Pro's left hand was positioned near the rifle's front and suddenly feels numb and lifeless. The space between the men is mere feet, just outside boxing range. Pro closes it by bouncing forward on the balls of his feet, charging across the ring. He sweeps his otherwise useless left arm across his body. His limb contacts the barrel of the still-firing AK-47 as if blocking a thrown punch, directing it up and away from him.

Quick as thought, he sends his tightening right fist in a

powerful right cross toward Montana's face. He feels a satis-fying crunch, and the man draws his head back in pain but doesn't go down. He is about to throw another punch, but the other man is stepping back, trying to get out of range. Pro starts to lose contact with the gun barrel and knows that he will be ripped apart when it comes back in line with his chest.

HONK.

His rifle lays on the ground. Montana is out of reach.

HONK. Flash-flash-flash. Fire spits from the barrel of the AK as it sweeps back toward him.

Pro's hand darts to his belt and closes on the pistol clipped there. He is only three feet away and has no time to aim.

HONK.

Drawing and pointing the weapon instinctively from his hip, he pulls the trigger as fast as he can.

POP-POP-POP.

BOOOOOM.

Jiggy doesn't feel the pain in his shoulder this time and focuses on bringing the scope quickly back on target. The crosshairs in the scope are clear in his vision now, as are the armed men 100 yards away. He doesn't realize it, but he has started breathing again. He does notice that his efforts are taking a heavy toll, however.

There are three Locos down now in the street. One is completely still, but two are crawling across the street, trying to escape the fight. He lets them go and is taking aim at another when the man suddenly jumps to his feet and runs around to the driver's side of the car.

Deuce curses, trying to get a shot but unable to find a target because everyone is moving. The vehicle in the back of the pileup jerks and starts moving, and he starts to realize what is happening. Locos run and dive into the car even as it backs in a wide arc, piling into it like sardines from all sides. It must have been able to slow slightly before the original collision because while the front has significant damage, the car is still drivable.

In his haste to leave, the driver backs over the legs of one of the crawling wounded, and Duece can hear the man's agonized scream even from his distance.

"Daaaamn." He takes his finger off the trigger, watching what is happening. Sirens suddenly sound very close. "They're running."

A couple men jump into the next vehicle, but it is less roadworthy. They have no choice, though, and drive off in the opposite direction of the first car. Sparks fly from the rim of a punctured tire, and steam comes from a cracked radiator. They manage to get up to speed just as the first of a stream of cop cars come screeching around a corner in the distance. The chase is on.

Seeing the red and blue lights, Deuce's priorities shift drastically. He bellies out from under the bush, exiting directly into the narrow space behind the apartments. Clutching the rifle with one hand, he sprints toward the apartment.

Pro picks his AR-15 off the ground and peers back over the edge of the concrete landing, but there are no threats left to shoot. He sees Deuce peering up from below, his gun trained on the stairwell where the gangster he shot in the leg is rapidly losing both blood and consciousness.

Sirens are getting closer.

"It's over! Go, dude!" Inarticulate from the adrenaline dump, Pro motions frantically to the younger man to run. Deuce gets the message and takes off toward their apartment.

Pro looks at the tangle of blood and bodies on the stairwell. *No way through that without leaving a trail.* With rising urgency to escape, he looks for other options. He spots the roof of the now wrecked van almost directly below his landing.

He takes a moment to attempt to scoop up all of the spent shell casings from his rifle that he can find, then he holds the weapon above his head and jumps.

CHAPTER EIGHTEEN

"They still out there?" Ice hunches on the couch, motionless other than the question leaving his lips.

Pro removes his hand from the curtain, letting the tiny wrinkle he was looking through evaporate. "Yep. Going door to door, trying to get people to talk, looks like."

The gang huddles in the near-total darkness of the unlit apartment, talking in half-whispers as the sun begins to brighten the sky outside.

Fade grips her daughters tightly on the opposite end of the couch from Ice, a fierce protective arm around each of them. "You think anyone will?"

Pro settles back onto the couch in the space Ice and Fade are leaving for him in the middle. He looks around the room slowly, still trying to process everything that happened, and considers the question.

"Probably not." *They'll be scared of us, of retaliation if they snitch.* He tries to focus on the positives. "We kept the Locos out. They would have torn this place apart, but we stopped them cold."

Grunts of agreement resonate in the darkness, then the room becomes still again.

The gang had raced back to the apartment as cops flooded the street by the gate. As he had hoped, the time it took the police to surround, clear, and process the battle scene had given them the time to maneuver they desperately needed.

He had forced a window open on the back of the empty apartment next door and hidden every single one of their guns in a utility closet. After the raging battle in which the guns had saved their lives, the gang had been reluctant to turn loose of the weapons. He had been adamant, though, that the most dangerous thing to do with all the cops going door to door was have a house full of guns —especially guns with ballistics matching bullets in bodies.

The next thing he had done was get everyone in the living room and get all the lights off. *Every indication anyone is home, kill it,* he had told them. *We are on vacation. We were never here tonight. Make them prove otherwise.*

A little while ago, the loud knock had finally come, and he imagined a stack of SWAT outside his door, ready to kick it in. It may have been Isa for all he knew, but they stuck to the plan. He had motioned for calm, for stillness, and kept everyone in the living room sitting with their hands clearly visible, praying the door didn't fly to pieces.

His plan worked, and without any specific evidence connecting them to the shootout, the cops moved on. Looking out just now, he expected to see the asshole gang detective who pulled him over, maybe Isa talking to neighbors, pointing toward his house, showing up with a warrant.

But none of that happened, and he could only assume that most of the cops chased the fleeing Locos when the tide of battle turned. *They'll be back.* He knows it is true and that sooner or later, they will have to say something, if only a flat denial, to the cops. For now, though, they are lying low, counting their blessings, and hoping.

The refrigerator kicks on in the kitchen, the slight hum piercing the stillness. Perhaps the sound awakens primal instincts. Maybe the natural rhythm of the morning begins to assert itself on the chaos of the night. Either way, it is a turning point.

"Mom, I'm hungry," four-year-old Seriah tries to whisper, but her unfamiliarity with not speaking in a normal tone betrays her effort. The gruff, half-croaking sound her little voice makes is totally incongruent with the tension in the room, and a couple of quiet chuckles float out of the darkness.

Fade's mind is still racing about what is happening outside, and she doesn't immediately reply. In the space her silence allows another older voice pipes up.

"I'm hungry too." Sitting on the floor nearby, Deuce tries to make his more manly voice gruff like Seriah's. He partially succeeds in his effort, but the sound comes out in a kind of barking falsetto mix that brings even more laughs.

Pro can see the sharp white of the little girl's smiles in the near darkness and feels some tension leave his shoulders. He plays off Deuce's voice, twisting it just a little further to sound like a certain ring-obsessed hobbit. "I'm hungry too. I wants to eat my precious!" He grabs at Seriah with clawed hands, wiggling his fingers into her ribs to tickle her.

She gives a little yelp, made all the funnier by the fact she tries to do it in a whisper.

Everyone is smiling now, unconsciously eager to have a distraction from the deadly battle.

Selena wiggles her way down and picks across the floor carefully toward the kitchen. "Ima get a pop tart."

"Careful, baby." By habit, Fade uses her left hand to illuminate her daughter's path with her iPhone. Her right reaches out to rest on Pro's arm. Her face turns toward him, her mind already forming a decision but clearly interested in his input. "We are probably good now, right?"

He feels himself nodding. They have been sitting in the dark for quite a while. No exploding door. No one turning the apartment inside out. The cops are circling outside. But to anyone but Isa and the gang detective, they are just another door out of nearly a hundred in the complex.

"Yeah." It is one word, but when he says it, people start moving. It is like someone pulled the safety pin out of a complex machine, and the parts all slowly start turning.

Deuce follows the girls into the kitchen and flips on the light. In short order, he has them organized into a pop-tart assembly line. Ice's shoulders relax, and he bumps sideways into his older brother in a silent show of camaraderie. Aliyah pulls out her phone and starts updating all her Snapchat streaks, returning to normality the best way she knows how.

"You got some for me, baby?" Ma stands a bit shakily, her question directed at Fade, who nods and heads toward the bedroom.

"Yeah, lemme get my purse."

"Yeah. We good." Pro repeats it, reassuring himself, and the words seem to take root in his soul as he says them. He pushes aside doubts about who *we* is. Liz lurks in his mind, but in the here and now, his family is what matters.

Jiggy flops down on the couch in the spot Fade abandoned and puts a big arm around Pro's shoulders. "This my dude right here." He winces slightly when the action stretches the growing bruise on his shoulder. "Next time, just give me a Glizzy, though."

Ice becomes enthused. "Yeah, man, you should have seen me with that shit." He holds his hand in front of him, turning his fist sideways and pumping it slightly. "Them Locos couldn't handle that heat. They gonna have to move around now."

Deuce comes back around the corner, a fresh pop-tart in hand. "You shoulda seen Pro, man. He must've put like twenty of them down. Straight G, up in here!"

Pro raises both fists toward the young men flanking him on the couch. His action both a silent acceptance of their approval and congratulation to them on the successful defense of their turf. He leans back, accepting their return fist-bumps as he reaches a broader realization about the new state of affairs.

They are all looking up to me. The feel of Fade's touch on his arm still lingers in his mind. *They accept me now.*

Ice rocks to his feet and throws signs for South Side with one hand and Neighborhood Crips with the other. "We're straight now. Stronger than *ever* now that Pro is back."

The other boys rumble their agreement, "Yeah, Big Homie knows how to run shit fo SHO." They stack their own hand signs toward Pro to show their respect and allegiance. All three are all looking toward Pro, waiting for his affirmation.

They are saying I'm family. The next part is a surprise, but he realizes it should not be. *They are saying I'm their leader now.*

Nodding slowly, he pushes one leg out and reclines further on the couch. "Yeah, we're good." Accepting their impromptu pledge of brotherhood, he extends his fingers and thumb in the hand sign they are expecting. "On the Set."

THE STORY CONTINUES...

PREVIEW OF BOOK TWO: CHAOS RISING

Rae stands up when she sees him walking out and can't help smiling when they make eye contact.

"Ayyyyyy!" He strides quickly to her and throws his arms around her. "Baby girl lookin fiiiine."

She feels him pressing against her chest and lets him. "Always for you, you know that."

He stands back. "Ice said you were making moves, but I wasn't expecting you to stack three grand this fast." He reaches around toward her backside playfully. "My girl must be tearing it up out here."

Clearing her throat, she dodges his hand and looks over at a sour-faced jail deputy who is glaring at the both of them. "Some shit went down. We gotta get out of here."

"That's what I'm *talking* about," Four nods his head emphatically and steps toward the double doors leading to the parking lot. He turns to exit the door backward, using his broad shoulders as a battering ram to open the portal. His reckless maneuver leaves both hands free, allowing him to flip the jail guard off with both of them. "I'm outta this bitch."

The jailer gives him a huge fake grin accompanied by mocking but quite sincere, "See you soon!"

Fade follows the energetic gang leader, maneuvering the red purse hanging from her shoulder to avoid the door as it swings shut. As soon as they are through the door, she pulls out her phone.

"Where's your whip at?" Four looks around the parking lot expectantly.

Still looking at her phone, her face reddens. "I've got an Uber on the way."

"A fucking *Uber*?" His voice is incredulous, and he continues looking around like he's sure he is being pranked. "An Uber – get the fuck outta here with that shit. C'mon, where the gang at?"

Stiffening, she starts walking away from the jail. "It's meeting us down the street."

"Are you serious right now?" When she walks on without replying, he starts following a few paces behind. "What the hell, did the whole gang start working at Walmart too? Why is nobody here but you?"

Scowling at her silence, he increases her pace to catch her. His jubilation at being bonded out of jail begins to fade as he realizes something is very out of place. He grabs her arm to stop her and addresses her in a serious tone. "Rae. Just tell me what's up."

Still nervous with the jail's close proximity but with no one around them on the sidewalk, she takes a breath and lets it out. "Locos pulled up again, and some shit went down."

He swears. "Everyone good? Tell me everyone is still good."

She shakes her head, trying to figure out how to spin her actions in a positive light. "I don't really know. I just knew I need to come to get you out."

He grabs her shoulders. "You don't *know*?" His voice

increases in volume, a mixture of fear and anger spitting forth.

"Yeah, I don't know! I'm on the outside, Babe." She puts anger into the words, needing him to believe her. "They making moves without me. I tried to stop him, but Pro's running shit now."

"Yeah?" Four's face darkens into something deadly. "Like hell he is."

ACKNOWLEDGMENTS

My good friend and former shift partner Tommie Johnson III, now Sheriff of Oklahoma County, grew up on the south side of Oklahoma City in the neighborhood where this story is focused. His stories about the challenges he faced growing up, the situations and versions of "normal life" he encountered as a teenager, and how he eventually broke free of the cycle were significant inspirations for the character Pro. A strong Christian and one of the best men I have ever met, Tommie feels an undeniable pull to help people, not abandon them. We have shared many lengthy conversations about what is helping inner-city problems and what isn't, and I applaud his ongoing efforts to have a wider positive impact.

Another massive influence on this book is the dozens of gang-involved young people with whom I was on a first-name basis as a Police Officer. When I was a rookie, I had a distorted, one-sided view of what justice and right and wrong were. A belief that I recognize now did not include the fact that everyone, in every situation, is a real person. The young people and their families I encountered helped me learn that. One of the reasons I left law enforcement was that I could not have the positive impact on them I wished I could. This book is an effort to tell the stories I saw on the street in a way that shows that regardless of which side of the law we are on, we are all just people.

My wife Schaine believed in me and this book so much that she sacrificed much to make sure I could write it. Far from the first time she has been my most ardent supporter and the best of all life companions, this is just another example of what makes her so awesome and why I love her. I could not write without her, so if you enjoyed this book, let her know how much you appreciate her!

Geoff Young is a pillar of my writing world and offered his exceptional talent of constructive criticism and problem-solving creativity to make this book way better than it otherwise would have been. A constant encouragement and inspiration, a writer in his own right, and a great friend.

Most importantly, I want to acknowledge Jesus Christ, my Lord and Savior. All that I am and all that I write is a gift from Him.

-Joel Cutter

ABOUT THE AUTHOR

Joel Cutter is a former Police Officer and Army Green Beret, and a Christian family man.

Having served the last few years as a Police Officer in Oklahoma, knee-deep, and face-to-face with America's criminal drug culture, Cutter has come to believe two things. All criminals are people, and ultimately all people are criminals. Redemption is the only thing that separates the two.

Joel Cutter writes stories that represent the hard edges of truth - taking readers on a journey inside the head of people who are embroiled in criminal lifestyles and of the cops bringing them to justice. A world where things are never as simple as 'good guys' and 'bad guys.'

Check out the official webpage at www.joelcutter.com and discover more of the best crime novels from Joel Cutter.